TOMORROW THEY ARE PLAYING GOD

Travel Tales from the South

Raccoon Sixty

Reciprocity Publishing
Victoria BC, Canada

🌑 Reciprocity Publishing
Victoria BC, Canada

www.reciprocitypublishing.com

Citation: Raccoon 60. Tomorrow they are playing god: Travel tales from the south. Victoria,
BC: Reciprocity Publishing, 2025.

ISBN
978-1-928114-67-3 (Hardcover)
978-1-928114-66-6 (Paperback)
978-1-928114-68-0 (eBook)

1. TRV010000 TRAVEL, ESSAYS & TRAVELOGUES

MORE OF WHAT PEOPLE
ARE NOT SAYING ABOUT THIS BOOK

"I recommend going in blind and falling down the rabbit hole." **Laura, Munro's Bookstore**

"A must-read for anyone who plays tennis, but I think even people who have never played will get something out of it." **Bill Gates**

"Oddly, I read the whole thing in a Bulgarian accent." **Camilla Long, Sunday Times**

"Lavishly filigreed as a Faberge egg, gleams with nostalgia for the golden age of Tolstoy and Turgenev." **O: The Oprah Magazine**

"I know words. I have the best words." **Donald Trump**

"Lyrically ebullient, charged with moments of magic and myth that betray literary influences as diverse as Colette and Garcia Marquez." **Amy Boaz, Elle**

"Everybody, wake up! You are all in the Presence of God." **Ruhollah Khomeini**

"A book you didn't know that you wanted." **David**

"One of the funniest travel writers in the business. The reader only has to worry about falling out of the bed, hammock, or deckchair laughing." **The Gazette**

"This is easily one of the worst books I've ever read. And bear in mind that I've read John Grisham." **Charleston City Paper**

"Contains four chapters consisting solely of haiku in transliterated Sumerian? **John Scalzi**

"Uproarious ... Stimulating enough to keep even an unmedicated narcoleptic awake." **The Washington Times**

"This book is a jewel and a must read for anyone who knows gin and loves it." **Arrigo Cipriani**

"A powerful and attractive man ... I predict he is going to be very popular in prison." **Gene Simmons, Kiss**

"I want the whole world to read this book. I know everyone is already pre-ordering, and if you're in a book club, you should read it together." **Oprah**

"There is so much to hate." **Mary McCarthy**

"A great book about a great horse." **Susan Richards**

"Whoever was the foremost authority on this topic is now the second most." **Bob Monkoff**

"A personal hero of mine." **Hillary Clinton**

"A mysterious survival saga that passionate fans describe as a fusion of The Lord of the Flies, The Hunger Games, and Lost." **EW**

"Heart pounding to the last moment." *Kirkus Review*

"Vastly entertaining ... If there is one book with which to get acquainted before departure or en route, this is it." *New York Times*

"A wonderfully engaging blend of wit, enthusiasm, clarity, and knowledge." **Bill Bryson**

"Readers who enjoy dystopian tales and unreliable narrators will find much to dissect." *Publishers Weekly*

"ya ochen' plokho govoryu po-angliyski." **Vladimir Putin**

"I took the manuscript to our little boys' room. The stories were so funny that I stayed there for an hour chortling to myself. My wife did an inventory of our medicine cabinet when I finally emerged." **Rufus T. Driftwood, CEO Boondoggle International**

"I found myself nostalgic for books plagued only by quaint defects." **Becca Rothfeld, *Times Literary Supplement***

"Messy and unhinged like a Twitter feud you can't stop trolling through."

Nash, Russell's Books

"We need to be super careful... potentially more dangerous than nukes." **Elon Musk**

DEDICATION

This book is dedicated to my last boss, Tom.
His favourite piece of advice was,
"The best predictor of future behaviour is past behaviour."
I never thought I would write a second book, but this is it.
So with that preface, there is plenty to be worried about.

Don't say I didn't warn you.

Table of Contents

MAP OF DESTINATIONS 8

INTRODUCTION 9

Part I MUZUNGU MUSINGS 13

Chapter 1 There's No Accounting for Rwandan Accounting 15

Chapter 2 Rwanda's Not Fake, Not News 25

Chapter 3 The Hokey Pokey on Mount Bisoke 33

Chapter 4 Haircut Consciousness 45

Chapter 5 Monkey See, Monkey Do 57

Chapter 6 The Hundred-Day Hell 65

Chapter 7 Method in the Madness Is Still Madness 73

Chapter 8 The Big Game in Tanzania 83

Chapter 9 Fair Is Foul And Foul Is Fair 93

Chapter 10 Just Visiting Greta Thunberg's Dream 103

Part II TERRA AUSTRALIS INCOGNITO FOR A WHILE 117

Chapter 11 Chile's Warm Welcome 119

Chapter 12 My Way Is Not the Highway 129

Chapter 13 Pat O'Gonia 137

Chapter 14 Dinner Time in the Argentine 147

Chapter 15 The Island That Shall Remain Nameless 157

PART III REEDUCATION RWANDAN STYLE 167

Chapter 16 The Beer Necessities 169

Chapter 17 Art For Art's Sake 185

Chapter 18 Measure If You Like, Cut Once 203

Chapter 19 Everyone Has A Story 225

Chapter 20 Overthinking the Last Supper 237

EPILOGUE	247
BE PREPARED	255
ABOUT FACE | APOLOGIA	261
WHAT DID WE LEARN - A QUIZ	267
GLOSSARY	271
BOOK CLUB QUESTIONS	276
THANKYOUS	279
ABOUT THE AUTHOR	280

Tomorrow They Are Playing God
Travel Tales from the South

 Selected destinations

INTRODUCTION

*"We are what our thoughts have made us;
so take care about what you think.
Words are secondary. Thoughts live; they travel far."*

—*Swami Vivekananda*

The problem with putting thoughts into words is that they can't be unsaid. Your own personal universe will never be the same, whether you are just talking to yourself, which prompts a whole different set of anxieties, or sharing your musings with someone else. The thoughts now have a life of their own, and the utterer's influence over where the words might lead rapidly diminishes. The scope of the possibilities, however, even more rapidly expands.

So, when, in the late twenty teens, I tossed out, "Wouldn't it be fun to go to..." in my wife Trixie's presence, the train was on the tracks and already leaving the station before I had even finished the sentence. Minor details like where the train was heading, how long the journey would be, how many stops there would be along the way, what we would do en route, and what we could afford would be but details to be resolved later.

As usual, how we thought about planning could scarcely be more different. Me, with my two dimensions, atlas on my lap; Trixie, at her knitting, nonchalantly optimistic, coming out with comments like: "Wonderful is what you make it." Sage advice that I would do well to remember, but not what I would call crucial input for our decision-making. Our mismatched stratagems took us down several interesting paths, all of which ultimately turned into dead ends.

Having full confidence that wherever and whenever we arrived Trixie would look after the "making it wonderful" part, I got us back on the pedantic, logical sequential track. Eventually, by process of elimination, we discounted several continents as potential candidates. Europe, Asia, Australia, and North America we'd travelled to or lived in. We ruled out Antarctica, which could uncharitably be described as "a few acres of snow;" a harsh assessment, words I've stolen from Voltaire, but it's how he described Canada. With that alibi, I feel that I am in safe territory.

Trixie had never been to Africa, and I had last stayed there over thirty years ago. Neither of us had visited South America. So, we would be heading south; that much we knew. That was the easy part.

And with that, the pivotal decision was made. We would be going somewhere new. With such an amazing variety of possibilities available to us, constrained only by the diminishing number of years left to sample those delights, where exactly would best tempt us?

Our trips to Asia, rather than clarifying why we liked to travel, had only succeeded in providing more reasons to do so. It could have been that we wanted a bit of luxury, a bit of pampering. The delights of Japanese cuisine and the decadence of a pristine beach in Myanmar will do that to you.

But just as revealing had been the satisfaction of having day-to-day interaction with the folks local to the places we had been. Specifically, we had found our time volunteering in Cambodia to be particularly rewarding. So much so that we decided to repeat the experience on our next trip.

In due course, I contacted the recruiting agency that I had previously used, Accountants for International Development (AFID). AFID specializes in matching volunteer accountants with non-governmental organizations (NGOs) in less-developed countries. Within a month, they provided me with a shortlist of three assignments to choose from. Due to the limited opportunities for English-only speakers in South America, they were all based in Africa. One in each of Zambia, Rwanda, and Uganda.

The choice between the three was not an easy one. A bit of research and lengthy discussions—fueled by many pots of tea—helped us to focus our decision-making. The clinching factor for us was the accommodation that would be provided by the charity-based school in Rwanda. This would give Trixie and I the opportunity to live in a schoolhouse on a farm in the community rather than in an apartment separate from village life. It would be a decision that would change our travel plans for years to come. As of this writing, we are planning our fourth trip to Rwanda.

Interspersed with those visits to the Dark continent, we did also manage to fit in a trip to the last remaining continent, notwithstanding Antarctica's bitter claims, the southern part of South America.

This book chronicles the escapades that ensued over the course of those separate sojourns. These stories of community, discovery, and travel, touch on six countries, on these two continents, not to mention one island in a parallel universe.

They also span a period of about five years, five difficult years, years that saw a global pandemic, a series of world leaders with dubious morals and even more dubious taste in hairstyles, the rise of AI, driven by a group of offensively wealthy AHs who think that they know what's best for us, and a planet that is rebelling against our demands on it. Who wouldn't want to take a time out from that?

I hope that you find these tales, of slithering down a volcano in the Virunga Mountains of central Africa, crime solving in a school classroom in rural Rwanda, and shopping for your eternal resting place in one of the world's top ten cemeteries, enough of an escape to ease those stresses.

Who knows, they might even provoke some thoughts, which start some conversations, which lead to some actions, which will see you on your way to your own next big discovery.

TOMORROW THEY ARE PLAYING GOD

"I've sucked way too much cement for this year. Bad juju rising off them city sidewalks. I need to babble with a brook or two, inhale starlight, make friends with some trees."

– Tom Robbins

Part I

Muzungu Musings

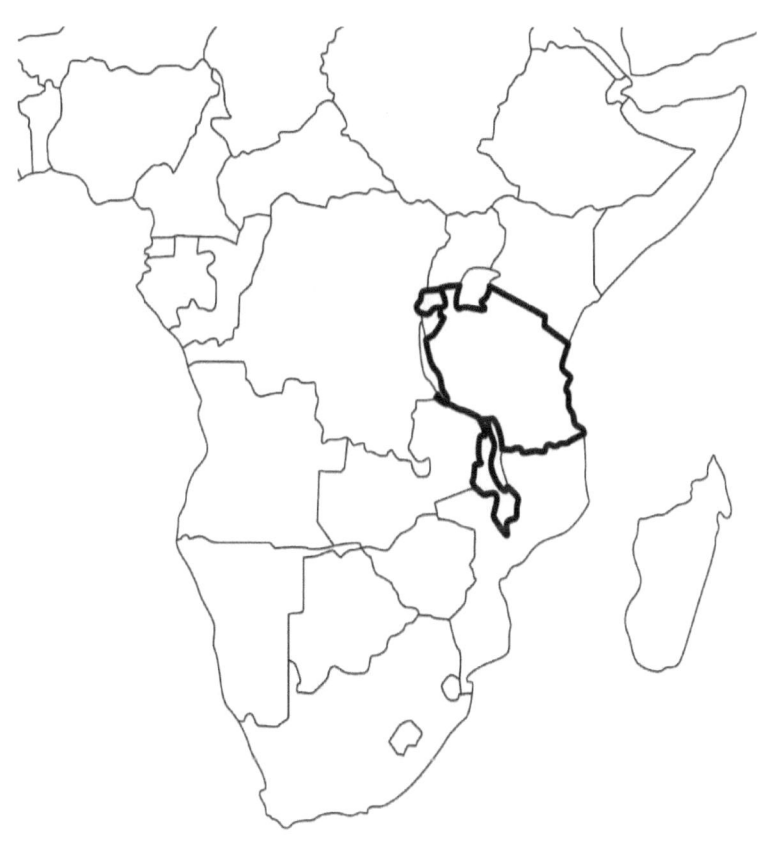

Chapter 1
There's No Accounting for Rwandan Accounting

*Sorry, but we are out of the Belgian
dry-hopped chocolate porter today.*

"HE WHO IS NOT CONTENTED WITH WHAT HE HAS WILL NOT BE
CONTENTED WITH WHAT HE WOULD LIKE TO HAVE."

– Socrates

"THERE IS ALWAYS SOMETHING FISHY ABOUT THE FRENCH."

– Noel Coward

It is half past dawn when I come to. It is a morning filled with regret and an acute thirst for black coffee. The string of events that have led me to this sorry state might best be told as a mini-series. So rather than skip to the end of the story, come with me, and we will relive the unlikely twists of fate that paved the way for that painful conclusion.

The name Rwanda probably isn't ringing many bells, a few images may spring to mind. Maybe gorilla trekking or there was that genocide thing some thirty years ago. More recently Britain has been trying to arrange to use it as a penal colony, somewhere it can park its illegal immigrants. That's about it.

To continue with the antipodean theme, the country can be described as roughly the shape of Australia but less than one-hundredth of the size. It is a land-locked island of relative stability surrounded by rowdy neighbours. A country similar to Israel, insecure about its place in a region that is armed to the teeth and ready for anything. A country that at the same time aspires to be the Singapore of Africa.

It is a speck of a country not even the size of Vancouver Island. And, I am sure that you are wondering where exactly the heck it is.

Smack dab in the middle of continental Africa, about five thousand kilometres from Cairo in the north and Cape Town to the south, and about as far from the Gulf of Guinea to the west and the Indian Ocean to the east.

It is hardly surprising that Rwanda is such an enigma. It was the centre of the world's attention during the 1994 genocide, but as soon as the carnage ended, the international media moved on to more dramatic pastures. Just as quickly as it shot to notoriety, the country sank back into obscurity.

I have signed up for another volunteer assignment, this time a six-week stint in central Rwanda, assisting a school in managing their finances. Do not despair, you will be just as blissfully

16

ignorant of the jiggery pokery of debits and credits by the end of this book as you are now. How to fly a kite, well that might be another story.

We arrive late at night. Why is it always night? The sense of anticipation when arriving in a new place is always a rush. The anonymity that the darkness provides heightens the feeling of being alien. Some of the most powerful memories and impressions are indelibly formed in those first few hours. Or might it just be the effects of sleep deprivation, it being thirty hours since we left Victoria?

We are greeted at the airport by the diminutive Belgian director of the school known to all and sundry as Mrs. Stella, and her driver, Roger. I am glad it is him and not me that is navigating the city streets, as the Kigali roadmap looks like the contours of the cerebrum. We are delivered to our cosy hotel in the downtown area of the capital. Coma-like sleep ensues.

In the morning, we are driven to the village of Kibuterama, a little over an hour away, the rolling landscape confirms the country's nickname "Land of a Thousand Hills." The verdant green flora contrasts richly with the brick red of the volcanic soil, a relaxing introduction to the country. Terracotta-roofed homes sprinkle the countryside, blink twice and you might think yourself to be in Tuscany. The mellow vibe turns out to be the norm.

As we near town, the plain mud-brick residences fringing the roads become fewer. Small-scale commercial buildings begin to proliferate. Business is alive and well and just like home, the beer and phone companies seem to dominate the marketplace. They don't hold back entire buildings are painted in one solid primary colour. Whether the colour coding indicates that any crossover marketing is happening is questionable, but you have to read the fine print before entering or you might end up coming out with a phone instead of a six pack. The big favourites are yellow (Skol beer and MTN phones), blue (Primus beer and KZG phones), and red (Mutzig beer and Airtel phones).

Not that the service always lives up to the hype. The little beer shack (blue) at the end of my street is well-supplied as far as choice goes, maybe ten different varieties, but alas only two bottles of each. It gives a whole new meaning to the phrase "shoestring operation." The beer girl dutifully tends the store from dawn 'til dusk.

We are provided with accommodation in a small house on the edge of town, where we share a mini-walled compound with three other smaller homes for out-of-town teachers who work at the school. There is also a small farm, which is supposed to supplement the school's revenues through the sale of eggs, a few vegetables, and milk, supplied by a couple of cows and goats. We buy the eggs; the watchmen eat everything else. I guess you could call it a sustainable model, except for the money that the school loses.

People are invariably friendly and gentle, but despite this and the relaxed atmosphere, all the buildings have barred windows. Although Trixie and I have never experienced any theft firsthand, it seems to be a concern throughout Africa. The school ensures that we have at least two elderly, languorous gents who qualify as our watchmen, who are always on duty. We make the acquaintance of our entourage. One is given the full-time responsibility to stand guard over, or more accurately doze in a chair next to, the clapped-out relic of a water pump that supplies our cottage. A third watchman, whose hat is bigger than his coat, augments the complement for the night shift. A technician (don't ask me, it's the least technical house I have ever lived in), Clavier, the elderly electrician, and a carpenter (who the others refer to as the "boozerman"), round out our retinue.

We gradually develop, or maybe adapt to would be a more accurate description, a daily routine:

4:00 a.m. the mosque announces its call to prayer.

5:00 a.m. a siren alerts the kids at the nearby boarding school that it's time to get up.

5:30 a.m. the church fires up some R&B gospel.

6:00 a.m. you are getting the hang of this, the siren again, this time announcing that breakfast is ready.

6:30 a.m. it is starting to get light, and the birds who have also been awake since four o'clock figure it is time to chime in.

7:00 a.m. the last couple in Rwanda still in bed get up, clamber out from under the mosquito net that drapes over the bed like some mutant jellyfish, and hit the cold shower.

Breakfast is a very Californian affair: coffee, tea, avocadoes, mangoes, paw paw, and guava are all local, delicious, and cheap. I head off, walking to work, arriving just after 8:30 a.m. The school is in full swing by 7:30, after having kicked off the day with a rousing rendition of the national anthem.

The work is fun. My un-airconditioned office sits adjacent to the playground. The secretary, the accountant, Jean Claude and myself occupy the small building. The temperature and humidity are rising as we approach the rainy season. We try and keep the space cool by keeping the doors and windows open.

A day at the office is unconventional, to say the least. At recess, soccer balls fly through the door, followed by careening bodies in hot pursuit. Giggling little kids play peek-a-boo at my window, a forest of small arms and hands reach in for high fives. It's like I am Justin Timberlake putting on a halftime show. The children are beautiful, happy, smiling, and proud in their smart school uniforms.

Things are chaotic on the accounting front too. Jean Claude apprises me of all manner of skullduggery that he has been tasked with sorting out. But when I try to get him to explain the crux of any problem, the discussion invariably degenerates into some sort of interminable verbal tennis match.

An abridged version of one of these Wimbledon epics goes something like this:

Me: serving up a juicy serve "So who owes us the 2 million RWF?"

JC: "The developer's widow, but she doesn't know it." Disguising his volley with heavy spin.

Me: "The who? So why does she owe it, but doesn't know it?" Caught wrong-footed by his unorthodox return.

JC: "Her husband was a bad man and the accountant before me too." This time his lob has me backpedalling in a hurry.

Me: "Wait what? Why were they bad?" Stretching to stay in contention.

JC: "They made the school pay too much money for the land for the assembly hall." His cross court forehand opens up all kinds of possibilities.

Me: "OK, how?" I grunt back.

JC: "The price for the land was 17 million, but the accountant told the developer that Mrs. Stella was willing to pay 19 million. So the developer sold the land for 19 million and gave the accountant 1 million." I am being outplayed, although he has probably never held a racket before.

Me: "OK, now I am getting it. But how did we find out? How did we know to record it as a debt?"

It has been a long time since I have played twenty questions, I am beginning to remember why.

JC: "The developer confessed to Mrs Stella before he died." Another piece of magic from his bag of tricks.

Me: "Wow, that's what I call a change of heart, but why did the developer tell her?" Desperate now to finish the point, I lunge in frustration at his drop shot.

JC: Silence.

I have "quarantined" us in the school's computer lab. With the drapes drawn and the door locked, we can hopefully find some peace and actually get some work done. He looks around the darkened room as if there might be ghosts hiding in the corners and listening. There is no one present but us two. He takes a piece of paper and a pencil and writes "AIDS" in big letters. Still dictating the play.

Me: "Sorry to hear that, but why did he confess?"

Leaning in confidentially, nervously scanning the room lest the deceased might leap out from the stationery cupboard, Jean Claude continues with his masterclass.

JC: "He was a Muslim man and when he knew he had..." He points to the piece of paper. "He knew that he had to repent. So he told Mrs. Stella just before he died."

There is a god who works in mysterious ways, and I am pretty sure that he is a she.

Me: "And?" My appetite for the rally rapidly waning.

JC: "Mrs. Stella fired the accountant, hired me and told me to get the money back, or else..." Game, set, championship.

"There are eight million stories in the naked city. This has been one of them."

Other episodes include a German ambulance driver touring through Africa on his bicycle, who obviously must be the ideal entrepreneur to turn the school's assembly hall into a moneymaking convention centre. He spends 4.5 million RWF on electronic equipment but attracts no customers, except for local football fans who come to get drunk and watch English soccer on the big-screen TV. Somehow, he manages to sell the beer at a loss and still is able to persuade the Rwandan courts that he has been swindled by the school. The court-appointed bailiff scoops the settlement out of the school's bank account and bingo, another case for JC to solve.

So how much money are we talking about here? Sure, one Rwandan franc is about the equivalent of three fourths of two fifths of bugger all or to be more exact .15 of a Canadian cent. But when you look at them in context the average annual GDP is around seven hundred and fifty US dollars—these numbers are huge.

Oh, for the quiet life of spreadsheets and budgets.

I gradually get familiar with the finances and hopefully become of some help. Money is the universal language and I am a philologist.

Day-to-day communications can be more stimulating. Rwanda's ethnic language is Kinyarwanda, and almost everyone knows it.

With the return of many exiled Tutsi from English-speaking Uganda after the genocide, English has eclipsed French. I have to think though, that when poetic phrases like "She has more certificates on the wall than stars in the night." or "It is raining too much in my heart" pop up in conversation, it has to be coming from the more traditional language.

Imported unfamiliar letter combinations cause tongue twisters the world over. It is no different here where there are almost Chinese sounding linguistic transpositions of the letters r and l.

When I quiz JC about the reason for this, he replies enigmatically, "It's because of the French", end of discussion.[1]

Strange, I don't remember "Vive ra Flance" pal exampre. It seems that the Flench are at the loot of any unexprained plobrem now.

JC and I often have interesting talks about the events that shape the current generation. I had been warned that it was too difficult for people to talk about the genocide, but that is not my experience. As long as the conversation doesn't wander into their own traumas, history and politics are popular topics.

In one of these discussions, JC states that a lot of the trouble goes back to independence from Belgium, back in 1962. "The West had thrown in the tower and decided that it should be majolity lure aftel arr." More on this later.

I settle into my role, something of a mix of therapist, guy Friday, father confessor, intermediary, and slave driver. (Sidebar: Using the word slave-driver, I feel that some equivocation might be prudent. This could be construed as a racially insensitive metaphor I guess, but maybe if I am thinking of JC as just another guy rather than a black guy it's OK. I am afraid that if I don't use it, I will be re-victimizing him by in essence whitewashing (Oh God, I fear that there must be something triggering about this word too!) the existence of slavery from common discourse. It's hard to keep up. (Please refer to the apology at the end of the book.)

Stella wants her financial statements and budget ASAP and if they aren't ready in time she will have someone's head, and mine is leaving in six weeks... still attached. If JC doesn't get cracking, he will be the lead character in the next curtailed episode.

---

[1] https://www.youtube.com/watch?v=64yianfGvzc

I would normally head home around five o'clock, at the end of each work day, perhaps stopping at the corner store on the way to pick up some utilities. This particular afternoon, I need to buy a twenty-five-litre jug of drinking water, so I hire a moto (motorcycle) taxi for the trip. Helmets are compulsory, but the one offered has no chin strap; in a flash, the driver offers me his pre-warmed one. Not wishing to diminish his gallantry, I accept.

I pay him three hundred RWF (forty-five cents), and he balances the jug on his fuel tank and away we go. I might have bought some electricity at the store too, if we had been running low. It's a pay-as-you-go system, kind of a cross between the old British shilling in the meter process and a scratch and win ticket whereby when you get home, you enter the secret code from the ticket you bought at the store into your meter and your power credit automatically grows.

Just because your scratch and win ticket was a winner doesn't mean you will automatically have electricity, though; every other day there is a power cut or water shut off. Such events would constitute headline-making news back home, but here in Kibuterama, it's common knowledge that there is no light without the darkness.

Chapter 2
Rwanda's Not Fake, Not News

Non-relatable alphabetical learning aids.

"AND THAT'S THE WAY IT IS."

– *Walter Cronkite*

"YOU WILL FIND TRUTH MORE QUICKLY
THROUGH DELIGHT THAN THROUGH GRAVITY.
LET A LITTLE MORE STRING OUT ON YOUR KITE."

– *Alan Cohen*

Being a news junkie, it takes a bit of getting used to not having on-demand access to the twenty-four-hour "feed." With frequent blackouts euphemistically referred to as "load shedding" and the poor and sporadic internet signal in rural Rwanda, staying informed can be an exercise in frustration.

Increasingly though, when I am able to tune in to the Western reports I find that it is mostly just dramatized sensationalized distractions catering to the lowest common denominator. An exercise designed to attract the largest number of "eyeballs." The top draw of course currently being the "Trump Show," which now in its second season still shows no signs that it will ever really be worth watching. A steady stream of new cast members really no better than a troop of disposable walk-on extras that have contributed nothing of value and the scriptwriters are as clueless as ever. With tanking ratings, the best that we can hope for is early cancellation.

However, here in Kibuterama, about an hour outside of Rwanda's capital Kigali, real news is happening. It is meatier fare and vastly more engaging.

By way of context, I should explain that my six-week volunteer assignment here is to assist preparing the financial statements for the independent school. As I mentioned, the school is run, literally, by Mrs. Stella, an eighty-five-year-old deaf, Belgian, firebrand ex-judge, who came here in 1995 as a part of the UN's legal team sent to assist with the judicial proceedings after the 1994 genocide. Then she never left.

She lives alone with her night watchman and cook, close to the school. Mrs. Stella makes trips to her home country Belgium twice a year to visit family and raise funds. There is no denying that she is an omnipresent force of nature, a vortex of energy, which is as likely to suck you in as hurl you aside.

The BBC would do well to have a news crew permanently located in the town. A typical newscast might go something like this:

Ditch the dramatic urgent staccato soundtrack intro and replace it with a more friendly Laurel and Hardy type theme, "Whoop de doo, whoop de doo, deedle de doo, deedle de doo..."

Pan to our newscaster, seated on a red plastic chair under a typical corrugated iron roof.

"And now the headlines."

"In overseas news, there is a report from Belgium that Basube, a thirty-two-year- old teacher who is being sponsored for training there, will not return to Rwanda as he had promised. Stella's covert operatives there have been activated with instructions to destabilize the situation by starting a misinformation campaign that Mr. Basube is in Brussels to arrange an arms deal. His extradition is at this point unlikely."

"In breaking news, eyewitnesses spotted Mrs. Stella's security guard cycling through town when he should have been at work. When questioned, Mr. Ildephonse claimed that "The housekeeper is crazy, she wants to kill me." He had gone home for lunch as it was unsafe for him to eat at Mrs. Stella's house for fear that the cook would poison him. One of Mrs. Stella's officials, speaking on condition of anonymity, confirmed that the reports were true, and that a replacement guard was being sought."

"Locally, the ongoing border dispute between Mrs. Stella and her neighbour Mr. Clavert has flared up. Mrs. Stella's watchman has apparently apprehended Mr. Clavert's goat which was caught eating Mrs. Stella's cabbages again. The goat has been relocated to the school's mini farm. Two Canadian volunteers, who have been feeding the goat, are implicated. They face possible charges of aiding and abetting a kidnapping. The school's accountant, Jean Claude, has been enlisted to unravel the mess, as Mr Clavert's daughter has a scholarship at the school and as partial compensation, makes classroom furniture for the school for free."

"The question as to how to value a goat, some cabbages, a scholarship, and some desks might be better solved by Solomon.

"Further afield, developments in the Bay of Rabbits standoff have seen Mrs Stella sell her recreational property on the shores of Lake Kivu. Rumours are running rampant that this signals the imminent withdrawal of the Belgian presence in the area. Talks regarding the final transfer price for the sale have reached a stalemate over whether the rabbits on the property are to be included in the compensation package. The school's accountant has once again been dispatched. The skills of a numbers man will be needed to match the rabbit's facility with multiplication.

"And now, let's have an update from Sally on the day's business news... Sally?"

Sally appears resplendent in a colourful African wrap, headscarf, a pot on her head and heels. (This is going to be a professional show after all.)

"Thank you, Rosie. The market saw very active trading today. Sales in perishables—avocadoes, mangoes, papaya, and cassava were brisk due to the markets being closed tomorrow to celebrate Umuganda* day."

"There are some black clouds on the horizon in the agricultural sector where goat futures were down sharply, due to the death of another goat down on the farm. This brings the death toll to two. The cause of the fatalities has yet to be determined and the names of the deceased are being withheld until the goatherd can be located."

"Over to you now, Johanna, for a look at the weather."

"Thank you, Sally. Well, as we all know, we are well into March so the rainy season is ramping up. Temperatures are easing off to the low mid-twenties—seasonal norms. Yesterday evening there were thunderstorms and heavy rains. There was serious flooding in one of the teacherage rooms down at the farm. Rescue crews, including other teachers and the volunteers from the neighbouring guest cottage rushed to provide assistance. Anderson Cooper in his T-shirt is expected on location shortly.

"In sports, footage of today's major event is unfortunately unavailable. In preparation for the Annual General Meeting of the school board, Mrs. Stella had the volunteer accountant, yours truly, provide a demonstration of kite flying. Mrs. Stella had enlisted the help of Trixie, my wife, in constructing the kite."

Pan back to our anchorwoman.

"And that's it from all of us here. Thank you for joining us and for choosing Kibuterama News. Goodnight."

More "Whoop de doo Whoop de doo, Deedle de doo Deedle de doo..."

In regards to the embargoed sporting event, it may be prudent at this juncture to provide some context as to the state of affairs regarding Rwandan airspace. For today, something timeless and more enduring is introduced. Exposure to the latest new-fangled innovations in aviation is on offer.

*Umuganda day is held on the last Saturday of every month. It was instituted after the genocide and its purpose is to rebuild a sense of community and trust between all Rwandan citizens. Every healthy Rwandan between eighteen and sixty-five is obliged to participate, working on some common community project such as park maintenance, drainage, etc. It is estimated that up to 80 percent of the population comply.

Many a technologic milestone has been skipped in Rwanda's development; phone booths, Blockbuster Video and the Atkins diet never had a chance to register in the national psyche.

This pace of evolutionary change leads to some interesting quirks in what is embraced as amazing and what is dismissed as passé. In particular, the evolution of aeronautics has had a few of its phases resequenced here.

Sightings of drones have become decidedly ho hum in Kibutarama. Located in our small town is the distribution centre for medical supplies for the region. Many of the roads connecting the communities in the area are washed out during the rainy season.

Innovation comes to the rescue in the form of aerial drops courtesy of drone delivery from the health centre—no biggie. [2]

And yet the few passenger jet flights, mere specks, that transit the sky high above the school send the young kids racing to the playground, hands clapping above their heads, chanting, "Aeroplane! Aeroplane! Aeroplane!"

And so, now to today's showpiece... the fine art of kite flying.

Having been taught in every kindergarten textbook that K is for Kite and kites being unknown in Rwanda, Mrs. Stella thinks that seeing a real kite will have much more educational value for the kindergarten children—not only the children as it transpires.

One of the kindergarten teachers and I are given the task of launching the kite. Not a great success. We sprint the length of the school soccer pitch, me with the ball of string and her with the kite held aloft, kids left in our wake, scattering in all directions. I yell at her to let go, but she stubbornly refuses to let go of the kite chasing after me the length of the field.

---

[2] https://www.youtube.com/watch?v=NBdB3G9Qvqs

Eventually, we both arrive breathlessly at the end of the pitch, the kite and string safely in our hands.

"Why didn't you let go?" I gasp.

"I think you saying 'yego,' she replies, this being the word "yes" in the local Kinyarwanda language.

Misunderstanding sorted out, off we go again, this time right on my cue she releases her grip, the kite takes tentative flight until the string snags on the crossbar of the goal post, and the kite then takes a nosedive into the red dirt of the pitch. The Wright brothers would not have been impressed.

The damage is minimal, but I manage to persuade my co-pilot that it will be smarter to wait for a windier day (and a faster string man), before attempting the next airborne spectacle.

So with kids and teachers being little the wiser, I suggest to Mrs Stella that it might be easier to have the educational publishers create a special Rwanda edition first alphabet book, where they have the letter K be for Kalashnikov. With AK-47s as common as cats sitting on mats, it has got to be a teachable moment. My suggestion predictably falls on deaf ears.

These events might not match the experiences of a year en Provence, but for six weeks these ongoing stories provide plenty of binge-watch calibre entertainment. Charming real-life community events with the good fortune to share in the intimacy of being there as it happens.

You have been treated to a glimpse into the future trends for news reporting. CNN, you have been warned.

For better or worse, we now return you to your regular programming.

Chapter 3
The Hokey Pokey on Mount Bisoke

YOU GOTTA ASK YOURSELF A QUESTION, DO I FEEL LUCKY?
– Dirty Harry

"IT IS TRUE THAT THERE COMES A TIME
WHEN I LITERALLY DREAM ABOUT McDONALD'S.
I DREAM OF SUPERMARKETS, DRUG STORES, POTATO CHIPS
AND THE SUNDAY MORNING PAPER."

– Dian Fossey

"I WOULD PREFER TO HAVE INVENTED A MACHINE THAT
PEOPLE COULD USE AND THAT WOULD HELP FARMERS WITH
THEIR WORK, FOR EXAMPLE A LAWNMOWER."

– Mikhail Kalashnikov

On weekends, Trixie and I take the opportunity to explore different parts of this compact little country. The school being based roughly in the centre of the ten-thousand-square-mile nation, we are never more than one hundred and fifty miles from one of its borders. Apart from using the mostly reliable local transport, we have been lucky enough to make contact with Gilbert, a parent of one of the children at the school and a bit of a one-man tourism conglomerate.

On this occasion, we have enlisted his services to take us to the far north Volcanoes National Park to the Virunga Mountains, really more of a string of freestanding volcanoes that straddle the three neighbouring countries of Rwanda, Uganda, and the Democratic Republic of Congo (the "DRC" or formerly Zaire). It is a peaceful border area. Who after all would want to fight a war halfway up a bunch of three to four and a half thousand metre peaks?

Gilbert is a larger-than-life character, a man with two modes of operation; one is of genial glad-handing sociability, the other of full-on action-oriented perpetual motion. In either mode his overriding attitude is one of positivity. He has a wide vocabulary but he has his favourites, "No problem... Fantastic... Sure... Exactly... Absolutely." He routinely also shares his philosophy for life. This he delivers with gusto in a rich deep baritone, emphasised with a punch to the air. "WHY NOT?!"

I never have felt more inclined to stride around handing out random back slaps and high fives in my life.

Today en route to the park he is in mode two, whizzing round hairpin turns, alternately hurtling down or crawling up Rwanda's countless hills. He gives us a running commentary on the rules of the road, then drops down a gear as he pulls out across a double white line, just before a blind corner, to pass a lumbering truck belching black exhaust as it creeps up yet another steep incline. It is a turtle race, with Gilbert's old but

34

serviceable Landcruiser gaining inches on the truck. Gilbert hunches forward, his chin extended over the steering wheel, like a jockey trying to get the last ounce of energy out of his faithful steed.

Pity the poor motorcyclist coming the other way, who ends up swerving onto the potholed shoulder to avoid him. In Rwanda, the only rule of the road that really seems to matter is that might is right.

On the way to the park we will stay overnight at a small seven-unit resort on the shores of Lake Kivu. The lake is one of the African Great Lakes, fifty-six miles long and thirty-one miles across. It forms part of the international border between Rwanda and the massive Democratic Republic of Congo (DRC). This is a precarious region in every way.

As we look across the lake to the DRC, the very existence of civilized life on the other shore is insecure. The UN's largest peacekeeping mission still to this day polices a fragile peace. The Congolese wars ended some twenty years ago but armed insurgencies are ongoing.

The country's wealth of natural resources has generated trillions of dollars in the worldwide economy and yet it has brought the average Congolese nothing but misery. It costs the UN over $1 billion a year to try to keep a lid on things. It is but a tiny gesture that does little to redress the decades of abuse that the people have suffered on our behalf.

The DRC is massive, a country the size of Western Europe. It's a country that I would argue, always a dangerous thing for me to do, anyhow pressing on, in for a penny in for a pound as they say, has had a bigger impact on the evolution of the modern world than any other in recent history, and yet its presence has scarcely registered in the world's consciousness. It is a nation that has paid dearly for our luxuries. In a period of a little over one hundred years it has suffered more than anywhere on the planet.

At the start of the twentieth century its jungles provided the rubber that provided the pneumatic tires that enabled the auto industry to flourish. This rubber would eventually become known as "red rubber." The harvesting of it would result in the exploitation of somewhere between five and thirteen million souls. They were fated to be enslaved, tortured, incarcerated and executed, or they died of famine or disease. The die had been cast.

In the 1940s the country provided 70 percent of the uranium that went into Oppenheimer's atomic bomb. The bomb that was dropped on Hiroshima. Thousands of workers died from mining accidents and radiation poisoning extracting the deadly isotope. Thousands of acres of land were contaminated.

The devastation of the mining processes would prove to be but a minor calamity compared to the victimisation that was to follow. The ensuing Cold War geopolitics would have tragic consequences. The region's uranium is extraordinarily pure and very easily mined. The readily accessible resource meant that the Belgian Congo (as the DRC was then named) was an irresistible temptation to the Russians and the Americans, who were in competition to source the uranium needed to prime their burgeoning nuclear arsenals.

To neutralize this threat, the US facilitated the assassination of uncooperative Congolese politicians. Pro-Western leaders were lavishly feted, praised for their "good sense" and provided with massive amounts of "aid" and corporate "inducements" no matter how despotic their behaviour. Fingers can be pointed in many directions.

The prime beneficiary of this largess was President Joseph Mobutu, who was in power for thirty-three years and accumulated a personal wealth of $15 billion USD. The citizens of the DRC saw nothing of the kickbacks he received from Western governments and corporations. Instead of the "aid" being a boon to the local economy, living conditions deteriorated, chaos reigned, and infrastructure collapsed.

More recently, the world's love affair with all things battery powered has seen the massive harvesting of DRCs abundant lithium and cobalt reserves. Approximately 65 percent of the world's production comes from the DRC. An estimated 40 percent of that comes from artisanal mining. Specious terminology that masks the truth about the primitive conditions involved. The mining is done with hand tools mostly in open pit, mud-filled holes. The distribution and marketing of these valuable deposits are ruthlessly controlled and frequently fought over by armed gangs and militia. A significant percentage of these artisanal miners are children paid slave wages. Pit collapses, disease and death are everyday occurrences.

And how has the country fared as a result of all of its contributions to our convenient lifestyles? It has one of the lowest life expectancies in the world, it has over 60 million people living on less than two dollars per day, government is dysfunctional and 6 million citizens are displaced due to ongoing internal armed conflicts.

You can learn more about these travesties online, of course. As you do that you might want to reflect on the fact that you, in all likelihood, have a little piece of the Congo right in the palm of your hand. One of the essential components in your cell phone is a capacitor, it contains elements extracted from a scarce ore known as coltan. Over 80 percent of the world's coltan comes from the DRC. Mined under the same atrocious conditions as the lithium.

The world would indeed be a much different place were it not for the DRC.

Things aren't any more stable underneath the lake. The world's tectonic plates continue to shift, Africa has no exemption. The continent is ever so gradually being torn apart. Lake Kivu is again on the front line. The symptoms rather remind me of having had giardia in Nepal. The water in the lake is being rendered permanently flatulent as it is saturated with the methane and CO_2 that seeps up from the bed of the lake. This creates conditions that scientists fear could cause the lake to expel lethal gases, which could lead to perhaps an extinction-level event. Tell me about it!

On the shores of the lake, things are more bucolic but dicey in their own way. Exotic bird life abounds, decked out in spectacular iridescent colours, singing their heavenly songs. They teeter on the tops of the reeds and bulrushes using their tail feathers like a tightrope walker's pole to keep their balance. With tail feathers as much as a ridiculous five times their body length, how do they mate, build a nest, or find a pair of trousers that fit?

To the naked eye though, everything looks idyllic. When dusk settles in, the flowers exhale their intoxicating fragrances and we are blessed with perfection.

The next morning, we arrive at the Virunga Park headquarters. It is now entering Rwanda's peak rainy season and March typically sees in excess of thirty inches of rain. Up on the mountain, three or four inches of rain in an afternoon is nothing remarkable, so we may be pushing our luck a bit with our plans to hike up to the top of the 3,711 metre Mount Bisoke.

The Virungas are not only home to three active volcanoes but also the last eight hundred or so of the world's mountain gorillas. "Gorilla trekking" is a major draw for wealthy Western tourists and a huge contributor to Rwanda's economy. Despite the soggy prospects we haven't seen this many white faces since our connecting flight from Canada took us through Amsterdam.

On this day, however, we are not here for the fauna but for the stunning view over the crater lake at the summit. You can't go wrong with a volcano.

We are mustered with a group of four middle-aged French tourists and their tour guide driver, and five recently graduated Rwandan university students. Our accompaniment consists of Ferdinand, the lead park ranger, his assistant, two armed soldiers and six or so seemingly superfluous porters. We feel more like Stanley and his expedition heading off in search of the source of the Nile than going for a six-hour hike.

Our group assembled, we head off on our ascent. It is about an additional 1,100 metre gain in elevation from the trailhead to the crater lake. The initial approach is a gentle incline through agricultural land, mostly planted with spuds, quaintly called "Irish potatoes" in these parts. As we enter the park proper, the trail steepens significantly and the vegetation closes in. With the exertion, altitude, and heat, our energy is sapped quickly. Then a welcome coolness seeps in as some clouds obscure the sun. We pass the turnoff to Dian Fossey's tomb, famous primatologist and hot babe in the movie Gorillas in the Mist (no wait, that was Sigourney Weaver). Share a joke or two with our head ranger Ferdinand.

"Maybe you can send a gorilla to carry me the last bit. Ha ha."

We give Trixie's day pack to one of the porters, named Innocent, to carry. Support the local economy, no shame in that. We reluctantly accept a couple of walking poles freshly hacked out of the jungle.

The column starts to string out, the driver from the French team calls it a day as his group pulls ahead without him. Thunder can be heard in the distance. The trail gets steeper. I decide to help the local economy too and pass my day pack to porter Thomas to carry for me. The vegetation doesn't pose much of a challenge for Thomas, shimmying and swerving like Pele between flatfooted defenders, meanwhile, I swim, wrestle, and snag my way through the clinging bush like Johnny Weismuller.

There are black clouds overhead, it feels like the first hour after sunset instead of mid-morning. Flashes of lightning now illuminate the jungle of trees, vines and giant ferns. I am now thirteen years old again and living out Conan Doyle's Lost World, King Kong could pop out at any moment.

The first big fat drops of rain inevitably fall, with loud splats on leaves like the sounds of seagull shit on pavement. Splat! Splat! Splat! We get the rain jackets out double quick. We are nearly soaked before the real deluge even starts. We have been walking for about an hour and a half but are determined to press on. The thick clothing I've worn, gardening gloves and heavy long canvas pants have been great protection against the nettles and thorns on the foliage, but they are rapidly sopping up water and weight. One of the Frenchies has thrown in the towel and we pass her as she and a porter take a breather before heading down. The weather takes a turn for the worse; marble-sized hail pounds down on us, and the temperature drops by ten degrees in an instant. It is a slog now and the muddy narrow path becomes a rivulet. Ferdinand joins me at the tail end of our little band. I ask him how far to the top and he provides his blunt assessment: "It depends how fast you can walk but we turn around at two o'clock." It is now around noon.

We continue on a bit less enthusiastically now. One of the students now passes us valley bound as he slithers down the slope, his water-logged sports jacket his only protection from the elements. We are really starting to feel the cold now. My pants are cold and heavy, like lead, maybe rain pants would have been the better choice. Each step is treacherous and the trail is now a full-flowing stream, the sheer volume of water and the steepness of the terrain having created a virtual waterfall. We are treading in water shin deep in some places. After another half hour of this stumbling along, the others are out of sight and Trixie turns to me and asks me what I think. I turn to Ferdinand, by this time a caricature of the Grim Reaper, his black face obscured by the hood of his military-style olive poncho, which sags low over his forehead and the sheets of teeming rain. Standing stock still with his staff in hand, the time for wisecracking over. He is a presence in the gloom, exuding a mute aura of disapproval. He obviously isn't going to make this decision for us.

Ah well, we achieved respectability three quit before we did. Chances are the top would be socked in anyway. Time to cut our losses. Ferdinand assigns one of the armed soldiers and the porters Thomas and Innocent to descend with us. Going down turns out to be more tricky than ascending. Once we gain momentum, there is no way of stopping unless we reach out and grab some unidentified piece of jungle. So on several occasions we end up unintentionally or intentionally butt first in the goo or more often than not, the river.

The most ambitious manoeuvre of the day is executed by Trixie: a maximum degree of difficulty snowboard "trick" performed in miniature and ultra-slow motion. I can picture her now imperceptibly, slithering down her 1/1000th scale mud ramp, desperately trying to arrest her progress as she nears the six-inch precipice. But to no avail... as a last-ditch attempt she tries to jam her toes into the lip, which only serves to provide vertical lift. She launches off the slippery slope, a good foot of big air between her and terra gloopa, executing a perfect, albeit involuntary, 180-degree toe loop and lands with a splat. Alas, she fails to nail the landing. Her feet slide out from under her and with a soggy sploosh, she ends up face down in the muck, and now facing up the mountain. As she slowly rises like the creature from the black lagoon, the last shred of any hope for dignity is cruelly stripped away by the blob of mud on the end of her nose. A chocolate Coco the clown for the ages.

Any illusions about decorum now truly dispensed with, we bumble our way downhill for another two hours of a Buster Keaton on banana skins sketch.[3]

I have to admit that I am not totally beyond caring as the armed military escort is slithering just as badly behind me. He doesn't have a walking pole to steady himself, only an AK-47 primed with live ammunition about eight feet from the back of my head. This ostensibly to protect us from potentially harmful buffalo or poachers. The weapon looks to be one of the first of the roughly 100 million Kalashnikovs made. These crudely efficient pieces of machinery are reputed to be responsible for more deaths than air strikes, rocket attacks, and artillery fire combined. I have no desire to add to that dubious tally—I hope that his safety catch is still working. I'd rather take my chances with the critters.

It is a slow process, alternately slewing down the mud banks or creeping forward like a blind man on ice, groping for hidden rocks and tree roots with the toes of your runners, your feet obscured by the slurry of earth being washed down the mountain. Eventually we make it to the bottom and mercifully the rain has eased to a drizzle. The mountaintop however, still reassuringly shrouded in black clouds. We arrive at the car park just in time to see our Landcruiser depart, slowly rolling around a corner, then lost to view.

It would be a gross exaggeration to say that I run after it, but I do summon up my last reserves of energy and take off in pursuit. If you can envisage a duck out jogging you've got the picture. I reach the corner to see our Jeep now joined by half a dozen or so running figures disappearing over the crest of a hill and out of sight.

---

[3] https://www.youtube.com/watch?v=UWEjxkkB8Xs

Evidently, they are attempting to jump start the disobliging vehicle, which I seem to remember, rightly as it turns out, is nearly impossible to do with a diesel engine. Chilled and still in sodden clothing, I head back to the parking lot. Arms out from my sides, knees apart and bow-legged, I waddle along with a rolling gait reminiscent of a gunslinger who has pooped his pants.

Grumpy now, I fish out my cell phone and write Gilbert a terse text: "We are down now, where is the car?" After a few seconds mulling whether to add an exclamation mark to the missive, I refrain and press send. It is seriously bad form to lose one's temper here in Rwanda, and I have to say that in the four weeks that I have been here I have yet to witness a raised voice let alone a raised finger. Beats me how in 1994 these gentle smiling folks could have slaughtered their own friends, neighbours, and relatives in the most frenzied, brutal ways imaginable. One million souls butchered in one hundred days.

Minutes later, a spiffy newish Nissan Xterra rolls up and there in the passenger seat is our new driver Thierry, Gilbert's assistant. Having failed to start the Landcruiser, he had flagged down this good Samaritan, there are many in this country, and come to pick us up. Climbing aboard and sitting on plastic bags so as not to ruin the upholstery, we are driven to the afflicted vehicle. The driver pops the hood of his Nissan, a gaggle of advisors, half the neighbouring village it seems, appear out of nowhere and swarm around the engine compartment. Someone produces a pair of pliers.

After much chatter and gesticulating, a few flashes of electricity and bodies leaping for safety, the battery is eventually excised and carried to the Landcruiser. A few moments later with a roar and a cloud of black smoke, it is back in business and we are on our way with nary a backward glance. Help anyone you see in distress seems to be another of Rwanda's rules of the road.

Thierry's driving is a lot less frenetic than Gilbert's, which is a good thing given the state of these back roads. Gilbert's approach would have been a pedal to the metal and a hoot of "Get ready for some fantastic African massage" as you are having your fillings shaken loose.

We are delivered to Gilbert's boutique hotel the "Villa Gorilla," where we are treated like royalty, or the royal family, really. We are literally waited on hand and foot. Hot towels to wipe the caked-on mud from our face and hands. Shown to seats in front of a fire and then despite our protests, our shoes and socks are wrestled from our feet. Braziers filled with hot charcoal are brought to warm us. A fine simple dinner is prepared for us and we are shown to our unit. A comfy thatched cottage with, luxury of luxuries, a bed pre-heated with hot water bottles.

"WHY NOT!?"

Chapter 4
Haircut Consciousness

Of course I can see your point of view.

"One believes things because
one has been conditioned to believe them."

– Aldous Huxley

"Television to brainwash us all
and Internet to eliminate any last resistance."

– Paul Carvel

Wherever you are you, might as well try and stop the sun from rising as try and escape the chores of life. After a hearty lunch of fea, a tasty thick stew made from plantain, peanuts, and tomatoes, prepared by Pachia the watchman at our cottage, we set off on our walk to downtown Kibutarama, fifteen minutes away. Presently, a pretty young Rwandan woman engages us in conversation. She is walking in the same direction as us and is heading for the college. She has probably pigeonholed us as Mzungus, the not unfriendly term used in East Africa for a certain stereotypical white. This Bantu word was originally coined to describe the first white explorers who "wandered around aimlessly, usually lost." I can see why it is still as popular now as it was then.

She has graduated from university with a statistics degree but now cannot find a job. The president says that the country needs more entrepreneurs, it must be so, she is now studying commerce. She hasn't even been as far as Lake Kivu an hour up the road, but her faith about her place in the grand plan is firm.

Cash is king in this town, so we head for the most imposing building in town, the bank and its ATMs. It meets all my requirements for making cash withdrawals in an unfamiliar country: it's daytime, the area is well-lit, actually adjacent to the bank, handy when the power goes out mid transaction or when the machine eats your card, and well frequented but without a big lineup. This one comes with the bonus of armed security guards. They are decked out in blue camouflage military style fatigues and each sport a pump-action shotgun. I think I would be happier if the thieves took my money than be in the vicinity when they start blasting away with those things. My withdrawal completed after deciphering the keypad, which has enough options to do a tax return, I stuff my pockets with the biggest denominations available, five thousand Rwandan franc notes (about $6.70 CAD), we go about our business.

It's time for a haircut. By now you will probably be wondering if I ever see a barber in Canada or if I am trying to fund my trips with the savings from cheap haircuts.

Setting forth on the exercise in a strange country does add a little novelty, a little dab'll do you. Standing on Kibuterama's rust-red dirt main street, I scan the surrounding buildings, mostly single storey, with the odd two- or three-storey mixed-use office blocks. Trix is with me en route to the computer store, another inevitable chore.

We stand out like two white beacons and might as well have flashing lights on top of our heads in the midst of the otherwise uniformly black throng. I cast my gaze about seeking a barber shop. A guy across the street on a second storey balcony waves and gestures at me. He must be fifty yards away and yet he somehow seems to know what my mission is. I take my hat off, point at my hair, and he responds with an enthusiastic thumbs up.

I negotiate my way across the street, climb the steps of the unlit staircase and enter under the hand-painted sign proclaiming the "Miraculous Hairdressing Saloon" eagerly anticipating my transformation, or maybe a cowboy or two. The salon is pretty basic: four wooden chairs and four counters comprise the stations. There is one other customer being attended to by a dreadlocked stylist. The only concession to modernity is one wall mounted modest sized flat screen TV that pumps out hip-hop music.

I get off to a bit of a rocky start with my coiffurist, Pierre. I am talking combien for the haircut, he thinks I am talking combien hair to cut off. There is only so far schoolboy French learned fifty years ago will take you. Misunderstanding hopefully resolved, we get down to business. There are no scissors involved, just a well-used set of electric clippers that feel like they have never been sharpened. They work well enough when moving with the grain, but it is a different experience when applied in the other direction and it feels like I am being plucked rather than groomed. Back and forth, back and forth, side to side, side to side, the repetitiveness of the passes makes it feels like my cranium is being sanded down rather than shorn.

This already lengthy process is prolonged by the involved use of many different plastic guards on the clippers. I guess they aren't as robust as the clippers as they are missing several teeth and there is only one set that the two barbers share as they work.

Having called a truce on attempting a conversation in French, I settle in and start watching the TV's reflection in my mirror.

Africa's Top 40 is on, although it might as well be its top two for all the difference that I can distinguish between them. The videos all seem to be staged in opulent mansions with swimming pools and luxury cars prominently placed out front. Foxy black women in heels, dressed in leather straps that make them look as if they are bound up like the Sunday roast, sip champagne and pout their ample booties. In the foreground struts the singer: gold chains, baseball hat, meticulously trimmed facial hair, baggy clothed, grabbing his crotch with one hand, waving the other with pinky and forefinger extended.

I think it is safe to say that they aren't singing "Count your blessings one by one" or "Love thy neighbour." It's nice to see that the youth of the continent is being coached to aspire to such noble goals. They just better be in a forgiving mood when they eventually figure out that all they are going to get are the two fingers.

White man speak with fork tongue and rapacious carpet bag.

I settle in and put my fate in the hands of my miracle worker. With my full belly, the midday heat at its peak, and the rhythm of the clippers lightly massaging my skull, I assume a broody, meditative mood, my mind idles in neutral. This detached state allows the subconscious to percolate up to the conscious level and thoughts start to coalesce into something resembling a cohesive train of thought. Judge for yourself how cohesive.

I have had the luxury of having gone "media light" for the past few weeks. The boss Mrs. Stella doesn't even do e-mail preferring to deliver her orders in person, they do carry a bit more urgency I have to say. Living this more muted reality I begin to wonder if some of what we do just does not seem to make any sense, is deliberately wasteful and lacks any altruistic or redeeming purpose. Waste is common all over the world, it's all around us and when we live amongst it, we become blind to it. When we travel, those blinkers tend to fall away. If we can fully disconnect ourselves from home, so much the better. The more detached we become, the more likely we are to find ourselves questioning what we would usually accept as normal.

We are all susceptible to confirmation bias: a trick that the mind plays on itself. Confirmation bias decides that what it is familiar with is actually the most sensible option compared to what it is unfamiliar with. These biases may develop over generations and be built on the basis of successes, experiences, and trial and error and so they aren't easily shaken, even when the current circumstances have changed and those biases deserve to be challenged. When different viewpoints, values and ways of life don't conform to the baked-in bias of the dominant culture, they are often dismissed as uninformed. And so it is in the developing world, where the developed societies boldly hold forth on what is needed for a healthy society. Its confidence outweighing its competence in actually delivering a better life for the majority of people. The endless quest for growth, the emphasis on quantity over quality, the assumption that change is the same as progress, is all starting to look a little shaky now.

Expectation management isn't part of the game plan; it is a constant stream of materialistic propaganda about a few getting rich quick. And I thought the missionaries were messing with people's heads. It remains to be seen how Africans will react when they realise that it is all empty promises, when the revolution of rising expectations degenerates into a revolution of frustrated expectations. Is it any wonder that the African political landscape is such a shambles? Those frustrations aren't unique to Africa and we are already seeing the beginnings of the end game starting in the US, Britain, Russia, and France, with more to follow. It is naïve to think that the poverty divide will be solved in Africa by emulating Western strategies, when that model is starting to unravel in the North.

The problem should be no surprise; it was anticipated decades ago. But we only hear what we want to hear and when President Carter tried to sound the alarm, it pretty much doomed his presidency. [4]

The myth that capitalism and democracy go hand in hand is being challenged. Money means power and as the money is shared by fewer and fewer, the power becomes more concentrated. There is no democracy in that.

Aid to Africa is often dismissed as a waste of money and an exercise in futility. There is no denying that corruption and failed programs are commonplace and serve to reinforce this cynicism. But there are successes too. Small volunteer charities are often the most effective at building lasting relationships. Seemingly modest initiatives that none the less bring tangible benefits. A rural village that we visited had been supplied with miniature wood burning stoves, a huge improvement to the old open hearth fireplaces previously used for cooking. Respiratory health issues are already improving due to the reduction in smoke in the homes. The forests are being depleted at a slower rate due to the efficiency in burning the wood and the villagers

---

[4] https://www.youtube.com/watch?v=dedzkxCQOag

can save a few RWFs by not having to buy so much of it. It's not a perfect solution but for as little as thirty dollars, a unit is a positive step in addressing a real problem.

Using wastefulness as an example, we find it a lot easier to spot it in others than in ourselves and yet I still stump myself when I turn over in my mind, "If there are hungry people the world over, why do we spend $600 billion a year on advertising?"

It is a mega business that predominantly preys on our human weaknesses, fear, greed, and envy. The goal is to exploit these frailties to the maximum extent possible and foment dissatisfaction within ourselves and about our lives. Then having created our discontent, we are offered the cure for our worries. All that is required is that we spend our money on the product or service that is being hawked. It is pretty hard not to view this whole cycle as a waste of money and emotion, especially when to add insult to injury, we have the cost of creating these elaborate deceptions embedded in the price that we end up paying. And if that isn't enough, everyone hates the imposition of advertising, yet we all tolerate it in silence, like car alarms, clam-shell packaging and Boris Johnson's haircut.

"Well, it is good for the economy." That is true and sadly the economy has become our master and a heartless one at that. By some estimates, there are 690 million hungry people in the world and the number is on the rise again. Someone needs to have a word with the economy. Someone should take out an ad.

Maybe WPP plc (the largest ad company in the world, with $17.3 billion in revenue, dwarfing Rwanda's national GDP of $10.3 billion) could spin something along the lines of: "Feeling anxious? Not getting enough sleep? Do we have a cure for you! Try giving up advertising for a year!

If we all do this together we will save $600 billion. Just think, no more ads for the Clapper, never see Matthew McConaughey again, and you can stop trying to figure out what jojoba oil is.

And that's not all! You will save, save, save! By giving up ads you could give every hungry person a thousand dollars a year for life."

Meanwhile until that happens, here in Rwanda, the youth in particular, with their increasing access to screen time, are the target audience. The timing of this phenomena could hardly be worse as the hype cycle reaches hypersonic levels. These young people are being incessantly baited with the promise of untold riches, the lure of bright shiny objects that dangle just out of reach. The celebrity wealthy are admired as role models by many of the impressionable, well-educated, and potential future leaders of the nation. Money is achieving the same status that it has in the West.

These luminaries would seem to be strange and worrisome idols to have in countries where even basic food and shelter aren't guaranteed. A motley crew of big shots, predominantly paternalistic, male, white, privileged, Harvard and Stanford educated.

These barons are probably nice, ordinary people, businessmen of course and vacuum cleaner salesmen. The Bezos (a digital shopkeeper), Zuckerbergs (social media developer, who got his inspiration from the creepy Hot or Not rating site), Gates (a computer programming geek), etc. All competent in their own narrow fields, but their only real genius was in their ability to create monopolies that would expand and dominate the global marketplace. Highly efficient economic vacuum cleaners that aim to suck up every available dollar from around the world. It's bad enough that these strategies entrench and exacerbate financial inequity, but more frighteningly, they indiscriminately and recklessly change the dynamics of society. Money has given them the scope to influence our lives far beyond their capabilities or wisdom. Using knowledge without wisdom, we are starting to learn, has a lot to answer for. And yet our governments continue to pander to their excesses, hob nob with them and solicit their advice. Asking the crew of the Titanic for tips on navigation would make as much sense.

This nouveau royalty is learning to be circumspect about their wealth and hide behind the walls of their estates and palaces, which are kept closed to the public.

Maybe it is time that we dusted off Plato's philosopher king concept and give it a closer look. Do we want our communities shaped by powerbrokers whose fundamental objective is profit and the power that comes with it?

It's a question that we would rather not face. As a result we have already unintentionally entered into a Faustian bargain, trading our essence for convenience and short-term savings.

The monopolies are in the business of selling convenience and they are good at it. Convenience: a stealthy seductress who has already started to eat away at what makes us unique as individuals. We have outsourced our taste in music to Spotify, our power of recall to Google, our memories to Instagram, our numeracy to Excel, our relationships to Facebook, our libido to Pornhub, our sense of direction to Google Maps and our storytelling ability to Netflix. Are we being reduced to the status of some sort of aimless receptor motivated only by instant gratification? What impact is this having on our brains? They are already shrinking in size.

Society is becoming smarter and more complex. But can the same be said about people? Is it reasonable to expect that we can continue to grow as individuals when our being is in danger of being drowned by our own feedback loops, virtual living, and a shrinking diet of real real-life experiences and interactions?

There is every reason to expect that the people here will be just as blind to the unintended consequences that come along with the quest for material wealth as the developed world has been. They can look forward to a building tsunami of depression, obesity, addiction, neurosis, slums, loneliness, widening inequality, increasing rates of incarceration, homelessness, pollution, soaring crime rates, Celine Dion Christmas albums, and suicide. Confoundingly, the dream destination for many Rwandans is the US, the world's richest country and a leader in all of these categories.

Pick any one of those problems in the US and have a closer look and it will reveal a society in deep trouble. Incarceration for example: the number of people in custody in the US is scarcely believable at over 2.1 million, growing by nearly four times from a little over half a million in 1980. There are another 4.7 million citizens on parole or probation. A total number equivalent to the entire population of greater Toronto: 6.8 million. Every man, women, and child subject to a fate even more wretched than being a Maple Leafs fan.

Income inequality also burgeoned during this same forty-year period. It would seem clear that the two trends are more than coincidental. And somehow, heedlessly, the solution chosen to address the problem is to imprison more and more citizens and let that inequality grow unchecked.

Yet the true cost of the mansions, the trophy wives, the fast cars, and the chains of gold never enters the conversation. The latest and greatest, the new and improved is hyped as never before, bedazzling us at every opportunity. For many a Rwandan, optimism trumps all and the promised land lies just across the ocean. We wouldn't dupe them again, would we?

Maybe Rwanda will be bypassed in the quest for development. Rwanda, just getting started may be better positioned being free of the scourge that has afflicted so many other African countries. The curse of natural resource wealth has been a mixed blessing that has devastated society in numerous other African nations: the diamonds of West Africa, the oil of Nigeria, the gold of South Africa, and Congo's rubber and coltan. How many civil wars, refugees, corrupt regimes, and how much inequality and ecological devastation has been fomented by foreign enterprises, white, black, brown, and now yellow? Of course, we are all complicit; it pays not to think too deeply about where our gasoline, wedding rings, and chips for our computers come from.

Phew, that was a lot to take in in one haircut. So what to do? What else but settle up five hundred RWF (about eighty cents), provide a generous tip of one hundred RWF. I pay in cash—no visa machine.Head back out into the sun, time to put my hat on, go get a beer, and focus on important stuff like:

What will the Canucks do now that the Sedins have retired?

Is there gluten in those cookies?

How did my stocks do this week?

Which brand of tooth whitening strips has the new active ingredient? Because I am worth it.

What kind of car should I buy when I get home? The old VW doesn't really say who I am anymore.

Better get some more toilet paper while supplies last.

Oh, and a new vacuum cleaner—the one that beats as it sweeps as it cleans.

Chapter 5
Monkey See, Monkey Do

Someone tell Monique to shut her mouth.

"IN THE HOPES OF REACHING THE MOON, MEN FAIL TO SEE THE
FLOWERS THAT BLOSSOM AT THEIR FEET."

– Albert Schweitzer

"I'LL LET YOU BE IN MY DREAMS IF I CAN BE IN YOURS."

– Bob Dylan

JC urges me to see as many of the highlights of his country as possible during our stay. The fact that he hasn't seen them himself is pretty much a convention world wide. At his suggestion, I tack on an extra day to most weekends. I have a suspicion he just wants a bit of a break from all my helpful advice, you know, so that he can absorb it better. Yeah, that's it.

Getting about is relatively easy. In many ways Rwanda is like the Switzerland of Africa, buses run on time, there is no garbage, the people are polite if somewhat reserved, there are more rules than you can shake a stick at and there is a functioning bureaucracy that is only corrupt at the higher levels. Hillsides are lovingly tended, there are orderly fields, dairy and honey are specialties.

The colonials instilled a very Catholic morality in the culture. The tables have turned, tourists those godless, strange smelling heathens from the West, with their tribal tattoos and shameless nakedness, are often just tolerated rather than welcomed. This too will doubtless change, but for now, better have a wash and cover up if you want to interact.

Modesty in action as well as dress is important too. It is not an "if you've got it, flaunt it" culture. Amongst the poorer classes it isn't proper to eat in public unless you are willing to share liberally. Whether this originated out of village tradition or as a survival strategy caused by the genocide I don't know, but it does speak well of being considerate to those less fortunate.

Confronted with a caravan of bus companies, Horizon, Omega and Volcano, all seemingly heading to our destination, we buy our ticket from the agent with the "We Go Deeper" T-shirt, having shunned the ticket seller with the black shirt emblazoned with "Drive for Thrills" above a skull and crossbones.

The rural routes are usually serviced by Toyota Coaster minibuses from the 1980s. They carry about twenty-four people when the dickey seats that block the aisle are folded down. We take the bus southwest to the Nyungwe Forest National Park. These trips are entertainment in themselves. They are social events, interaction amongst strangers is commonplace, singing along with the bus radio is an everyday occurrence.

I might be viewing things through grey-tinted spectacles as I enter the last quarter of the game of life, but in situations like this, I can't help wondering if there are not lessons to be learned here. The developed world teaches the developing world to aspire to be bigger and better, without at the same time acknowledging that the world is collapsing under the weight of those advances; it is the not so obvious elephant in the room. Is there not a lesson here that the teacher should be attempting to relearn, this time from the pupil? How to appreciate the small things and take pleasure in the simple.

Rural roads are quiet, there are more cyclists than vehicles. Rwanda's two-wheeled Sherpas are everywhere and this terrain is brutal on them. The downhill sections are the most lethal; the riders lower their jewels onto the crossbar, one flip-flop skimming the ground. It is the only compensation for the brakes that wore out years ago. All manner of cargo is transported by these two-wheeled truckers: three milk churns, lumber crossways, four crates of beer, hay, and a passenger or sometimes even two in the city. They aren't above hiring additional help en route, it is common to see collaborators pushing their load up hills, two to a bike.

The buses often only leave when all the seats are taken, so they usually are full. It's not chaotic but certainly intimate. On one side of my middle seat I have a mom breastfeeding her baby. With every swallow, the babe reflexively prods me in the ribs with her foot. Her leg motion is like she is trying to kick-start some invisible miniature motorcycle.

An elderly lady villager, who seems a bit unfamiliar with the whole setup, a first time rider, I suspect, sits on my other side.

The mountainous serpentine roads and combination of bald tyres and intermittent deluges make for some tense moments. The senior citizen pulls her scarf over her head, for a nap maybe. Ah nope, that doesn't sound like any snoring I've ever heard "ralf, urgh, blugh."

We are nearly there, and I try to occupy my mind with pleasant thoughts but keep coming back to the logistics, like hoping that the little plastic bag she has dug out is at least as big as her stomach.

Footnote for those of you that like to plan ahead: one litre is a stomach's normal capacity but depending on how much of a piggo you are, it can distend to up to four litres.

I try humming songs but can't shake Gerry Rafferty's "pukers to the left of me, pokers to the right, here I am, stuck in the middle with you."

Thankfully, without further ado, we arrive at our destination and disembark from our Volcano bus to be greeted by Monique, our twenty-something guest house manager and general factotum. She is a giggler, with a smile that could melt an iceberg from where we are standing one hundred miles south of the equator. I have never seen a set of teeth like these, perfection in every aspect: uniformity, number, spacing, and the colour, a blinding white. A battery of halogen lights on high beam that dazzle and mesmerize. As her lips close, shuttering the laser beams, my eyesight readjusts to the more tolerable lumens emitted by the sun. Her raven hair gradually comes into focus, spectacularly gleaming and braided into serpentine coils, a Medusa's nest framing an angel's face.

This kid is going places, she plans to go to university so that she can "earn a lot of money."

It is only fair that I share my worldly wisdom, so playing the philosophising old buffer, I sagely counsel her that "money isn't everything."

She pauses for a moment, then thoughtfully replies,

"If God helps me, it will happen. I need that money so that I can open an orphanage."

Well hush my mouth.

Monique helps us hire a Jeep to take us to our chimp trek. The park ranger takes us and another five trekkies into the bush in search of our closest living relatives. I am not sure that that is quite true; I am pretty certain that my son shares more than 98 percent of my DNA, unless my wife isn't telling me something?!

We are in luck. After an hour or so of traipsing through the jungle, we beat the fifty-fifty odds of sighting our cousins. Firstly, it is the pant hoot, the soundtrack to every Tarzan movie ever made, that helps us zero in on them. Then like an inverted terrestrial version of Moby Dick, our guide spots the spout, and THAR SHE BLOWS! The golden shower. With all the vegetation that the monkeys eat, they are prodigious peers and it pours down from on high. We spend the rest of the hike eyes peeled on high alert for active shooters.

Not surprisingly, given that the chimps spend 95 percent of their time up there in the trees, there isn't much in the way of eye-to-eye contact. Aw shucks, a couple of furry specs twenty-five metres above us and a few decent peeks through the binoculars is the extent of our family reunion.

Our knowledgeable guide fills us in on the scandalous swinging dynamics of the group to keep us interested. Apparently, the Alpha male gets first dibs with the females and may copulate up to twenty-five times a day... Much shuffling ensues as everyone simultaneously grabs for their binoculars again. Lenses lift skyward, but no... we are too slow and have caught Big Butch just after a dalliance. He is stretched out on a branch, one arm behind his head, an ankle crossed over his knee, smoking a cigarette, looking pretty satisfied with himself. Of course, having missed the "act," I may just be revealing my binary gender biases. At this distance, I may have totally misgendered him/her/they. This could be the kind of linguistic mistake that might have the virtue vigilantes setting their hair on fire.

Here are a few tips for the unenlightened.[5]

Other non-X-rated entertainment is available. We add on an eco-tour visit to a rural village. It is lots of fun, more like joining in on a kibbutz type operation than a typical show-and-tell experience. Jean, our guide and translator, hands us our plantation mattocks, which he jokingly refers to as Africa's laptop and has us join the ladies in the field digging up our lunch: cassava. It is a full-cycle activity whereby you plant the next crop as you are harvesting the current one. The Portuguese brought the tubers from South America in the 1600s. It is still a big hit and is the major source of food for the Sub-Saharan continent and may be eaten as many as three times a day.

For lunch we are having a special treat. The maize is also ready for eating and we are given the job of roasting it over an open fire. After lunch we learn to weave baskets, like we are contestants on an Amazing Race challenge. We are spared the prospect of elimination, as we are the only competitors and there are many legs still to be completed. Our teachers are a female ensemble of all ages, complemented by a troop of young children. At the end of the day, we share a cup of tea, sing a few songs, dance a bit and relax.

---

[5] https://uwm.edu/lgbtrc/support/gender-pronouns/

As evening approaches, it is time for us to return to our guest house. We chat with the matriarch of the group, a grandma, who thinks that she is around eighty years of age. She is reading the Bible to her six-year-old grandchild, her own daughter Deveen is illiterate. The Belgians left a nascent education system behind when Rwanda was given independence in 1962 but many of Deveen's generation were deprived of the opportunity to go to school when the country's internal strife escalated during the "lost" decade. We say our thank yous and take our leave.

The sun bursts into our room on the last morning of our extended weekend. Up early our muscles stiff but eagerly anticipating a jungle trek into the nearby unspoilt rainforest. More often than not, you must hire a government naturalist to accompany you on these walks. Fabrise will be our guide for the day. He is well trained, well informed, and rightfully proud of his parks. Sure, we might end up on some slippery neck-breaking paths, but they are still better than the routes that you could find yourself on. Well worth the investment.

At over two thousand metres, it is cool here despite the sun. Incongruously, Fabrise escorts us into the park via a tea plantation, tea being Rwanda's second largest cash crop after coffee. Jungles are like no other places. Everything has a smothering three-dimensional claustrophobic intimacy to it. Dank greenery envelops you, chokes off views and obscures the sky. You have the feeling that you are walking inside something not just alive but animate.

Lush vegetation, beautiful birds, and complete solitude, what more could you ask for? At this particular trail's end is a magnificent waterfall. We, like so many explorers before us, pretend that we have found the source of the Nile. We are on the continental divide, just the wrong side; this particular river will flow into the mighty Congo River and travel west to the Atlantic.

"This is an amazing place," I say to Fabrise.

"Yeah," he agrees, beaming proudly, "it is, you know."

Arguments still rage over the actual source of the world's longest river but since 2005, it has been accepted that it does originate in another part of this forest before travelling over 6,700 kilometres to the Mediterranean Sea at Alexandria.

This geographic connection also fed the tenuous theory put forward by hate propagandists that the Tutsi ethnic group were essentially foreigners originating from Ethiopia. Just one of many false truths used by the inciters to whip up the hatred that led to the horrific events of 1994.

The scars of that tragedy are still evident to this day. Whether you are a Rwandan or a visitor, the reminders are inescapable.

Chapter 6
The Hundred-Day Hell

"Nearly all men can stand adversity, but if you want to test a man's character, give him power."

– Robert Green Ingersoll

"There is a higher court than courts of justice and that is the court of conscience. It supersedes all other courts."

– Mahatma Gandhi

Before a trip I feel the need to do a bit of homework about the destination, especially one like this one. None of the usual sparks of memory are logged. Capital? Location? A mountain? Ancient civilization? Resort? Celebrity may be the closest contemporary point of reference. That would be their current president, Paul Kagame or His Excellency, as many a man in the street refer to him without a hint of irony.

But there really is only one thing that Rwanda is famous, or rather infamous, for. So we watch the movie Hotel Rwanda, read Shake Hands with the Devil, and take in a documentary or two. Mercifully, the quality of the videos' witness to the atrocities is poor, blurry figures in the middle distance performing unspeakable acts, butchered bodies littering roads. The first genocide filmed by bystanders as it was actually happening.

No matter how long or short your stay might be you cannot escape the presence of the genocide. It seems that every one of the villages or towns settled amongst the terraced hills and green banana plantations has a memorial. Where to start?

It goes without saying that it is possible to do too much research. What you learn from media will shape your preconceptions or in this case cause me to frame my initial impressions in the context of the genocide. During the first couple of days after arrival, my mind would try and reconcile those media images with the current reality. On my early morning walks to work, it would be near silent in the town, the chirp of bird song, the sweep sweep, sweep sweep of twig brooms getting kitchens ready for the day. Then I would hear the swish whack, swish whack of a machete. The machete, also known locally as a panga, is Africa's multi-tool and in the villages, they are more prevalent than cell phones. As I approach the sound, I see a middle-aged man hacking at the thick scrub that was growing on the verge of the road: an unmistakable motion. He pauses, looks up at me for a moment in silence, the eighteen inches of broad bladed rusty steel dangling down from his hand, then bends back to his chore.

Neurons involuntarily firing in the brain, I find myself thinking, "What was this fifty-year-old guy doing twenty-five years ago?" Further on, I pass through road construction, courtesy of the China Land and Bridge Company, and see various layers of exposed strata of earth. The red earth in places is flecked with white specs resembling crushed sea shells or gravel. I think that they must come across the remains of victims, who, if they weren't left to be consumed by packs of dogs who had gone feral, were often left to rot or be buried where they were killed.

The next day, rounding the corner from the small lane where our cottage is located onto the main road, I see a dead body in the middle of the road. I freeze on the spot, too big a jolt to the brain to formulate any coherent thought. As I slowly draw near, I see a truck with a smashed in grill and the outline of the corpse becomes clear. A dead calf that foolishly wandered onto the road during darkness and was hit by the truck, I assume.

Three mundane commonplace occurrences, yet my awareness is primed with images of genocide-elicit dark thoughts, giving me severe, though temporary, cases of the heebie jeebies. But what about the same sort of trivial events that the Rwandans experience every day? What real life lived through horrors are triggered in their thoughts? It is a whole country with post-traumatic stress syndrome (PTSD). One wonders how much has been repressed, pushed to the furthest corners of consciousness and yet life must go on. When the choices are few, that may be the only available coping mechanism.

Ten thousand people a day slaughtered for one hundred days so some estimates go. Nearly one million victims of the genocide that started in April 1994.

The majority militant Hutus had gone on a rampage in an attempt to eliminate all the Tutsis, who comprised about 15 percent of the population, as well as all the moderate Hutus. Tens of thousands, possibly hundreds of thousands, participated in the butchery. The regular army, militias known as the Interahamwe, bloodthirsty mobs, and regular citizens all played a part. Friends, classmates, neighbours, children, strangers, even relatives if they were moderate or not extreme enough in their views were prey. Neighbours shoulder to shoulder, cheek to cheek in church, praising the Lord, "Hallelujah," one week, then chopping each other up the next.

There were no extermination camps, mass roundups, or killing fields. This was a hunter and hunted scenario, which saw people literally fleeing for their lives. In all too many cases, people were slain in their homes, cut down at road blocks, massacred in their churches, besieged in their schools, or hacked to death in the streets. An ever diminishing band of terror struck survivors trying to stay alive in a literal zombie apocalypse nightmare.

The horror would continue until July 1994, when the rebel Rwanda Patriotic Front (RPF) army, which had invaded from neighbouring Uganda, captured the capital Kigali.

The town we are staying in, like most in the nation, has its own story. The Catholic Kagbayia Cathedral had become a place of refuge for thousands of fearful Tutsis. Churches had been spared as places of safe haven during previous times of unrest. It would be different this time.

A group of government soldiers encircled the church grounds, ostensibly to protect the refugees from the blood thirsty militia. Once the complement of soldiers and militia swelled sufficiently, they went about slaughtering captives. The clergymen reported that approximately 1,500 of 30,000 were killed.

The cathedral's clergy and Red Cross representatives were Hutu and were unharmed only to be executed later by the advancing RPF rebel army. And so it was to be for one hundred days.

The post genocide fallout was ongoing. The population of the country fell by over a quarter from seven million in 1990 to five million by the end of 1994, as a result of the genocide, refugee exodus, famine, and disease.

Western help started to appear, a bit late you might say. A UNICEF study at the time estimated that 57 percent of children had seen someone either killed or injured in a machete attack, a tragic 82 percent had seen dead bodies.

The return of Paul Kagame's triumphant RPF Tutsi army reputedly showed a surprising amount of restraint. Accusations of retaliatory killings in response to the genocide are few. But the fog of war can obscure much, as Hitler is quoted as saying, "The victor will never be asked if he told the truth."

Calm, shrewd, and polite, Commander Kagame had received military training at Fort Leavenworth in Kansas, and he was well-known as a pragmatist and tactician. He was well aware that his army and the Tutsi themselves were hugely outnumbered by the Hutu populace and he knew full well the worst thing to do would be to alienate the moderates or seek revenge on the perpetrators. Who knows, it may have been purely out of humanitarian ethos; he wouldn't be the first front line military leader to be repelled by the futility of killing.

In short order he went about reconciliation and building goodwill. Pasteur Bizmiungu, a Hutu, was appointed president, with Kagame as vice president, though clearly the de facto leader. A new national flag was unveiled, English replaced French as an official language, all references to ethnicity were outlawed, dogs having reverted to packs of wild animals that survived by feeding on human corpses were banned, corruption was punished, and capital punishment abolished. A constitution was introduced in 2003, which mandated a minimum of 30 percent of the seats in the legislature be filled by women. As of

2016, 64 percent of the seats were filled by elected women (the US had 19 percent at the time).

None of this alone could raise Rwanda from the ashes without justice and reconciliation and the faster the better.

In the aftermath the courts were clogged. Many of the judiciary were implicated in the crimes and had to be tried, so they fled the country. The legal system was in a shambles. Jails built for twenty thousand housed six times that number. It was expected that the case backlog would have taken two hundred years to address.

In 2001, an innovative approach was instituted, a grassroots justice system called Gacaca courts. These local hearings were administered by respected citizens of the villages where the alleged crimes took place. Even then problems arose. Twenty-seven percent of those chosen as Gacaca judges by their fellow villagers ended up being disqualified when it was discovered that they in some way participated in the genocide. By the time that the system wound up in 2012 over one million Rwandans went through some form of trial. Over 80 percent of the trials resulted in a conviction, tellingly none of the RPF army were even prosecuted.

As far as the truth goes, it was determined at a Gacaca court in 2009 that the priests and Red Cross workers present at the massacre at Kagbayia Cathedral had been complicit in luring the Tutsi into a trap. The actual death toll was finally revealed to be a much higher estimated 64,000, men, women, and children, many simply buried alive.

This grassroots approach to justice was criticised but had obvious benefits evident when contrasted with the more traditional court proceedings instituted to try accused Cambodian genocide perpetrators. A judicial system established in 1997 had as of 2014 cost over $200 million and completed just one case.

There is no doubt that the Rwandan process was badly flawed, but it did contribute significantly in finding out the truth about what occurred, making justice timely, providing a safety valve for victims to have their suffering heard, and most importantly, for the community to confront its own problems. They would continue to be neighbours after all.

Kagame's reputation continues to grow, he is undoubtedly a charismatic leader. His pride in his country and bold visionary plans make him popular with the citizenry, and he is careful not to over promise.

There is a price to pay for all this single-minded determination to better the nation. It is out of the question that everyone will agree on how to go about reform. There are increasingly voiced concerns about his intolerance for criticism, influence of the press, the suspicious deaths of political dissidents living overseas, the heavy-handed restrictions imposed on religious activities. There is no doubt, though, that his formula thus far has been good for the nation.

The standard of living has steadily improved; Rwanda consistently ranks near the top of the least corrupt and best places to do business lists for Africa, health and mortality indicators are improving, society is peaceful in a very troubled region, it is all very "normal." The means so far seem to have justified the end. And yet it does raise the interesting philosophical question, "Is it better to have a generally benevolent dictator than a corrupt democratic government?" One thing is for sure, democracy isn't a panacea.

But what of the future? Kagame has effectively been in power for twenty-five years and has as yet resisted the temptations available to an autocrat. He is no post genocide kleptocrat, the likes of Cambodia's Hun Sen, but still power does have a habit of corrupting. What if the power as in this case is bestowed by the populace?

He had made it known that he wouldn't run again when his term expired in 2017, but in response to the outcry from the public for him to remain, caused the Rwandan constitution to be amended by plebiscite in 2015, to allow a president to sit for three terms instead of two. Kagame duly won a seven-year third term by a 98 percent landslide victory in 2017. At fifty-nine, he is still a relatively young man and his successes to date must further cement his faith in his own infallibility. But what happens when confidence morphs into arrogance? The country has no real Plan B.

The unvoiced question as to whether enough progress has been made that another genocide cannot happen again here still haunts the national psyche. There may be more clues to be found to answer that question by looking back rather than forward. Why did the genocide happen in the first place?

Chapter 7
Method in the Madness
Is Still Madness

Let us know how it turns out.

"I DO NOT WANT TO MISS A GOOD CHANCE OF GETTING US
A SLICE OF THIS MAGNIFICENT AFRICAN CAKE."

-King Leopold of Belgium

"THE BITTER HEART EATS ITS OWNER."

– Bantu Proverb

Rwanda generally went about its own anonymous business until the late 1800s. Being as far away from the oceans as possible meant they were safe from the Arab slavers on the east coast and the European slave trade on the west coast. Explorers Stanley and Livingstone came close to being the first Europeans to set foot in Rwanda, when they travelled through the region in 1876. Why? Because it happened to be close to the source of the Nile, the goal for their expedition.

Duly noting its existence, the insubstantial information was relayed back to Europe, where its ownership was magnanimously assigned. During this period the scramble for Africa was full steam ahead. Establishing commercial trade routes and extracting resources was the name of the game. As the opportunities became more apparent, the nations of Europe became more interested, empire building was the mindset of the times.

Wise men there were put to work doing the tedious job of drawing international boundaries on a map that didn't yet exist. It wouldn't be the last time that the Rwandans own means of governance would be used against them. So at a conference in Brussels in 1890 a few dudes decided to add it to German East Africa, though the first German to set foot in Rwanda wouldn't do so until four years later. The Rwandans were of course oblivious. Next time my buddies and I get together after a round of golf, we can have a beer or two and decide how we would like to divvy up Mars between us. Yeah, I know, it couldn't happen again. But wait no, the Musk, Branson, Bezos empires have already started cluttering up our atmosphere without so much as a by-your-leave.

Things cruised along with little change for the next twenty or so years. Little did the Rwandans know that the gunshot that was heard around the world would take its deadly toll even in this backwater. The assassination of Prince Ferdinand in Sarajevo would truly put them on the road to hell. WW1 came and mercifully ended in 1918. And as is usual, to the victorious go the spoils. In 1919, the League of Nations entrusted Rwanda to Belgium.

A curious choice indeed, based on which criteria it is hard to fathom. Belgium a scant fifteen years earlier had been tagged as an international pariah for its abuses in its only colony, the vast Congo, Rwanda's neighbour to the west. [6]

'Abuses' is putting it mildly. In a money-driven frenzy to exploit the huge mineral wealth of Congo and satisfy the world's new love affair with the automobile by harvesting the huge forests of rubber trees, morality went by the wayside. Any and all means were used to coerce the local inhabitants into the work. Kidnapping the wives of the subjugated plantation workers, whipping underperforming indigenous people, amputating hands, and generally enslaving the locals. Estimates of the death toll between 1895 and 1908 range from four to ten million. All this after the Western world had agreed to abolish slavery some one hundred years earlier.

Meet the new boss, worse than the old boss.

In any event, Belgium had so many lucrative irons in the now Democratic Republic of the Congo to devote much time to "developing" Rwanda's meagre resources. And besides, the Rwandans already had a handy governance structure in place that the colonists could readily adapt for its own purposes.

Rwanda, small but the most densely populated country in Africa had three communities of coexisting peoples. Literature describes the situation as being more of a class system than a strict tribal delineation, maybe like the distinction between our urban and rural dwellers. Whatever the anthropological terminology might be, the groupings were: Tutsi, 15 percent

---

[6] https://www.youtube.com/watch?v=FhPZZqp9cp8

(tall, cattle herders), Hutus, 84 percent (generally stockier in stature, farmers), and Twa, 1 percent (pygmy forest dwellers). As with any class system, there were elements of envy, rivalry, and distrust. A pretty normal simmering tension that would doubtless have taken their society through the usual push and pull of the evolutionary process.

The Belgians, however, were to stack the deck in the Tutsis' favour and in doing so, turn a simmering dissatisfaction into a pressure cooker of resentment, which would eventually explode with a huge toll. The Tutsis were to be the Belgians' agents, their government in absentia. Giving the Tutsi a few weapons would also help to solidify their power status. They would be given preferential treatment in all walks of life. All the plum administrative assignments including tax collection went to the Tutsi, and educational privilege was systemic; about 80 percent of the children in school were Tutsi, and eligibility for education was often determined by the children's height or the number of cattle owned by the family. So to use a metaphor, the Belgians put the lid on the pressure cooker, lit the gas under the pot, then left the kitchen.

In 1935, the Belgians further reinforced this apartheid-like discrimination by requiring the populace to carry ID cards stipulating their "race." Owning one of these cards was still compulsory when the genocide happened in 1994. The Tutsi were in effect carrying their own death sentence in their pockets

In the 1950s and 1960s, a wave of Pan-African independence movements swept the continent; self-rule was the order of the day. Colonial powers had no choice but to surrender their control. The story in Rwanda was no different.

Belgians had started to try and redress the imbalances that their system of Tutsi privilege had perpetuated and exacerbated, but to little effect; by this time, ethnic violence had started to surface. By now, things had come to a tipping point.

Over time it became clear that it should be majority rule after all and that it was time for Belgium to throw in the towel, cut their losses, and get out. And so with a tip of the hat and a, "You guys can take it from here, mon amis. We think it's time you guys had a democracy, how about the Hutus? Good luck with the election, anyway we're off." That was that.

Elections were held in 1961, and the Hutus swept into office. The Hutus, bitter from the decades of subjugation under Tutsi governance, enjoyed their new found power. The shoe was on the other foot now and of course the Tutsis, like everyone everywhere, didn't want to give up their perks, still they would have to take the full brunt of the changes. Tens of thousands of Tutsis fled to neighbouring countries, among them a three-year-old boy and his family who crossed into Uganda. His name was Paul Kagame. Revolutionary forces of a kind were already evolving.

Over the next three decades, Rwandan government was formed through coup or elections, with a one-party-only ballot. For a while the economy made small improvements but corruption grew and as progress faltered, the populace became impatient and a Hutu Power movement was established and gained momentum.

The French, who had edged out Belgium as Rwanda's most influential ally, were predisposed to support the Hutu government, even though their human rights abuses were becoming well known. The English-speaking Rwandan Patriotic Front (RPF) were seen as another Anglo-Saxon threat to Francophone influence in the region, an echo of the US sentiment in South East Asia, when they supported the genocidal Pol Pot regime in fending off the North Vietnamese.

The superpowers "my interests are the most important interests" mentality still as pervasive as ever.

The French obliged the Habyarimana government, hoping to achieve two things, keep some Francophone allies in the region and stabilize a democratically elected government. Neither of these things as we now know worked out in the long run. The French supplied the regime with a surfeit of arms, the impoverished nation spent $112 million on weapons and military training in the three years before the genocide. The joke making the rounds at the time was that it was easier to come back from the village market with a couple of hand grenades in your basket than pineapples.

Many of the Tutsis displaced by the purges in the 1960s were still exiled refugees in neighbouring countries, and they wanted to return home. They formed militia and in the late eighties and early nineties, they made incursions into Northern Rwanda, ostensibly to force the Rwandan government into having meaningful democratic elections. These raids had the opposite effect and created alarm amongst the Hutu, who feared that the Tutsi were making a grab for a return to power. The president at the time, Habyarimana, something of a moderate, had been in talks with the RPF, with the goal of establishing a peaceful transition to power sharing. These negotiations resulted in both parties signing the Arusha Accords in 1993. The hardliners in the president's coterie saw an opportunity to divert attention from their own incompetence by a change of tactic. They would weaponise the familiar lightning rod of ethnicity.

The Rwanda catastrophe has often been simply dismissed as a run-of-the-mill tribal hatred gone out of control, an oversimplified and wildly inadequate explanation. Each genocide has its own core issue, whether it is religious like the Nazi hatred of the Jews, ethnic like the Serbians hatred of the Muslim Bosnians, or ideological like the Khmer Rouges hatred of the bourgeois, but they have common root causes too. So what are those common causes? How did things come to this in Rwanda?

Economic deterioration, political confusion, pathological authoritarian leadership, unresolved previous conflicts, an assumed ideology of superiority, tradition of obedience to authority, toxic media, and fear of loss of power. All of the conditions for disaster were coming together. None of these problems were being addressed. Yikes, does this sound like any neighbours near you?

The hardliners instead singled out one factor as the root cause of all the country's problems—the Tutsi. The anti-Tutsi sentiment was fostered at every opportunity. Us and them rhetoric was rampant, cartoons and graffiti caricaturing Tutsi proliferated, dehumanizing name calling became commonplace, the term inyenzi or cockroach was commonly used to refer to the Tutsi. For months radio stations' broadcasts were almost exclusively devoted to racist propaganda, fear mongering, conspiracy theories, and scapegoating. Real news and debate were impossible to find. I'm really getting nervous now!

As hysteria and paranoia grew, mobilization plans became feasible. The organisers got busy. There was distribution of free weapons by the Hutu government, machete supposedly in the name of civil defence. Militia were formed. The most radical supporters were given the task of preparing hit lists of prominent Tutsi and moderate Hutus. Anxious village officials were co-opted into directing their citizens to inform on the whereabouts of their Tutsi neighbours, and ultimately to participate in the slaughter.

Peace and order were hanging by a thread. On April 6, 1994, President Habyarimana was flying back from a conference in Tanzania, when his plane was shot down just before it was about to land in Rwanda's capital of Kigali. He would not survive. To this day, no one knows for sure whether it was the hardline Hutus or Tutsi rebels who fired the rocket that brought about his demise, both groups had motives to do so.

The death of Habyarimana was the spark that set in motion the final phase of the plan, mass extermination of the Tutsi.

And where you may well ask were the colonisers and opportunistic exploiters who were the cause of this toxic brew?

The UN had dispatched a peacekeeping force to monitor the implementation of the Arusha Accords, a rag tag contingent of 2,500 who arrived in dribs and drabs in the country over a period of five months up to February 1994. Poorly trained and equipped and hamstrung by the constraints of the mission's mandate, any hopes of being a moderating force in what was to transpire was thwarted before it even began. Ten soldiers from the Belgian complement of the UN force were slain the day after the president was murdered. Shortly thereafter, the Belgians withdrew their remaining four hundred troops.

The commander of the UN contingent had plead with the UN bureaucrats for reinforcements of five thousand well-equipped soldiers. The international community dithered and debated and eventually decided instead to reduce the UN presence to only 450. These few brave souls did save many lives by creating protective cordons around a few defensible locations, sheltering Tutsi and moderate Hutus. Other than that, they were abandoned, destined to be impotent observers of the horrors going on around them.

Belgium, Britain, and the United States evacuated their citizens, well aware of the misery they were leaving behind, and lacked the political will to do anything to stop it, either independently or jointly through the UN.

France also rescued their compatriots but had a bigger plan in mind. Their goal was to establish a safe zone in the southwest corner of the beleaguered country. No one else was volunteering, so the UN gave them the green light. A questionable decision given France's cosy relationship with the government that was the driving force behind the genocidal rampage. Nonetheless, Operation Turquoise was launched and 2,500 French troops, jet fighters, armoured cars, and helicopters arrived in late June and secured the region.

We visited one of the country's most poignant genocide sites at Murambi, also located in the southwest of the country. Sixty-five thousand Tutsi had gathered at the technical school, lured there by promises from the mayor and bishop that French troops would provide protection. The protection evaporated and all but a dozen of the sixty-five thousand were killed. According to our guide, the French later brought in bulldozers to dig mass graves. Many of the bodies were later exhumed, the heat of the decomposing corpses had effectively mummified the remains. Thousands of the cadavers are on display, stacked in spartan, bullet-pock marked classrooms, thigh bones piled like kindling, bodies preserved in lime, plaster of Paris-like skeletons, ghostly white mummified bodies, twisted and grimacing in their last moments of terror. The paratroopers had paved a volleyball court over the top of one of the burial pits. A literal attempt at a cover up? Our guide seems to think so.

Resentment towards the French still lingers nearly thirty years later. Who did they create the safe zone for? Why didn't they take any action until their Hutu associates were on the run? Were they really only motivated because they wanted to prop up the regime and prolong their standing in the region?

The Tutsi had already been decimated before the safe zone was conceived of never mind established. The safe zone came to be a refuge for the Hutu genocidaires, who were now to become the refugees in front of the advancing RPF army. Immune behind French lines, they reactivated their radio station and continued to incite more hate and more killing of the Tutsi. Not one of the killers was arrested. As it became apparent that the RPF would prevail, the Hutu, now fearing the end, began to flood across the border into Zaire (now DRC) in the hundreds of thousands. The French disarmed the regular soldiers and militia men at the crossings and passed the weapons to the Zairean authorities, who promptly gave them back to the perpetrators.

The French had long cemented their influence in the region by being the second biggest supplier of arms to Africa. This Franc-Afrique stratagem presumably developed in the belief that a strong government is a stable government. Strong governments armed and trained by the French had opened the door to many lucrative trade deals. Zaire, a former Francophone colony, was also a huge arms customer.

The madness finally ended on July 15, 1994, when the RFP announced victory and a ceasefire.

Twenty years after the genocide, Ban Ki Moon, Secretary-General of the UN, delivered an address in Rwanda's national stadium in Kigali. It was packed with foreign dignitaries (the French were not invited), and solemn Rwandans. His closing words were the all-too familiar,

"We must not be left to utter the words 'never again, again and again."

Chapter 8
The Big Game in Tanzania

Shuka cloth with all the trimmings.

"ONE MORNING I SHOT AN ELEPHANT IN MY PYJAMAS. HOW HE GOT INTO MY PYJAMAS I'LL NEVER KNOW."

– Groucho Marx

"WHERE IGNORANCE IS BLISS, 'TIS FOLLY TO BE WISE."

– Thomas Gray

We take our leave of friendly Rwanda via a short flight from Kigali to Kilimanjaro International Airport in neighbouring Tanzania. Dense clouds obscure our view of Africa's iconic highest mountain. It is the beginning of the rainy season so this is not a surprise, but a disappointment nonetheless. After a comfortable hour's ride by minibus, we arrive in Arusha, known as Tanzania's safari capital, a town of about half a million. It's an "outpost of the West" where English and the US dollar are ubiquitous, as it acts as a gateway to the local attractions, namely Kili, the Serengeti, the Ngorongoro crater, and Massai villages.

It's easy to spend a couple of leisurely days sampling the various ethnic cuisines available, lounging by the pool and making arrangements for our five-day safari (a word meaning "journey" appropriated from the local language Swahili).

Before heading off, we opt to spend an afternoon taking in the sights of old town Arusha, modest as they may be. Pre-warned about the bothersome "flycatchers" as the touts are known here. We decide to run the gauntlet and set out on foot. Before we have even left our street, one of the aforementioned latches on to us. At first, we engage in friendly pleasantries, but inevitably the conversation steers in the direction of his sales pitch. Our polite refusals are less and less politely received, until finally he tries to shame us into giving him a "gift" by saying that only racists would deny him a few dollars. It is an uncomfortable ten minutes or so before he finally relents.

As we approach the Old Clock Tower in the centre of town, we are tagged by another tout, who introduces himself as Sedu. Before Sedu gets a full head of steam, I pre-empt him with a fiendish defence.

"Establa Espagnol" I blurt out in mock bewilderment, shrugging my shoulders by way of added Iberian authenticity. At the same time, we exercise cunning ploy number two by ducking into the corner convenience store, before I have to use my only other Spanish phrase: "Tapas Ole!"

Our stalker does an about-face and heads off, tail between his legs. After a few minutes browsing the predictable merchandise in the store, Johnny Walker whiskey, Pringles potato chips, tacky tee shirts etc., we emerge onto the sidewalk. Before walking two steps we are again confronted by Sedu, this time with an accomplice known as Hombre. Hombre now takes centre stage and engages in some long diatribe, would you believe it, in fluent Spanish! The game is well and truly up, smooth move, now we have two limpets to contend with.

Conceding defeat, we each now have a personal guide and given that they are both affable, knowledgeable and the fact that of course they don't want any payment (because they are just proud to show off their city and practice their English) helps. Uh huh.

Anyway, we are treated to an excellent walking tour of the city, the produce market, the museum, the bat tree, the Uhuru monument, and the old bus station. Irritatingly, a visit to the one site we really wanted to see, the Massai craft market, is last on their list of priorities and seems to be forever deferred.

These guys are reassuringly well known in the neighbourhood; jokes and handshakes are exchanged with various stall owners and citizenry. Sedu and Hombre's Wikipedic knowledge of the history and politics of the country and area are well worth whatever price we will eventually have to pay (we hope).

Not that the information flow is one way; boy can these guys pump you for info.

"How long have you been here? How many children? What kind of souvenirs are you looking for?"

They missed their calling; they should be working at Guantanamo Bay. They fill in any dead air time chattering away in Swahili on their cell phones. By some extraordinary coincidence, we bump into Sedu's brother, a taxi driver, who happens to have a parcel for Sedu to deliver.

Finally, we head for the Massai market. As we come within about one hundred metres of the entrance, Sedu stops he tells us that because he isn't Massai, he isn't welcome here; it's an awkward moment. We prepare to say our farewells; we've been with these fellows for close to two hours by now. When I offer them a few dollars for their expert guiding, they flatly refuse, affronted that I should pay given that we are now friends. I have a hunch that this isn't going to be the end of our relationship.

Just as we are about to go, Sedu says, "You did say that you are interested in Tinga Tinga paintings. I am an artist and my brother just gave me back some paintings that he was trying to sell for me. It would be an honour if you would look at them for me," unwrapping the parcel as he is saying this.

So ten minutes later and after much conflicted haggling, we are seventy-five dollars lighter and the proud owners of three rare Tinga Tinga paintings. These paintings are a Tanzanian specialty, surreal caricaturish, stylised, and totally distinctive. It seems like a good compromise, we have a nice keepsake and they get some cash, with their pride intact.

Conscience salved, we carry on to the market, curious to see what exotic wares they may have on offer. We walk through the entryway and are stunned with a vast array of birds, elephants, giraffes, and fish, all in startlingly bright primary colors. Tinga Tinga paintings, each and every one of them. Every imaginable size and style available for as little as five dollars.[7]

I should watch more of the Mission Impossible series.

---

[7] https://www.youtube.com/watch?v=pJhSfGzjEck

The next day, looking to do something where we don't have to be quite so alert, we head into wild animal country. Our ride rolls up to the front door of the hotel at the appointed time. Introductions complete, we clamber aboard the vehicle. It's a Landcruiser, one of thousands specially customised in Tanzania for the tourism industry. A pop-top roof, fridge coolers, chargers for your cameras and gadgets, radios, GPS, spare water and tyres, reinforced crash bars, comfy adjustable seats, all spic and span.

Our first stop is at a Massai village, several of which are dotted along the highway en route to the parks. We aren't the only visitors, this obviously is a well trafficked attraction. There is no doubting the authenticity of the setting or the living conditions, but it is a commercial operation, which includes an entry fee and plenty of opportunity to buy trinkets and souvenirs.

We are treated to the Massai war dance and a tour of the coral, or village. Our guide Wilson is a Massai warrior, one of the chief's sons. He is dressed in the traditional Shuka cloth, a sort of wrap-around shawl with a plaid check design of bright reds, blues and blacks. Body piercings are de rigueur, silver medallions, chains and amulets dangle and sparkle. Men and women dress alike. It makes an awe inspiring sight, like some blinged-out Highland gathering, which might not be too far off the mark.

Wilson is an absolute riot and a patter merchant. When I ask him if it is difficult for the Massai to move about freely when their traditional lands encompass parts of Kenya as well, he tugs on his Shuka and says, "This is my visa."

When he shows us the tight little mud sleeping quarters, he offers that we can stay the night "at a better rate than on Expedia." Other special offers include his mother, who is available for "a very reasonable price, only fifteen cows." It is common knowledge that the actual going rate for a bride is only ten cows.

One of the theories goes that Scottish missionaries tried to convert the Massai to Christianity and trade their cow skins for cloth. However, the conversation is reputed to have gone along the lines of, "Nah, not interested in the Christianity thing, but we'll have those blankets tho' and now if you know what is good for you- beat it."

So you are probably wondering, commando or no? All I will say is that draughtily, the same undergarments are worn under Shuka as are worn under the kilt.

The haute couture may not be the only thing that was left by the Scots that the Massai value, there seems to be some culinary crossover too. Their whole diet seems to be based on some sort of "I dare you to..." challenge.

Raw blood, milk, meat, maize and porridge are the staples.

It wouldn't be fair to dismiss this nascent theme park feel as a crass money grab at the expense of their heritage. It seems to me to be more like a pragmatic solution, which may serve to extend some of that traditional way of life. Not much different than the need to open the grand estates of Britain to the public in order to survive, except that the exhibits here are larger than life, living, breathing, proud people rather than suits of armour.

Our first night is spent in a very upscale resort carved out of the bush, private bungalows surrounded by spectacular manicured tropical gardens. This really is a theme park, a lake and waterfall will be installed within the year to complete the jungle's transformation into an international destination wedding site. The question to me is, why come if the only time you feel like you still might be in Africa is when the watchmen walk you back to your house from the dining room?

The well-heeled guests are a newish cosmopolitan mixed tribe, the 1 percenters. No longer is there the preponderance of nationals from countries experiencing economic booms, first the Americans, then the Japanese, then the Germans. Now Russian, Hindu, Spanish, and Arabic are all audible in the dining room. Wealth has gone global as it has been shared less.

All the opulence seems a bit silly after our visit with the Massai. We need a bull horn to communicate with each other across our cavernous bedroom, where it's all imported this, thread count that, granite countertop the other. Our en suite bathroom has gone to the extreme absurdity of having its own en suite, where the throne sits in isolation. We each have a massive bed bigger than the square footage of a Massai sleeping room, none of it really our style or as you probably have guessed, our budget. Sleep like babies.

The next morning, our driver Moses whisks our baggage away and shows us to our newly washed and vacuumed 4X4. He's a very likeable guy; he resembles a middleweight version of the boxer George Foreman, solid and powerfully built but with a charming almost cherubic demeanour. The impression is reinforced by his mannerisms, he is a hand talker, particularly when he drives. He lifts his mitts up to his temples, like he is fending off jabs to the head.

We are lucky to have him, it is only thanks to this being the off (wet) season that he is available. The less senior seasoned guides tend to be laid off at this time. Fortunately, but for a few spectacular distant thunder and lightning displays, the weather holds for us. As a result of the rain, the grasses are longer and thicker, which makes spotting the wildlife more difficult. This and the fact that this isn't the season for the wildebeest migration prove to be no more than a potential excuse for us to go back for another visit.

The spectacular lush vistas, lack of dust, absence of traffic jams (it's true it happens in the dry season!), and price more than compensate. Nevertheless, it does seem an expensive vacation, park fees alone of seventy dollars per person per day. That is until you think about what you get: three million living attractions in a 15,000 square kilometre lost world that is magnificently suspended in time, including the massive Ngorongoro volcanic crater and the endless plains of the Serengeti (Serengeti means endless plains in Swahili). I guess we could be spending $160 a day for a Disneyland pass.

The days touring the parks are rewarding. The big five natch, and as a sampling, five hippos swimming, four lion cubs a laying, three kori bustards, two dik diks dicking, and a partridge in a Baobab tree. Me in my conning tower, binoculars around my neck like Rommel, scanning the horizon for my quarry, a lull in the action - nothing out there.

As Moses, typically speeding along pot holed rutted roads, swatting at tsetse flies, informs us, "That smudge on the horizon is a heart wildebeest; you can tell by the shape of the horns, and that is a warthog and some more lions on the right."

I raise my binoculars, which are actually useful here, not just the extra baggage they have been on so many other trips, and focus.

"Yup, that's a wildebeest. How did you know that it is just not a rock?"

He replies, without a hint of irony, "I know all the rocks out here. And there isn't a rock out there."

Why do I even bother when we have Moses? Of course, it is the thrill of the unexpected. Every moment is a cliffhanger, who knows what we will see, or where, or when.

Then, with uncharacteristic urgency, Moses spots a cluster of Jeeps all painted the usual Afrika Korps khaki in the middle distance, jostling for prime position beside a lion. Rather than take the direct route toward them, he takes a longer loop, which brings us in front of the direction that the convoy is heading, perfectly timing his arrival so as to rendezvous with Leo, who is effectively being herded in our direction by the gaggle of vehicles. He walks right by our window, close enough to see his breath condensing with the cool morning air. He is a solitary male bearing the scars of a fight, probably with a dominant male. If you want the girl in the lion world you have to prove your cojones in battle, if you lose you are destined for a lonely life (except for all the photographers). With a turn of his head and sniff of the air, he turns off the road into the thick grass and vanishes. Within a couple of minutes the convoy melts away as they head off in different directions looking for new targets.

Moses now backtracks, he espied something curious as we were making the dash to the lion. This time it was a lump on top of a rock that shouldn't have had a lump on top of it. As we near, it becomes apparent that the lump is a beautiful lioness. Moses kills the engine and we coast the last one hundred metres right up underneath the rock. She is about fifteen feet from us and four feet above us. An easy hop for a hungry carnivore like this. We timidly pop our heads out of the roof of the Landcruiser, take picture after picture, speaking in low tones like we are David Attenborough, thinking maybe she won't notice us. Duh, she is staring right at us!

Moses reassures us that no one has ever been attacked when they have stayed inside their vehicle, he figures she is taking time out from shopping, enjoying a bit of free time sunning herself on the rock. The lionesses are the ones that get the groceries for the hubby who gets first serving and then the kits. The lion spends his energies being macho and chasing off other males who might come sniffing around his women folk.

It is a signature moment from the safari, the three of us have ten minutes alone with her, it is an image never to be forgotten. Soon enough, another Jeep spots us and the throng reassembles. Our time starts to wind down, I get antsy and frequently check my watch, not out of impatience rather a reluctance to see the last minutes drift away.

Our drive back to Arusha is uneventful, passing through rich agricultural land and rolling hills, catching glimpses of the foothills of Mount Meru, which at 4,566 metres is no shrimp but Kilimanjaro, its loftier (5,988 metres) more famous neighbour, remains stubbornly shrouded in mist and cloud.

"Hakuna matata" as they say round these parts. Which I am edified to find out is Swahili for "no problem." I hope that Disney is paying copyright to someone for that!

Chapter 9
Fair Is Foul And Foul Is Fair

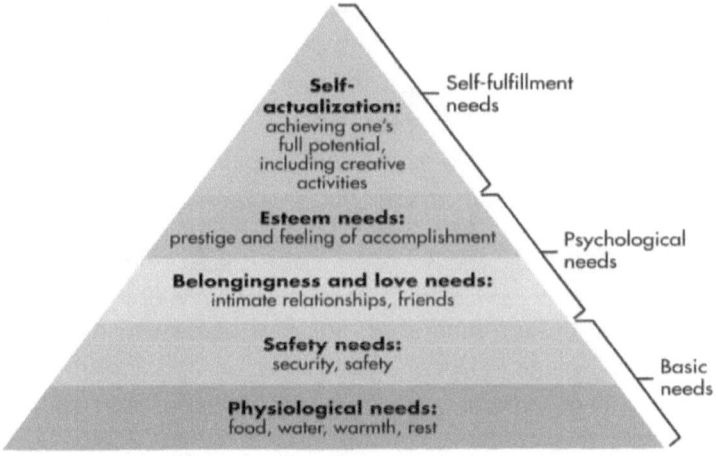

It's all about periwinkle this year.

"IF MEN WANTED TO LOOK GOOD IN A SKIRT, THEY WOULD NEED THE BODY OF AN AFRICAN. AND THE COLOUR. A SKIRT WITH WHITE, SKINNY LEGS. HORRIBLE!"

– Yves Saint Laurent

"PART OF BEING OPTIMISTIC IS KEEPING ONE'S HEAD POINTED TOWARD THE SUN, ONE'S FEET MOVING FORWARD."

– Nelson Mandela

Two years after our first visit, we are again back in Africa, memories of our last trip are the bait that lure us there. The big smiles, the youthfulness, the vitality, the unexpected experiences of daily life in a foreign land.

Trixie set off two weeks ahead of me, and is staying in a small village in rural southeastern Rwanda. It lies adjacent to the Bugasera River, which was chillingly known as "the shortcut home" during the genocide. A grotesque metaphor attesting to the thousands of Tutsi corpses that were dumped in the river, which were then carried by the current back in the direction of their mythical ancestors in Ethiopia.

On our last trip, Trix had befriended a group of young Rwandan men who had established a local NGO called Journey House Actions (JHA). As a fundraiser, she had been working with a number of village weavers who were creating basketry to be sold in North America. The funds have been used to help support a local early childhood development facility, where local kids get some basic schooling, a nutritious cup of porridge once a day, and it also provides a safe welcoming place for the mothers to meet and drop off their children so that they can work in their fields.

It's mainly an agricultural way of life. Things may change, as Rwanda's new international airport is in the process of being built about an hour's drive away. Sixty percent of the funding is being provided by Qatar Airlines, with an opening date scheduled in advance of the commonwealth conference due in June 2020. An interesting turn of events in itself, Rwanda never having been a colony of Britain. The Rwandan government changed the official language from French to English in 2008, and as a final thumbing of the nose to France, sought and was granted membership in the Commonwealth of Nations in 2009 (The British Commonwealth until 1949).

There are important lessons to be learned here, most of the lessons are being learned by us as visitors. The majority of the JHA founders work as part of the team whenever they have spare time but also have regular jobs in the city. As an ongoing presence, there is Marcus, the executive director and three assistants, young Rwandan women on twelve-month work experience assignments. It's a low overhead operation, the staff quarters would be considered very modest in the West, but a concrete floor and an inside toilet are very chi chi by local standards. Appointments include two wooden chairs, a one burner stove and three bedrooms with basic bunks. A plastic garbage can, replenished daily with buckets of water filled at one of the community water wells, is used for flushing, washing and cleaning. Meals are taken communally, sitting on a woven mat on the floor, eaten from a large plastic tray and whomever is there at the time is given a fork and everyone gets to tuck into the shared food. Trips to and from the city are taken either by bus or rented car, the society doesn't own a vehicle. Pets aren't really a thing, although every morning just before dawn we are woken by a colony of bats returning to the attic above our bed. Animal to human transfer of viruses via bat has yet to become much of a concern.

Everyone pitches in. The team, as they matter of factly refer to themselves, seem to unthinkingly lead by example. Whether the toilet needs cleaning, the steps need sweeping, the garden needs digging or the dishes need washing, it could be anyone who takes on the task. The founders, now men in their thirties, were pre-teens when the 1994 genocide happened, raised by single mothers with many children, not always all their own. Marcus recalls his mother saying, "What's one more mouth to feed?" when taking in an abandoned child. He already had seven siblings. Their characters have been shaped by knowing what it is to be hungry and homeless but at the same time seeing what compassion and determination can achieve. These fellows all seem to have some sort of a Ugandan connection; they have either lived, been raised, or were born there. Refugee camps for displaced Tutsis were established there to deal with the collateral damage of earlier civil wars and attempted revolutions. Those conflicts go back as far as the 1960s. Now "home" in Rwanda, their passion is to be involved in building a better inclusive country for all its people.

There is no glamour in the day to day, year to year commitment of these young leaders but there are rewards, huge rewards, in the smiles and gratitude that the villagers have for them. The modus operandi seems to be that laughter is easier to share than power. I am sure that these examples of goodness are universal and that there are those in our own communities that are just as dedicated and just as anonymous, but it sure brings it home seeing it first-hand.

The village itself is unremarkable. I try to get tech savvy and do some research via the "Maps Me" app on my phone, not that helpful. It proclaims, "no points of interest found." What a fantastic endorsement, it sounds to me like the twenty-first century equivalent of "there be dragons here." The fact that there is nothing worth seeing here must surely make it worth seeing. There are no monuments, geographical landmarks, unique wildlife, imposing buildings, fancy shops, tours, etc., but there are a lot more than two and three dimensional experiences to be enjoyed.

We visit the home of the head weaver, Vestine, to see how she prepares the dye for the baskets that they are weaving. Invasive water hyacinth is harvested from the nearby lake and will be dipped into the vats of dye before being transformed into beautiful pieces of art. Her husband machetes limbs of wood into manageable sized logs and feeds an open fire in their back yard. Atop the fire sits a large cauldron of water, which she brings to the boil. It's a scene from Macbeth.

Double, double toil and trouble; Fire burn and cauldron bubble.

Her expertise is plain to see. Without the benefit of scales or measuring cups, she confidently adds dollops of dye from a variety of bags into the vat. Dunks sample sheaves of sisal into the boiling brew and flawlessly matching every colour sample that Trix provides.

As the alchemist and her devotee descend into the finer points of lilac versus periwinkle or maybe a half shade lighter powder blue, I am rescued by the teenage son, Evode, who offers to give me a tour of their home. Although it is close to midday, it takes a few moments for my eyes to grow accustomed to the dimness of the unlit interior of the house. Inside, the three room home is clean and tidy, the hard packed earth floor is spotless. Evode shows me around his humble home, it doesn't take long. He proudly shows me his kettle, his parents' room, the bedroom he and his three siblings share and the living area, which features an immaculate but threadbare couch. On the way out he points to the heavy padlock on the door, which looks like the most expensive possession in the house.

Back at the cauldron, the debate continues. Perhaps another dab of "eye of newt," a little less of "toe of frog," "wool of bat and tongue of dog" will provide the magic combination. In any event, it falls to Marcus, showing remarkable endurance, to provide the translation services. While the controversy regarding the market trending toward arctic blue and away from Capri are debated at length, Evode and I settle in for the long haul. I teach him how to play tic-tac-toe. He provides a piece of wood to write on and I provide the pen.

A few more laps of the chromatic spectrum later and it is time to take our leave. Although I have barely met Vestine and we know maybe a half a dozen words of each other's respective languages, I receive a hug like I've never had before. I'm not sure if I am getting a reverse version of the Heimlich maneuver as I am squeezed so tight that I can feel the air being evacuated from my lungs. Simultaneously, my back is being kneaded like a piece of dough, an intense massage given by powerful hands used to digging in the fields and weaving baskets for hours at a time.

I have to admit that it wouldn't be the only time on this visit that I would get a little misty. I can try to write it off as the jet lag, the smoke from the fire, or the declining testosterone levels. Apparently, the average guy in his sixties will only have levels of about 60 percent of what they had in their thirties. I suspect that there is some sort of Invasion of the Body Snatchers scenario going on, where testosterone is being transferred from men to women during the night, hence the confusing later in life phenomena of women mustaches and man boobs.

The homes are mostly made of local mud, shaped into brick and baked in the sun. Very eco-friendly and recyclable. If neglected or abandoned, the heavy rains in the wet season will eventually dissolve them back into the earth. Where there are few opportunities to make money, sustainability becomes a factor in much of the activity.

Kitchen gardens have been built next to many of the homes [8]. To look at their state of dilapidation and neglect you would expect the JHA guys to be discouraged. Maybe that is just my Western mindset at work? "Let's get on with it, why can't you see what a good idea this is and just do it?"

But then how do you measure progress? How do you distinguish progress from just change? Anything that's easily measured— deadlines met, units produced, dollars invested here—wouldn't

---

[8]   https://www.echocommunity.org/en/resources/825acc09-8402-4b59-9fb9-58c611efdd6c

impress a management consultant. But there are strong fundamentals at work. Community buy in, collaboration, sharing in successes and failures, joint ownership and mutual experience. Seemingly small principles that we all are supposed to have learned in kindergarten, but that seem to have gotten lost in our quest for growth.

Such distinctions are pretty low on the list of priorities of daily life when you are at the base of Maslow's hierarchy-of-need pyramid. When worry about water, food, and shelter is a daily reality and the weather can make the difference between eating or not, it's not surprising that health, education, plumbing, and electricity aren't at the top of one's mind. Self-actualization—what's that?

The JHA feeds 120 preschoolers every day and there are another 140 on the waiting list. The kids are proud and enthusiastic about their learning. The school uniforms are sewn by local tailors and we have the privilege of helping the new pupils put their new clothes on for the first time. A chaotic but happy event for the noisy confident youngsters, but probably a form of child cruelty for the shy ones getting their small heads stuck in the too tight head openings in their uniforms. Help is on the way, the JHA recently sponsored an apprenticeship for a bashful orphaned teenager to become a tailor, she's now proud as punch and never seen without a tape measure draped around her neck.

The volunteers don't work all the time, they often take to the local pitch for a game of soccer. This evening they are playing a team of refugees who are housed in a camp known as the Emergency Transit Mechanism (ETM).

The camp is situated on the fringe of the village, it's a tidy facility resembling an architectural mashup of a 1980s school and motel. Built in the last five years, it houses roughly seven hundred refugees, who have been flown here from Libya.

The complex is surrounded by barbed wire and the gate is tended by military police armed with AK- 47s. The purpose of the security is unclear. Whether it is to keep the refugees in or unwanted lookie-loos out is anyone's guess, people seem to come and go as they please. After a half hour of general milling about, we wander inside.

The internees are almost exclusively young men who have volunteered to be relocated to the camp which is run by the Rwandan government on behalf of the UN. They have already made dangerous overland journeys from their homes in Eritrea, Chad, Nigeria, Sudan, etc., to Libya and now they have opted to go through official channels and have their eligibility for asylum assessed here in Rwanda.

While they wait, they linger in the ETM, in the relative comfort of four solid walls and are favoured with indoor plumbing, regular meals and a small allowance to spend. It is safer than undertaking their original plan which was to make the perilous voyage across the Mediterranean in the hopes of slipping into Europe. To date, some fifteen hundred of the refugees diverted here have been successfully relocated to North American, European and Scandinavian countries.

It's a model that the UK government was hoping to adopt before human rights activists raised concerns. It is an irony not lost on the local villagers that the ETM residents enjoy basic benefits far beyond what are available to them in their daily lives. The transients' funky haircuts and unblemished clothing are extravagances beyond their own meagre means.

The game itself is competitively played in a collegially sporting manner. Dodging the odd goat and an honour system on agreeing where the invisible sidelines of the playing area are, add a bit of unique flavour to the proceedings.

On the last weekend of our visit, the team and the beneficiaries have a campfire in the evening, where we listen to some music, dance and relax with a bottle or two of banana beer. Very relaxing given that the banana beer comes in at a hefty three-for-one punch, 15 percent alcohol level. Apparently, the party wound down at 3 a.m.; a couple of the intern girls who are Muslim are up in time for prayers at five o'clock!

The room grows hotter, it's another cassava sunrise. Today we will head back to Kigali where we will spend our last night before flying out. Justin, another of the volunteers, despite our protests, has vehemently insisted that we stay with him and his heavily pregnant wife. Their first child is due on March fifth. It is March fourth today.

The first notes of Marcus's morning anthem stir the silence. Ryan Shupe's "Dream Big" at full volume on his cell phone. It's time to get up and be on our way.

Chapter 10
Just Visiting
Greta Thunberg's Dream

Every home should have one.

"IF I AM A DICTATOR, IT IS BECAUSE MY PEOPLE WANT ME TO BE. I AM A DICTATOR OF THE PEOPLE, BY THE PEOPLE, AND FOR THE PEOPLE."

– Hastings Kamuzu Banda

"EVERYBODY WANTS TO SAVE THE EARTH; NOBODY WANTS TO HELP MOM DO THE DISHES."
– P.J. O'Rourke

Here we are.

In a land of free-range cattle and organic fruit and vegetables. The sky is blue, unblemished by carbon emitting aircraft. The people are young, smiling and beautiful. Heavy goods are transported by bicycle, people travel mostly on foot. The corn grows tall, towers over your head and is ubiquitous. A holiday of a lifetime might be an epic one-hundred-kilometre drive to the eponymous lake. Community is everything and everyone knows your name. Homes are biodegradable, renewable mud brick. It is just after the rains, everything is lush vibrant greens.

Are we in Eden or maybe in Greta Thunberg's dream?

No, we are in Africa's warm heart, Malawi.

We have flown in from Rwanda and I am here to volunteer with an NGO, which gets its funding from a mixture of sources including a charity based in England and the UN. The needs are familiar, as are the programs to address them. Food security, health, education, job skills, and environment are the priorities. My assignment is scheduled for six weeks.

I won't be offering any tips on environmental responsibility. Malawi lies about 1,300 kilometres southeast of Rwanda. Such is the state of the infrastructure and lack of direct flights that our route entailed a mini air tour of Africa. Kigali (Rwanda), Entebbe (Uganda), Addis Ababa (Ethiopia), Lubumbashi (DR Congo), Lilongwe (Malawi). Or put another way, 4,900 kilometres, or for each of us about 486 KG worth of CO2. All I can say is, it's a big continent.

Before being too judgmental, try calculating your own carbon footprint before you book your next trip. [9]

---

[9] https://www.icao.int/environmental-protection/Carbonoffset/Pages/default.aspx

Well maybe instead I can give them some wise advice about controlling birth rates now that I am done with procreation. Nah, I am on some pretty shaky ground there too. The average Canadian produces about 15.1 metric tonnes of CO_2 a year, the average Malawian .083 metric tonnes. Or to put it more bluntly, 360 Malawian kids would produce less CO_2 than my two offspring. So controlling birth rates alone isn't going to be enough to curb our impact on the planet. Still, I vote Green, does that count?

It is a young country and it does feel a bit like you have stepped into an Afro Shangri La, with the average age of a citizen at only eighteen years of age (compared to forty-one at home). And yet Malawi is pretty typical in this respect, its population having grown five-fold from under four million in 1960 to over nineteen million now, again like Africa from 250 million to 1.25 billion. Five times the number of people coming to dinner as there were in 1960.

A large swath of this area was claimed by the British after expeditions, explorers, and missionaries had charted the land in the mid/late 1800s. The mega region was initially administered under the umbrella of the British Central Africa Protectorate. The area unbound itself into its current component parts comprising what is now Zambia (formerly Northern Rhodesia), Zimbabwe (formerly Southern Rhodesia), and Malawi (formerly Nyasaland). The whole region gained full independence in the 1960s.

My assignment starts out in the usual fashion. The NGO is based just outside of the country's biggest town, Lilongwe. It has a million or so inhabitants and serves a district of about ten thousand square miles. Day one includes introductions with the staff, then Ceetay, a nurse at the NGO, takes us to the local mall, all very modern glass and steel, to buy provisions for our comfortable self-catering hotel unit. Day two, is a a jet lagged, doddering attempt at defining the scope of the assignment. Day three and four, the weekend. Monday, Day five, is spent visiting a trade school that the NGO has built a couple of hours drive into the rural areas. The carpentry shop being the most memorable, with its focus on renewable consumer demand items—coffins. Tuesday, Day six, the real work commences, interviews with key staff, data and information gathering.

Day seven is working from home. A general protest has been planned at the parliament buildings and the citizenry have been advised to stay home. The current government controversially "won" the last election back in May 2019. But in early February, in a striking show of courage, the Malawian courts ruled that the election be annulled due to the "integrity of the result being severely compromised" and new elections be held within 150 days. Thus far, the ruling party has taken no steps to schedule another campaign. Everyone we meet is proud of their peacefulness and civility but their patience is being tested and the question is becoming "how much longer will they be tolerant." The electorate are growing more restless and getting ready to let their leaders hear their frustrations.

The political landscape is similar to several other African nations. Dr. Hastings K Banda, the founding prime minister who took over from the Queen in 1964, is still held in high regard by many. He ran the country essentially as a dictator for thirty years. Fostering his cult of personality, his control was far reaching, no detail was too unimportant. Standards of decorum were strictly enforced, female visitors were banned from wearing short skirts or pants, men were not allowed long hair or flared trousers.

Not all of his initiatives were quite so quaint, Dr. Banda had no tolerance for any questioning of his authority. It is estimated that over six thousand citizens were killed for alleged subversive activities during his tenure. Only one radio station and one newspaper were permitted, both were closely monitored and censored. No national TV station was available until 1999. Dr.

Banda was peacefully ousted from office at age ninety-four and died four years later, having amassed a personal fortune of over $300 million.

He was one of a crop of new leaders in Africa in the 1960s as most of the British colonies were granted independence. Like his contemporaries, Kenyatta of Kenya, educated at the London School of Economics, Nkrumah of Ghana, similarly educated at the LSE, Nyerere of Tanzania, educated at the University of Edinburgh, and Khama of Botswana, educated at Oxford, Banda studied to be a doctor in Britain at the University of Edinburgh.

The first taste Africa's new "big men" had of Europe was in the upper middle-class realm of the professions and academia and probably gave them a favourable impression of what was possible under post-war industrialism. Had their experience been gained in the coal mines of Wales, the shipyards of Glasgow, or the factories of the midlands, it may have had a different influence on them as to how to go about bringing prosperity to their own countries. To then return home and try to emulate that model in countries formed less than one hundred years ago that were comprised of multiple languages and customs, where some of the citizens didn't even know the name of their country, was a tall order. Those leaders, though not puppets of their former colonial masters, were to an extent moulded by their Western experiences and had as much in common with the Brits as the people that they now represented. These same characteristics, combined with only fledgling democratic systems and laws, paved the way for descent into dictatorship and corruption. Much less an inherent flaw in the African make up, as a blueprint adopted from the colonialists' playbook.

There were of course benefits and some good was done. Pride in country was resurgent as independence was enjoyed, peace, education, and general health improved, these achievements are still celebrated. Many a street, building, or monument bears the name Kamuzu (the "K" in Hastings K Banda).

The mixed blessings will eventually be recognised, revisionist wokery will hold sway and the rewriting of history will begin. Statues will be taken down, landmarks will be renamed. Maybe it's time we realize that our leaders are human just like us, with the same failings and strengths and instead of putting up and tearing down edifices, we recognize the good and the bad rather than air brush out the past. How will we learn anything if we descend into some form of conversational muzak, where no controversial issues can be voiced, challenged, and debated? Without nuanced dialogue, the loudest voices will drive the new dogma, bandwagon activism will flourish and we will be on our way again to creating a new set of problems.

Day eight, I am back to work after the protests have passed peacefully, but concerns on the home front are beginning to surface. Our kids alert us to the spread of that Wu Han flu thing, a minor news story before we left. They are recommending that we should come home. Their tone sounds vaguely parental. There is some kind of subtle shift in the relationship happening. We are accustomed to them being vaguely interested in our pursuits, but this feels more like them assuming some responsibility for our well-being. It is a strange hint at the inevitable reversal of roles where the parent becomes the child. A shift we are not quite happy about or ready for. Anyway, a sign from God soon confirms that their worries are well founded, I hear that the National Hockey League season has been shut down, virus interruptus alles. No trip is complete without a pandemic in the middle of it.

Day 9, Friday, I share the news with the staff that we will be leaving next week, sometime after we have figured out a suitable flight path home. Even after I explain the significance of civilisation without hockey, they are still bewildered as to what all the fuss is about. I also fill in the treasurer in London on our plans via Skype. It was to be the first of our planned virtual meetings, a weekly progress report (laugh that one off). Another productive day under my belt, I knock off at 1:00 p.m., as is the Friday convention at the office and head for the beach.

Or to be more accurate, to Lake Malawi. As prearranged, I borrow the office's little Nissan, our destination Cape Maclear, a resort town about two hundred kilometres from the capital, Lilongwe. More of a no name destination than a bucket list trophy, but in local circles, it is a treasured gem. For most of the folks here, a trip to the lake would be the equivalent of us going to Machu Picchu and as for Cape Maclear itself, I have heard of it as being the Vegas of Malawi. Thankfully, we soon find the comparison a bit of a stretch, the first clue being that the last thirty kilometres into town is on an overgrown single lane dirt track.

The lake is beautiful and the small lakeside resort has a low rise unrefined charm to it. The village is rustic to the point of austerity, it's all very relaxed. The guest houses line the beach, each one separated from its neighbour by a pathway from the beach into the village, with a head-high bamboo fence on either side of the path for privacy. We spend a couple of nights in our cabana, modelled after the straw house in the "Three Little Pigs" fairy tale. We take leisurely strolls along the beach and generally chill out. In the evening I buy local—a couple of MG&Ts—the Malawi gin for the economy, the tonic for the antimalarial properties, and watch the sun slowly set as I dip below the mosquito net.

The nights are hot, the unit unairconditioned, so I rise early at 5:30, as the first glow of morning light arrives and faint murmurings begin. A sporadic drip, drip, of humanity as the women dribble out from the bamboo corridor, where it reaches the beach. Eventually, the trickle becomes a flow as more and more young women appear, swinging empty pails. Bright splashes of colour: red, orange, blue, white, yellow and green twenty-five-litre buckets, figures silhouetted, contrasting against the dusky predawn lake. They commence giving them a good scrubbing and rinsing. What could they have been used for the previous night that they needed such attention?

The cleanup complete, the girls fill the pails with lake water and sometimes with the help of a friend, hoist them up onto their heads for the return trip to their mud-brick homes. They then disappear back behind the bamboo walls invisible again but for the virtual conveyor belt of disembodied pails that surf past our patio like a scene from Disney's Sorcerer's Apprentice. It will soon be 6:00 a.m. Many of the men are already at work in their dug-out canoes, fishing on the lake.

The midday shift will begin later, when older ladies will tread the same path, bringing their kids and wide washbasins filled with dishes for washing and the day's laundry, socializing as they work. Life revolves around the lake, it all seems sublime. Greta would be happy.

Necessity being the mother of invention is at work here. You don't have to worry about ethically sourcing your next ensemble, sweatshops they don't have. You can pick out a piece of fabric, talk to your own personal tailor, design your own custom pair of pants and have it all whipped up on a treadle sewing machine in less than an hour. While you wait, there are a couple of funky post-apocalyptic-styled boutiques to browse. Maybe pick up chic new kitchen shelves made of welded together hollowed-out microwaves, or lamp shades made from the recycled wire cages of desk fans finished with the colourful local Kitenge cloth woven through the grills. Or go for a boat trip, the local guides have figured out a rota, whereby each guide has a shift allocated to him for a particular guest house for a given period of time. It's all very free and easy, none of the incessant hassling by touts common in other locations, none of the turf wars either. Although when I hear that a portion of all the proceeds go to the guides' widows' fund, I can't help wondering if they couldn't also form a boat maintenance co-op.

We pay a visit to the site of the Livingstonia mission, now preserved, just about, as a national monument to Dr. Livingstone, I presume. Livingstone was a Scottish doctor turned missionary turned explorer who brought the three Cs of Christianity, Commerce, and Colonialism to the country in the 1850s. He is still fondly remembered for his humanitarianism, in particular his efforts to bring an end to the horrific slave trade being plied by the Portuguese and Arabs in the region at the time.

It is beautiful, idyllic in some ways, but of course that is only part of the story. There are signs everywhere of the problems being confronted, like abandoning the landline telephone system after wire thieves looted them for resale. Indoor plumbing would be nice, there is no health care to speak of (one coronavirus testing kit for a population of eighteen million seems light), life expectancy is sixty-three years; electricity and internet is only available sometimes, a 90 percent decline in fish stocks in the last twenty years, drought sometimes, famine sometimes, 10 percent of the population suffering from AIDS, deforestation, what little wealth there is, is grabbed by a corrupt elite.

So this is where the dream comes in. Can we expect everyone to have paradise and the material benefits of the West at the same time? Is it even possible? Are our advances the solution? Or is it the hubris, that we can show how clever we are by making fire without recognizing that we have cut down the last tree to demonstrate how beneficial it is? Can we continue to make withdrawals from the Bank of Mother Earth to bring the have nots up to our standard of living or is the BOME teetering on bankruptcy and some sort of equilibrium can only be reached by the "haves" levelling down to "have not" status? Is growth and global trade just one giant pyramid scheme and these folks are just unlucky to be the last to join the Ponzi just as it is about to collapse? It's the laws of simple arithmetic.

Is there any measure whereby we will know when we have reached peak material satisfaction? Just to give an example of an order of magnitude, how about when everyone on the planet, all seven and a half billion of us, has their own swimming pool? Let's say a really nice Olympic-size pool. Of course, we would need somewhere the size of the US—9.4 million square kilometres—to put them all, while we are at it, we would have to drain the Great Lakes in order to fill those pools. But just think of the economic stimulus it would all create, who could argue with that? We have the ability to delude ourselves that we all can still have it all.

Self-sacrifice isn't really part of the discussion at the moment. All is not lost though, community has risen to the occasion before. When something as nebulous as faith in king and country can have millions volunteering to die in a hail of machine gun bullets, it tells us that somewhere deep down we have the capacity to care about the greater good and have the willpower to do something about it. Whether it is giving up bottled water, SUVs, air travel, or whatever our personal environmental trigger might be. There are promising signs, conspicuous consumerism is losing its cachet, malls are closing, young people especially are moving to buying previously loved merchandise. Charity work, activism, and giving are becoming the new symbols of social status. We will know that we are making real progress when actual sacrifice is in vogue.

As far as now goes, we are being told that we have reached the proverbial tipping point. We have a choice to make. Do we tinker around the edges, make token gestures to "reuse" and "recycle" and put our faith in technology to save us from ourselves? Or, do we get serious about "reducing" our demands on Mother Earth until we know that technology can come to the rescue?

I'll keep going with the recycling and technology thingy, it should see me right for my remaining years. But for you young folks, I think the reduce-now approach is the only long-term bet. After all, us wrinklies haven't got much of a track record about getting things right so far.

The last night of our stay isn't restful, checking the invaluable information on our embassy's website: "wash your hands" and "watch the news." We realize that we are on our own and that flights home must be booked pronto. Being in Greta Thunberg's dream is not an ideal spot to attempt this. The frustrations of power cuts, intermittent internet signal, flat batteries, emails blocked due to "unreliable server," internet subscription fee expiry, not to mention the mayhem on the booking sites themselves, cancelled flights, reroutings, travel bans and soaring prices make for many stressful hours. Time is too precious to waste trying to find bargains on the internet, but we are talking thousands of dollars here, so midnight oil must be burned.

To nearly top it all off, Trix comes down with a bad bout of diarrhea and has to head for bed. Bookings finally complete, I head for the bathroom and a tooth brushing before turning in. As I go to reach for the brush I see that it is moving. What the?! There resting on the bristles is a cockroach, antennae twitching in that peculiar way reminiscent of the backstroke. Odd thoughts pop into my head, "Is it just having a last minute buff up before it goes for its six month checkup and cleaning?"

But then the frustrations of the day finally erupt in a frenzy of Tarantinoesque violence as I fling the offending bug on the floor and do a deranged Tarantella dance atop it, cracking his carapace, scattering limbs, exoskeleton, and splattering goo. Glorious climax and bliss but for the slow realization that I still wanted to brush my teeth. So what to do but boil the brush in a pot of water, I figured that five minutes would be enough.

Extract said brush from pot, allow to cool, observe deformed swizzle-stick-shaped plastic implement now sprouting Tina Turner-like tufts of spiked bristles, apply toothpaste, make a face like Quasimodo and start brushing. A perfect end to a perfect day.

Our mini holiday passes all too quickly and we head back to the capital. The roads are busy for the drive home and not so much with motor vehicles. Non-wheeled traffic populates the shoulder so alertness is essential. For some reason the roadside vegetation seems to provide the best nutrition for cattle and we pass scores of mini herds on the verge. Just how much confidence should you put in a couple of pre-teen kids with bamboo poles, who have the responsibility of corralling forty or so steers at a time, when you are barrelling along the highway at ninety kilometres per hour? Also, this being a Sunday, everyone is out on foot, heading to or from visits to church or family, nose-to-tail pedestrians, like there is some sort of well-dressed mass migration going on.

Back in the office on Monday, I let folks know about our departure on Wednesday, explaining that because of my age I am in the high risk COVID-19 category, blah blah, thinking to myself, "The average Malawian would die to live long enough to be in the high-risk category," if you get my drift.

We say our farewells. Social norms are changing quickly. Various substitutes for the handshake are tried out. The toe bump didn't last, it doesn't meet the six-feet distancing requirement, unless you and your toe bumping partner can simultaneously execute a Bruce Lee-style karate kick. The non-contact Nepali namaste surprisingly hasn't gone viral yet, though they do have one of the lowest infection rates. I do suggest to Trixie that she might like to test drive a Burqa. Her response is a modernised take on that other famous veil wearer, Queen Victoria's quote, "We are not amused."

Instead, awkward aborted half-handshake wave gestures are delivered at six-feet's distance. There's no way to disguise the whiff of privilege. I have a feeling of sheepish guilt that I have the ability to just bail on the situation and retreat to the relative security of a country with a comprehensive medical system in place. It is in situations like these that you most value the handshake or a hug for its flesh-to-flesh contact, its absence makes the whole situation more uncomfortable.

Back at the now near-deserted guest house, we pack, say goodbye to the last remaining guest, a young Spanish woman who figures that any place is better than Madrid right now. We provide the housekeeper with an unexpected bounty of provisions from our fridge. She has been our everything, resort plumber, electrician, and font of local knowledge. On this occasion she is tending to her wildlife-control responsibilities and is on her way to deal with an intruding dog with her rifle.

Departure day duly arrives. What can you learn about a country after a visit to the capital, checking out an NGO, a drive to a resort on the lake, only twelve days in all? Well, it's enough to know that I like the place and the people. At the airport we sit well spaced in the departure lounge, with a half dozen other passengers waiting for the flight. Our airliner sits lonely on the tarmac. There isn't even one other private plane or jet to be seen. Our flight is called and we are ferried out by airport bus, I guess to observe protocol and keep up appearances. We could walk the one hundred yards faster in complete solitude. We have escaped by the hair of our chinny chin chins.

The first leg of our trip home takes us to Joburg, where we spend a night in the airport transit hotel. As I close the door of the hotel room door, I can't help but feel that I can also hear the sound of borders being closed behind us. I wonder if the ones in front of us will stay open long enough for us to complete the remainder of the seventy-hour, six flight, 22,000 kilometre journey home. The prospect of being stuck in transit in perpetuity a la Tom Hanks in *The Terminal* an even more worrying thought.

Part II
TERRA AUSTRALIS INCOGNITO FOR A WHILE

Chapter 11
Chile's Warm Welcome

GOALLLLLLLLLL!

"I WANT WOMEN TO BE LIBERATED AND STILL BE ABLE TO
HAVE A NICE ASS AND SHAKE IT."

– Shirley MacLaine

"MY MOTHER THINKS THAT I AM THE BEST. AND I WAS RAISED
TO BELIEVE WHAT MY MOTHER TELLS ME."

– Maradona

We have loved our adventures in Africa and Asia, but it is a big world and there are a lot of empty pages in our mental atlas. So why not expand our horizons? Ay Caramba! South America!

A trip to the hypothetical continent known as Terra Australis Incognita would seem to promise an illuminating experience. This "Unknowable Land of the South" existed only as intellectual conjecture in the fifteenth century. No one knew what to expect south and west of Cape Horn. And so this mysterious peninsula now shared by Chile and Argentina temporarily laid claim to the alias.

The logic of the geographers of the time implied that there must be a southern continent, one with a landmass large enough to provide a counterbalance to the lands of the Northern Hemisphere. It wouldn't be until 1770, when Captain Cook landed on the East Coast of what is now called Australia, that this portion of South America finally surrendered its title as the fabled Terra Australis Incognita to its antipodean neighbour to the west.

Be that history as it may, what draws us here are the big horizons that abound in Patagonia and the Pampas, not to mention good food, stunning hikes and culture. So we make plans to head south, well not as directly south as I had assumed. Santiago, Chile, our first port of call is actually due south of Boston, about three thousand miles east of us here in Victoria. Checking the map, I see that if we are to travel due south from our home, we will end up roughly two-and-a-half-thousand miles west of Santiago, which will put us in the neighbourhood of Easter Island, one of the most remote islands in the world. As far as rationalisation goes, it's a pretty flimsy premise but it provides us an excuse, not that we needed one, to go there too.

Santiago is a modern hustling, bustling city, but in some ways, it has a mid-twentieth-century feel to it, a throwback compared to its North American and European relations. Surprisingly, it is more monochromatic, a younger, unicultural population, more smokers than cell phone users; black, brown and yellow faces are few, the lack of ethnic mix more like a Seoul or a Prague than a Vancouver or Paris. Folks are friendly, courteous, even a little reserved. Not at all the hand-waving, hot-blooded Latin caricature attributed to South America. Chile is older than Canada but seems to have peaked early. It is expensive, comparable to home and yet minimum wage is just six hundred dollars a month, less than a third of Canada's equivalent.

The attitudes seem to be of social consciousness, unflappability, practicality and community mindedness. The Scandinavia of the subcontinent, if you will.

Geography has shaped the national character of the people. A 4,300 kilometre long (as long as the US is wide), 350 kilometre wide, string bean of a country wedged between the Andes Mountain range to the east and the Pacific Ocean to the west. Extremes abound, the forests surrounding Santiago have just been hit with Chile's worst fires in history.

A victim of the climatic conditions that they refer to as the Triangle of Fire or 3 by 30. Thirty days of drought with thirty plus degrees of heat combined with thirty-kilometre winds. Just four days before we arrive, the not-so-distant snow-capped Andes had been hidden by smoke and ash. This is followed a month later by flooding and mudslides, which leaves millions without water. Combine that with the ever present seismic tremors which hint at the overdue "big one" and the choking smog that regularly shuts down the capital (sounds a lot like I could be talking about California these days). It is perhaps predictable that it takes a lot to ruffle feathers down here.

The downtown city centre is blessed with some magnificent classical architecture intermingled with modern buildings, which tell a tale of faded prosperity mixed with fledgling promise. Beautiful cathedrals seemingly on every block, the Catholic

Church knew a thing or two about creating an inviting ambiance—cool, quiet and peaceful, before Starbucks perfected the model. Of course, those were just the introductory offers, once hooked the unsuspecting parishioner was subjected to some heavy fear-of-God marketing. The gallery of the Iglesia de San Francisco we visit has a massive art collection. Biblical freezes on wall after wall. Floor-to-ceiling artwork, intimidating six-feet by twelve-feet paintings. Scenes in the style of Bruegel but with none of the conviviality. Every form of savagery imaginable depicted—decapitation, flagellation, crucifixion, pillory, leprosy, stoning, burning at the stake, starvation, etc. The message, all too clear, "Don't mess with the big guy."

Graffiti is rampant and in some trendy areas, Bellavista for example, it is so sophisticated as to have been elevated to an art form/tourist attraction.

It is a dog friendly town and dogs (not all friendly) are everywhere. Occasionally the caring goes too far for my liking. Picking a ratty looking Yorkie stray up off the street, putting it on the restaurant table and feeding it hot dogs, is a bit past my comfort zone. Food safe and cannibalism taboos notwithstanding, you have to admire a city that has a dog sterilization initiative underway. Santaguinos being who they are, there is also a typically informal grassroots movement at play, where individuals or buildings or businesses adopt their local stray.

We soon learn that the open heartedness isn't limited to our four-legged friends. One of the things I love most about travel is the random acts of kindness that are so commonplace, it reaffirms my faith in the goodness of people. On this trip for example, we've had shop owners personally deliver us to restaurants we've been struggling to locate, had Grandpa Filipe invite us into his home of fifty-six years for a drink, after he spotted us admiring the graffiti on the walls of his house. We had a nice chat for about an hour him using only Spanish and us only English. Had a bank teller offer to launder our money through his own personal account to prepay our hotel which didn't take Visa and bank transfer wouldn't work. Had a stripper share her Pisco Sour with us on an overnight bus trip.

Q: What do you use for a conversation stopper?

A: Ask a stripper what she does for a living.

I perform a few mental contortions, simultaneously attempting to suppress the mind's wish to visualize the tempting distractions while at the same time trying to formulate some fatherly advice about prostituting her body, although a very nice body it appears to be. Then figure I have probably got some dubious skeletons in my closet investments wise, in sweatshop companies, arms manufacturers, petrol giants and the rest, and it is not like my survival depends on them. So on reflection, taking your clothes off seems quite noble and anyway, as it turns out, she is an anthropology graduate, so maybe it is just part of her doctoral research.

We've had harried housewives hail cabs for us, students interpret bus schedules (nearly missing their own connections in the process), had waiters map out walking tours of the most impressive buildings.

And the gravity defying architecture isn't limited to bricks and mortar. Booty is much on display. There appears to be some sort of mass scientific experiment being conducted into the breaking strength of fabric in this city. In order to qualify as a guinea pig (and this is entirely the wrong metaphor), each participant must be female and sport a draught to beam ratio of at least 1.5 in the aft quarters. The ratio is more important than overall displacement, but that's not to say overall tonnage isn't often considerable. The "cargo" is then leveraged into pants, frequently white and at least three sizes too small. The object of the exercise seems to be to inform the observer (and there is no doubt that anyone would possibly put themselves through these contortions to be ignored) of the exact type of underwear being worn. The thong, the sumo, the French cut, the slingshot, the pirate's eye patch, the hipster and the spanks (although this must surely be part of a control group study), and yes, even the humble brief.

The fabric is stretched to its absolute breaking point, to the extent that it is often possible to read through the material to the label, "agua tibia lavable a maquina" ("machine washable warm water" if you prefer it in English).

Vanity or inhibitions don't seem to come into play; it's all about the engineering. Whether it's the ripest, firmest, plumpest fruit or the translucent white glow of the Moon's Sea of Tranquility lumps, bumps, craters and all, in the end it's all about the science. How many cubic inches can you pack into a finite two-dimensional constraint before explosion?

Before any female readers feel too victimised, it should be noted that the men suffer as much from this arrangement as the women. A few years of sensitivity training isn't going to instantly change hardwiring that's been in place for centuries, so be patient with us as we attempt to reorient the male gaze. When you see a spike in the number of cross-eyed men, you know that efforts are really being made. In the age of Harvey Weinstein, we should all know what an unhealthy interest in the opposite sex looks like, but can anyone... dare anyone... define what constitutes a healthy interest without invoking someone's wrath?

Better that we keep any ideas of sharing such notions safely buried in a lead-lined container. How far do we go before we end up with some unrealistic lowest common denominator, which re-establishes the hypocrisy of Victorian prudery, I wonder?

Anyway, as I was saying, it's all about the science and it is hoped that the new fabric tensile qualities will have revolutionary properties. Proposed applications include new sails for Chile's entry in the America's Cup, new parachute material for the army, and as a replacement for spider thread [10]. The most innovative development is for use as a new artificial skin. Apparently, Cher is already planning to use the membrane the next time she has her face reupholstered. Expect to see her celebrity endorsement soon on The Shopping Network.

Thank you for your selflessness ladies.

Food options abound in the city, but if you love seafood, you must have all your lunches at the Mercado Central, the city's fish market. A frenetic hive of activity, with every imaginable type of marine produce there for the eating. The eating isn't the only treat, the general vitality and mayhem is mesmerizing. Fish shop owners display magician-like slights of hand as they fillet the catch. Perpetual motion composed of confidence, precision and flair that would be the envy of any surgeon. Blood soaked aprons, fish flying through the air, barrow boys ploughing their tubs of ice through the shoppers, like they are starring in The Fast and the Furious, buckets of entrails, flashing steel and good-natured banter and laughter are the order of every day.

This all takes place in a Victorian style building, formerly used as the city garbage facility. It takes up a whole city block. The space is flooded with natural light, provided courtesy of the glass and cast-iron roof prefabbed in Glasgow and shipped out in the 1870s. Kind of weird to think that at the same time in Vancouver, development only comprised a saw mill and a few loggers' huts.

A dozen or so locally owned restaurants line the perimeter walls of the market. Each has their own regular diners, but competition for the tourists and out-of-towners' dollars is

---

[10] https://www.youtube.com/watch?v=U58lP25HKhM

fierce. The eateries all have a greeter, whose job it is to rustle up customers. We spend an excellent three-hour lunch supping local Sauvignon Blanc, eating conger eel soup and downing ceviche at a second-storey bistro, watching the antics of one such rainmaker.

It would be an effrontery for any Chilean to be named after an Argentinian soccer god, but in this case the similarities are just too indisputable for him to escape us dubbing him Maradona. There he is, stocky, barrel-chested, grey curly-haired, pacing in front of his restaurant doorway, like an expectant father outside the delivery room. He is a basket of pent-up anticipation. He owns the strike zone, as opponents approach, he blocks their path, jinks one way then the next, pleads, clowns, cajoles, intercepts a fish-laden plate from a passing waiter in mid delivery, wafts it under an unsuspecting passersby's nose. He finds a chink in the defence's armour, prays to the heavens, arms outstretched like he's been felled in the penalty box and steers the adversaries through the door.

There is no time for celebration, he's back patrolling his wing in short order, signals that he is open to a distant prospect, but to no avail, they baulk and head down the opposite flank. Maradona plants his fist of God into a pile of Styrofoam fish crates in disgust. As the final minutes tick away, his teammates pat him on the back, give him hugs as they shuttle back and forth between the kitchen and the tables, he is their star player and money maker and they know it. As 5 p.m. and the final whistle approaches, the cute counterpart from a neighbouring restaurant comes to mid-field to chat with Diego, compares notes, puts her arm around his neck, pretends to slap him on the face. (They do everything but swap jerseys, but not quite.) The second leg is scheduled for kick off at 11 a.m. the next day.

Fortunately there is nothing really tempting souvenir wise, our best bargain is a visit to the touring Picasso exhibit at the Centro Cultural, for four dollars. At this rate, the holiday will soon be free, as we had planned to see the same show at home, price forty dollars. Although severely tempted, we couldn't justify delaying our departure by a week to see the James Taylor/Elton John double bill for a mere fifty dollars. Traces of jet lag fading and acquisitions avoided, it is time to move on.

Heading west for an hour and a half by bus, we arrive at Valparaiso, Chile's major port, a somewhat dilapidated historic town, which has suffered over the years from earthquakes, tsunamis, and the desertion of marine traffic since the opening of the Panama Canal. The town is perched atop, well more "clinging to" really, the side of steep hills, which drop straight into the open harbour, a collage of aged historic buildings and modern rooflines that cut the vista with their colourfully tagged faces. The city's renowned street art is unsurpassed. It has recently been added to the list of cruise ship destinations and its UNESCO World Heritage Site status has spurred a surge in interest.

With hills steeper than San Francisco, getting around the city presents significant challenges. Streets are narrow, parking scarce and privacy minimal. (I have to close the curtains in our guest house when the tour groups amble by as I am putting my pants on.) Geography dictates where things are built, town planning does as it is told.

There are fifteen or so ascensores (funiculars), which crank and clank twenty foot passengers at a time from the water side up to the lofty neighbourhoods towering above the docks. These one-hundred-year-old antiques were built to last, even after bouncing down the hillsides during the 2010 earthquake and tsunami, they were repaired and to this day continue to provide eye-to-eye insights on day-to-day life on a cliff as the track threads its way up between houses, shops and apartments. If you fancy a more panoramic experience, the micro bus number 0 or 612 whips you around the rim of the town and down into the frenetic market. A heart stopping thrill ride that is part Monaco Grand Prix and part Coney Island roller coaster.

Having had our fill of these elevated experiences, we pack our packs and prepare for the next stage of our journey, which will take us off the beaten tracks and south, south, and further south.

Chapter 12
My Way Is Not the Highway

Do you know where I put my car keys?

"NOT ALL THOSE WHO WANDER ARE LOST."

– JRR Tolkien

"THEY TRIED TO MAKE ME GO TO CATHOLIC SCHOOL. I LASTED
A VERY SHORT TIME. WHEN THE PENGUIN CAME AFTER ME
WITH A RULER, I WAS OUT OF THERE."

– Frank Zappa

TOMORROW THEY ARE PLAYING GOD

The few days we spent in Santiago this southern capital of this southern continent, haven't had the impact on my epidermis I had hoped for. It is time to head further south in a last-ditch attempt to baffle the migratory instincts of the hairs on the back of my skull to relocate to my shoulders and to invert the gravitational pull that drags the jowls and buttocks southward. It's a long shot, but still I look forward to my first makeover, my own personal hole in the ozone having grown alarmingly over the last decade. Perhaps it has something to do with the proximity of the CFCs emitted from my shaving foam can.

After ten hours on a sleeper bus, a comfortable inexpensive way to travel, we arrive on Chiloe, the fifth largest island in South America. It is a picturesque spot, with a temperate climate. The dramatic extinct volcano Mt Osorno opposite us on the mainland provides a perfect white-topped Hershey's Kiss backdrop to the view.

We make our way to the even less busy West Coast of the island. It is nice and rural, with long sandy beaches, excellent for hiking. Mostly it is pretty quiet, you might come across a herd of cows out for a day at the beach. But change is slowly happening. As is typical, the young backpackers are the pioneers, then the gray hairs pick up the scent, you know the end is near when pickup trucks laden with packs and partiers are driving up the sand to the campsites. Even in this semi-wilderness, humanity must demonstrate its deference to the machine and step aside to let the cars past. Why this hierarchy still exists, especially out here when we now know the negatives associated with the combustion engine, especially compared to walking, is a mystery.

En route from Castro, the main town on the island, we pass by showy displays of hydrangeas, fuchsias (native) and roses (introduced), growing wild by the roadside. Several derelict churches are in evidence, a couple still with flocks. Sheep bowing down reverently eating the grass on the overgrown front lawn. Supposedly the population of the Mapuche peoples, whose land included Chiloe, plummeted from a half a million to a little over twenty-five thousand in the late 1800s.[11] Guns, germs, and steel and religion, (at least they brought wine) at work.

There are lots of tourists and most of them are Chilean. It is a country of young people and it is February and summer break, so everyone seems to be on holiday. Don't they know how difficult they are making it for us to find accommodation? How dare they.

We are staying in a hostel, however, these are not the dark dank dorms of our youth. More a glorified BnB style, usually with your own room and ensuite, plus communal kitchen facilities and a common dining/living area. They are a great source of up-to-date information when travelling. Ergo we make use of "the war room." Maps, computers, bus, boat, and plane schedules and routes, pincer movements, provisioning, and logistics are all part of the mix.

It soon becomes apparent that our (well, my) plan to overland to Punta Arenas (population 125,000), the most southerly city in the world (for now), won't quite pan out. The end-to-end Chilean highway isn't actually a highway end-to-end yet. There is a surprising gap in the middle, one of several obstacles that results in you zigzagging across borders.

Turns out that the bus to Punta Arenas goes through Argentina and is an epic thirty-four-hour ride. A boat, bus, then another boat route is an option, but ruled out. The royal treatment from our Nepali hiking compadres has softened us up over the years. The distance from the arrivals carousel to the taxi stand is our limit for hefting a fully laden backpack these days. Plane it is.

---

[11] https://en.wikipedia.org/wiki/Mapuche

Many a celebrity of bygone eras visited the area: Magellan, Shackelton, Cook, and Darwin. Punta Arenas, which translates to Tip of Sand, was on its way to becoming the next Cape Town. A grand town square and imposing ornate nineteenth-century granite buildings flag those auspicious beginnings. However, its destiny was to be determined by its geography. Roosevelt (the first one) had other ideas, and the Panama Canal, opened in 1914, put the kibosh on PA's boom.

For being this far south, the climate isn't very cold. But then at fifty-three degrees south, it is only the same distance from the equator as Dublin. The land is low and flat, the Andes having gone subterranean for the last seven hundred kilometres of South America before popping up again as Tierra Del Fuego, the island about one hundred kilometres to the south.

Strolling the streets of Punta Arenas one is oblivious to the fact that if you were to continue on for roughly one thousand kilometres, across the Drake Passage, there sits the massive continent of Antarctica, nearly twice the size of Australia. Up north, all we have is a big but rapidly shrinking ice cube.

Where the weather extremes come in is in the wind; the furious fifties are well named, the bleak landscape is testament to that. Gnarly trees bent to leeward, victim to the prevailing easterly winds. Sir Francis Drake may have had the honour of naming the strait after himself, but never had the satisfaction of actually making passage through it, heavy winds and strong currents forced him to take the slightly more northerly route through the strait of Magellan. Three hundred miles and sixteen tempestuous days later he and his battered ship, the Golden Hind, emerged into the Southern Pacific.

The town's suburbs give a taste of that desolation, our walk back to our Airbnb is a dismal, depressing trek. Corrugated iron houses, threatening dogs, steel-shuttered shops and car wrecks give off a Belfast during "The Troubles" vibe, yet ironically enough, we never felt ill at ease.

We will never forget this our first Airbnb experience, primarily due to the incredible hospitality of our hosts, but also due to the peculiarity of our accommodation. Immediately upon entering the home, as we shoehorn ourselves onto the interior steel-spiral staircase, an overwhelming sense of claustrophobia envelops us.

Not that it is a small house but every available square centimetre is occupied by things living and inanimate. Birds, cats, plants, flame-breathing gas stove, mothers, suits of armour, diving helmets, stacks of twenty-year-old issues of Life magazine. I am sure if we look long enough, we might find Excalibur buried under the rubble.

It's a one-hundred-year-old house that looks like it's three hundred years old. I feel like we might bump into the Addams Family on our way to the bathroom. Although having said that, we need a map and a machete to answer the call of nature. Camouflaged by potted plants, it's behind a sliding door doubling as a coat stand in the living room. It does have a shower, it's like having a coffin inside a phone booth. In order to do any business of any kind, it is necessary to lower one's garments while standing fully erect, pirouette 180 degrees clockwise so as not to knock the figurine of Napoleon off the toilet roll, and reverse into the niche under the stairs while simultaneously lowering oneself onto the porcelain— bullseye!

Once finished, extrication isn't any easier, with every possible handhold in view occupied the only option is to put your hands above your head, grab the underside of the stairs, like you are about to do some chin ups, rock back and forth three times on the throne and on the third pitch launch yourself into the upright position. This is the kind of tip that should earn me super status on Airbnb.

Apart from being a jumping off point for Antarctic trips the attractions here are mainly in the fauna department. We aren't too successful on that front. The tour boat to the nearby Isla Magdallena doesn't run on the weekend, we are there on the weekend. Presumably the sixty thousand resident penguins send their tuxedos to the cleaners on those days. As an alternative, we try to access the nearby land-based colony of a mere six thousand nesting pairs of Magellanic (as you might expect them to be called) penguins. Alas, with the recent increased coal mining in the area the penguins have moved out, or as some have rumoured, "have been disappeared." Shades of an avian version of General Pinochet's purge in the 1970s when around three thousand political opponents conveniently vanished, fate unknown. Pinochet was a Chilean dictator who came to power via military coup overthrowing the socialist government of Allende. The Central Intelligence Agency (CIA) were suspected of being part architects of the affair, this having taken place during the "stop the commies" era of US history. Chatting with several Chileans, they have not forgotten or forgiven this interference.

Less controversially, the cormorants are however still here (perhaps they are sleeper CIA assets?) Decked out white shirted and with their pot bellys so different from the skinny all black version we have here in Canada. The sight must have added more stimulus to Darwin's thoughts about evolution. It doesn't take much imagination to speculate that some eons ago one particularly tubby or perhaps vain cormorant figured that it was just too difficult or humiliating to continue flying. Way ahead of his time, he decided to choose the environmentally responsible option and give up air travel altogether. Presto, the first penguin!

I haven't reached that level of obesity or consciousness yet, so pass the burger and fries and fasten the seat belts.

It may of course be that Darwin had missed this connection, due to the distractions of domestic strife at home. When departing Plymouth harbour he mentioned to his wife, Emma, that he would be home late from work, "1836" to be exact.

To which she replied, "That's rather precise, Chucky dear, twenty-four minutes to seven."

To which he frustratedly retorted, "No, you silly bint, the year 1836!"

"I don't care. It is still jolly late, so don't blame me if your dinner is burnt." she blubbed in response, it was then 1831.

She may have wished that he had been even more tardy—after he returned, they had ten children together.

And talking of departures, those broad horizons are calling...

Chapter 13
Pat O'Gonia

How many times do I have to tell you?
The organic tofu you dimwit!

"WHO WRITES YOUR NAME IN LETTERS OF SMOKE AMONG THE STARS OF THE SOUTH. OH, LET ME REMEMBER YOU AS YOU WERE BEFORE YOU EXISTED."

– Pablo Neruda

"HI-HO, SILVER! AWAY!"

– The Lone Ranger

We head north from Terra Australis, which seems to be the tourism marketing brand down at this nub end of the sub-continent, the Austral highway, Austral beer, etc., it doesn't seem like the locals have gotten over the Aussies stealing their name yet. It's a relaxing five-hour bus ride through the panoramic, empty, flat windswept vistas of Patagonia. These back roads through this steppe are in good repair. The semi-arid planes supported huge sheep farms at one time, but with the resulting overgrazing, we pass thousands of acres of empty fenced ranch-land. Empty that is except for wildlife with a decidedly Australian outback character, wild dogs, rheas (an emu-like flightless bird), and guanacos, a cousin of llamas but with a head like a kangaroo and a stout heavy body like a hairy deer, no puma, though.

We arrive in Puerto Natales, a small touristy town that is the jumping-off point for hiking and visiting the nearby fjords and glaciers and the Torres del Paine (TDP), otherwise known as the Towers of Blue Mountains, billed as the eighth Wonder of the World. It must be thirty times I have heard the claim for eighth place being made. Can you name the first seven? Nyah. TDP soon slips down to ninth place when I find a plug for the sink in our hotel room—the first since arriving in South America—now that was a wonder.

With tourism comes more eating choices, we opt for parrilla, a local traditional open fire type BBQ. In this case the whole lamb is split in half and lashed to a kind of an iron crucifix called an asado. The foot of the cross is stuck in the ground at an angle over the hot coals. Once cooked the lamb is taken down and hacked into hunks with a cleaver, slapped on a plate with maybe a boiled potato or two, and you get stuck in.

It is a brutal but delicious recipe taken straight from the ISIS edition of the Joy of Cooking. The meat tends to be well done, but it is still chin dribblingly good and delivers a viscerally satisfying experience that tofu just doesn't equal.

Rapacious appetites savagely numbed, we prepare to leave town, rent some camping equipment and a car to take in some of the sights. The cerulean Towers unveil themselves after a misty rain shrouded night and they are undoubtedly unique and a constantly mutating treat for the onlooker. The interplay between the ever-changing clouds and sun provides endless compositions of shapes and colours. You can be gazing at a three-thousand-metre-high white granite cathedral one minute only to see it transformed half an hour later by overcast skies into hulking grey battlements the next, with jet-black cloud plumes streaming from the tops of the columns like smoke from a Dickensian factory. The park is seven hundred square miles in area and it is possible to hike the circuit around the base of the spires in eight days. The park is "protected" by a necklace of azure glacial lakes so that access can only be gained via catamaran or park bus service. In the meantime, we content ourselves with distant views from the tour bus route on the far side of the lakes. We join the shuffling masses on the walk to the lookout two hundred metres from the car park. The passengers spill out of the coaches, decked out like they are prepared for the final assault on the summit of Everest. A trekking-gear fashion show.

Definitely a mixed experience, there is no way to be disappointed in the raw beauty of the surroundings like that, but the conveyor belt-like processing of people has it feeling a bit like going to see the Washington Monument rather than a wilderness experience. And of course, if it is a bucket list type destination, there will be many businesses there to generate buckets of money. The market is being geared more and more toward the wealthier and therefore older tourist. A stay at an estancia (ranch) will run four hundred dollars, a modest hotel, two hundred dollars; a hostel, one hundred dollars; and a tent, forty dollars a night. Yes, we are older... but also frugal... our rented tent does the trick.

The mountains' silhouette is like no other—iconic, a gift-wrapped brandable logo in waiting. And yet, peculiarly, the state emblem is a giant prehistoric sloth, its remains discovered here in 1896. Replicas of these three-metre-long one-thousand-kilogram creatures known as Mylodons are evident everywhere. These beasties were around the earth sometime pre-ten thousand years BC. A relative newbie compared to when the dinosaurs roamed the planet tens of millions of years ago. My guess is that the roaming fad had run its course before the Mylodons came on the scene.

Yet does anyone outside of Puerto Natales care? For that matter, is there even anyone from Puerto Natales that cares? I have a queasy feeling that you don't even care, I'm a bit ambivalent myself.

We give the Mylodon taxi company the cold shoulder, tag line:

"As slow as a sloth dinosaur but always with a smile."

We go independent with a rented Renault and hit the open road. Map in lap we zero in on the only car-accessible free campsite, miles from anywhere. Predictably, under an unrelenting rain we find ourselves on the wrong side of a cattle grid, locked gate and barbed wire trying to translate a faded sign written in Spanish. Frustratedly, we retreat to the car, break out the sandwiches and consider our options. Before even tossing out the first trial balloon (sleep in the car—that would have been mine), a dog runs up, puts his paws on the driver's window, looks in, and just as quickly takes off again. No sooner has he done this than out of nowhere, actually the lake behind us, a gaucho rides right up to the side of the car. I've never been in a Western before let alone a South American one. This fellow has the full gear, the hat, poncho, bombachas and facon (knife) on his belt. No cigarillo but the requisite stubbled chin and the scowl, it is all "For a Few Pesos More." It is still pouring rain, but this guy has his own force field around him.

Not a word is spoken, from high in the saddle he glares down at us with a face like a branding iron. I start the engine and hightail it like we have been run out of town.

We spend a pleasant night in the nearest regional campground. The regional thing is a bit confusing too. Some bureaucratic (and they do love their bureaucracy here) bright spark in the 1970s decided to carve up the country into administrative districts, with numbers rather than provinces with names. I found this out when making small talk with a Chilean on the bus. When I asked him where he lived, he said twelve. It took an age to figure out it wasn't his lack of English or my lack of Spanish that was at the root of the problem. These soulless descriptors don't sit well with the Chileans, who hold poetry and poets in high regard.

The next day under clear skies, we climb up to the nearby condor lookout. At times the wind is so strong that we have to hide behind rocks in order to avoid being blown over. Even the condors have cancelled all their flights for the day. The views are still spectacular, though, the mountainous park to the northeast and flat plains to the south. An end-of-the-earth destination, a long way from nowhere, with not much but scrub for cover and yet it has attracted many escapees over the years. The Welsh to escape their coal mines, the Scots escaping the Highland clearances, Butch Cassidy and his gang on the run from the Pinkerton detectives, sixties children of the Cold War getting as far away from the nuclear threat as possible and finally now, travellers on the run from all the redundant distractions of life in civilization... "Your business is important to us...," "For your own safety we recommend...," "Today, President Trump tweeted...," blah-blah-blah.

Adventure options are many and tempting, but pricey. We make our budget stretch to a two-day kayak/camp/power boat excursion. It is a lot of fun despite a challenging start. Fifty kilometres an hour winds mean we can't launch on Lago (lake)

Grey (grey), which is a bit of a bummer because it means we can't paddle around the icebergs that have calved off of Glaciar (glacier) Grey (grey) at the far end of the lake (lago). We put into Rio (you should be able to figure this one out) Grey about a kilometre from the boca (mouth—there will be a test). Our guide kits us out in dry suits, which I think is a bit of overkill, until she shares the story of Doug Thompkins, one of the pioneers of the adventure sports movement and co-founder of The North Face sports equipment empire. Alas, poor Doug went paddling down here in 2015 without a dry suit. He capsized into the four-degree Celsius water and died of hypothermia, even after being hospitalized. His legend as they say lives on, his foundation owns over two million acres of land in Patagonia and is dedicated to conservation.

The canoe trip down the river is a treat, the mountain backdrop is spectacular and the paddling easy going as the freshet carries us toward the sea. In the evening, we feel pretty smug as we settle into our campsite for the night. In the next tent, our neighbour is an affable Santiaguino on a camping trip with his three kids. We should have anticipated what comes next. He is built like Hoss Cartwright out of Bonanza.[12] Ground shaking, guy wire trembling and otherworldly groaning like calving icebergs rent the tranquil night. Hoss is a snorer. His poor kids are probably wishing they had a cork to put in his boca.

We spend the next day relaxing, strolling the adjacent prairie, wildlife watching, gazing at the shadows of the clouds on the hillsides that look like quilts being fluffed as they morph and scurry across the pampas, you would swear the hills are moving as the colours change, spotting guanaco and flocks of white ibis heads bent down in a line stalking across the fields, like some forensic crime team searching for clues. Condors soaring in the

---

[12] https://www.youtube.com/watch?v=iQjb_QiFbJE

air. Don't tell me they are trying to spot a mouse from an altitude of anything up to 15,000 feet, it looks to me that they are just having fun. They glide effortlessly, motionlessly above the landscape as if suspended from an invisible zipline.

At the appointed time on the morrow, ourselves and a family of New Yorkers, chipper from their five hundred dollar a night hotel room sleep, are whisked by zodiac down the Serrano River to the Serrano Glacier. Our timing is perfect as the tour boats coming up from Puerto Natales have yet to arrive. We have the place to ourselves for a spectacular hour. For the remainder of the voyage back to town, we are transferred to a tour boat, which is the perfect way to enjoy the scenery in its quintessential state, torrential rain. Spirits are lifted when the boats pull in at a tourist stop estancia (ranch). The feeding of the five thousand ensues. Massive waist high barbecues ten feet square are laden with lamb. The chefs tend their flocks with extended tongs.

There should be a health warning alert, as any vegetarians amongst the throng would surely have a seizure at the sight. I quite enjoy it.

After a night back in town in a cosy guest house bed, we are ready to get our boots muddy. We pack our backpacks and catch the bus out to the trailheads.

TDP's Instagram cred continues to burgeon, iconic to South America. Like the Eiffel Tower is to France. It attracts hundreds of thousands of people to Patagonia, tens of thousands to Puerto Natales, thousands to the circuits around the mountain spires and the lunatic fringe climb up the outside of them. I am reminded of one of the six Shakespearean quotes still accessible in my grey matter after twelve years of schooling. As he said of the multitudes' awe of Julius Caesar:

"And walk under his huge legs and peep about."

I've waited forty-seven years for an opportunity to use that. And bugger it if it isn't a perfect fit, so it's staying in. We are going to peep about for four days and nights.

The advertising hints at a packaged away-from-it-all escape, but the TDP has become more of an attraction than an outdoor experience. If you invest the time, the crowds thin out as you get closer to the mountains. Even at the trailhead, however, it is all there in a glitzy ski village type community, the latest fashions in trekking clothes and accessories the first time out of the box—down vests, spandex, hiking poles, bright primary colours and cocktails a mere arms length away. Inside the lodge the surround sound pumps out an adrenalin broiling sound track while wall sized LED screens spin vertigo inducing aerial shots of the mountains, which sit impassively just on the other side of the window pane. Wilderness it ain't but with the majestic backdrop, you can easily mute the fashion show overload.

Finally, out on the trail it doesn't take long to get away from the St. Moritz aspirations and into the raw untouched beauty, not a scrap of trash anywhere, empty skies, miles and miles of pampas vistas, not a house, a road, a power pole or a sign of civilization in view—virgin land. The ring of glacier-fed lakes act as a moat, stops the park from being overrun by visitors, the only boat you might see is the four times daily catamaran run that brings the hikers in and out. The sounds of TDP range from eerie silence, eerie because it is so seldom quiet, to a rumbling low roar like a distant jet engine. Unless it is one o'clock and the daily Punta Arenas to Santiago flight really is overhead, the noise will actually be emanating from a gale blowing over the next ridge, a glacier calving in the next valley, or a waterfall around the corner.

The wind is the most persistent and impactful of these, its strength and unpredictable direction are forever playing havoc. The few stunted and gnarly trees give no clues as to whether there actually is a prevailing wind. The best gauge is to scan the trail ahead and see what the hikers in front of you are holding on to. Or where they are scurrying after hats, sunglasses, toupees, etc., blown off their heads. Taking a tinkle presents its own challenges. As the wind swerves and swoops from all directions, it is advisable to adopt a relatively narrow stance so that you are able to rotate your torso all the better to employ a sweeping tank turret type motion and keep the trajectory of flow at exactly 180 degrees to the wind direction lest you be hit with friendly fire. I am too afraid of getting soggy pants to try for the rainbow effect.

The wind at times is so strong that it will whip up a fine mist of water droplets on the surface of the lake. If the sunlight hits the mist at the right angle, you might be lucky enough to experience a unique spectacle as an other worldly rainbow coloured silk cloak materializes and speeds across the turquoise lake.

The scenery is spectacular and the skies amazing. We are treated to the rainbow of a lifetime, which hangs in an arc over the mountain. Vibrant and unchanging for over an hour and after developing a blister on my shutter finger, I began to believe that it is somehow permanent, a high-tech hologram employed by the Chilean tourism department to attract visitors.

There couldn't be a more fitting end to our visit to Chile, well that and downing a last glass of Carmenere before heading into Malbec country.

Afterword by Bernardo O'Higgins

Here we are in Pat O'Gonia after goin al over Chile and yer fookin eejit of an awter has greviously omitted de Oirish and meself yet. Oi may have been debt since 1842, boot me name is al over de country bein as Oi liberated oos from de Spaniards. Doze paella eatin' poirates. And tanks ta may da Repooblic ah Chile was proclaimed in 1818. Yell foind dat nearly effry main drag in effry town is named after me Bernardo O'Higgins and they're al' designed in the classic European stoile, built outwarts from da central Plaza Des Armes (army square).

Course I'm naht the only Oirishmin tuh be shapin da heritage aff dis glorious cantinent, ass da nixt revolutionary chaptur whill reveal.

Chapter 14
Dinner Time in the Argentine

Don't go asking how you'd like your steak done.

"FOR AN INSTANT GOD OPENS HIS DOOR AND HIS ORCHESTRA
PLAYS THE FIFTH SYMPHONY."

– Jean Sibelius

"THE ONLY TIME TO EAT DIET FOOD IS WHEN YOU ARE
WAITING FOR THE STEAK TO COOK."

– Julia Child

Instantly on arriving in Argentina I have the feeling that I am going to like the place. Going through immigration seems an odd way to foster the warm and fuzzies.

Three hours into our ten hour bus ride to the other side of the Andes, we arrive at the border control, a little bureaucracy in a foreign legion setting. Two buildings under two flags surrounded by forsaken fields as far as the eye can see.

The strangeness lingers inside too as the customs sniffer dog dawdles from passenger to passenger, seeking out who is most likely to give him a belly rub. Welcome to the Argentine.

Folks take the opportunity to use the internet, we are all writers now. It's comforting to put it out there into the electronic echo chamber in the hope that someone may be listening or even interested.

All duly documented, we continue our journey through mile upon mile of overgrazed landscape, flimsy fencing, and derelict estancias, abandoned except for long distance cyclists taking shelter from the unrelenting winds. Few vehicles and just as few livestock.

Finally, we arrive at our destination El Chalten, a frontier town plonked down in 1985 as a way for Argentina to remind anyone and everyone, especially the Chileans, of its ownership of this land. The embarrassing defeat in the Falklands war of 1982 was no doubt still fresh in the politicians' minds.

The town planners had a field day, wide boulevards, wheelchair ramps and municipal infrastructure, then dubbed it Argentina's Trekking Capital and gateway to the majestic Los Glacieres National Park. Except no one came.

Thirty odd years later, with its population still only a couple of thousand, only a quarter of that in the winter, it has settled into its niche as a scruffy little town catering to the hikers and climbers wanting to access the spectacular Fitz Roy range of mountains. The clientele is kind of rag tag, no bling, clothing is of a more muted colour, younger folks, bigger packs, dreadlocks, dirt on the boots and fewer hiking poles—funky.

Our shared hospedaje (lodging) is ineptly designed, a bit like the Alamo, with a kitchen situated on the roof, like a guard tower perfect for repelling bandits with designs on our rice and salami dinner, it is comfortable enough. The woefully appointed kitchen also looks like it had also been plonked down in 1985. Ill-equipped, with a two-burner camp stove, incomplete sets of mismatched cutlery, and the crowning glory is a battered tin teapot with a melted spout.

The folks are an interesting mismatch too, mostly kids (i.e. under thirty) and not of the "tick off my bucket list" "passionate about fulfilling my dream" mindset. They seem to have more of a John the Baptist in the wilderness disposition, what is it all about, what does it all mean, what does the world have to offer, maybe it will come to me if I meet it halfway. World politics is a frequent dinner topic. A young Argentinian couple sensitively questions if we are worried about having the current US president right next door. You have to know that you've reached the bottom of the barrel when the Argentinians are appalled at the iniquity of your government.

We spend some days hiking in the area of the Fitz Roy range, a string of mountains with the profile of a paper crown taken out of a Christmas cracker. Fitz Roy itself, the centrepiece rising to 3,405 metres, is listed as one of the ten most difficult mountains to climb in the world. Truly a runt amongst the giants. Annapurna, the most difficult, stands at 8,091 metres.

There are none of the issues of oxygen deprivation or the necessity of long term endurance posed by the monsters. The challenges of Fitz Roy are its sheer verticality and treacherous weather. Conditions that can change without warning from one minute to the next. The mountain wasn't conquered until 1952, the year before Everest.

We are all slaves to our own endorphin prompted addictions, whether its drugs, food, alcohol, sex, gambling, even travel has its compulsions. The longer you travel the more you drill down for the ultimate high, the impalpable perfect destination.

"You must go to South America." "You can't miss Patagonia." "TDP is amazing." "Fitz Roy is so much less touristy." "Nobody knows about the hospedaje outside El Beson." "You've got to hike up to the refugio between the glaciers." Then inevitably, you reach your own personal point of only return, back track and satisfied for a while, journey home. The appetite is only temporarily satisfied and after a suitable spell of detox and withdrawal, you start the process all over again.

Like visiting any destination, deciding on the timing is important, maybe more so when visiting the Argentine. It isn't just the seasons and weather that are important as much as the financial climate's impact on your budget. While we are here sixteen pesos to the dollar is the exchange rate, double what it had been when I first started cogitating about a visit back in 2014, so I thought that we should be getting a bargain. Wrong, the inflation in the country for that same period significantly outpaced the devaluation of their currency. The prices were no cheaper than Europe.

The economy here is mystifying, but maybe the wonks down here are just trail blazers. The US seems to have adopted the same "print money like it is going out of style and cross the fingers that nobody notices" type of, I hesitate to use the word, strategy. The haves here also seem to be doing quite nicely from this flim-flam.

Meanwhile, the regular punters get the shakedown for every nickel and peso. There are some obvious signs of the ongoing desperation: maximum ATM withdrawals of two thousand pesos at a time (about $125 CAD), which costs you seven dollars for the privilege, strange rituals like having to show your passport when using your credit card in a grocery store or six dollars to mail a postcard. I hear that the government's next plan to balance the budget is a giant bake sale.

And don't get me started about that postcard, it took three months to arrive. Maybe they should have the Mylodon as their next commemorative stamp.

Enough of the rant, having completed the ascetic physical legs of our trip, we are now in the mood for some serious self-indulgence, and what better place to be in than Buenos Aires or B.A. as it is familiarly referred to. It is alive in all ways, an assault on all five senses in contrast just to the sights and sounds of Patagonia. Named for its fair winds, it does have a good air to it, there is lots to see and do on our three night stay.

The greater city is home to nearly 13 million citizens but for a start, we will limit our activities to the downtown core, which houses 2.9 million. Our hotel is in the Recoleta district, which has beautiful buildings in the neoclassical style of architecture brought by the Spanish, Italians, and French.

Many of the sights are within walking distance for us. On our second evening in town, we set off for the Teatro Colon, the city's renowned concert hall. Built in 1908, it is replete with rococo ornamentation trimmed in scarlet and gold. Seven storeys of seating rise vertically from a horseshoe footprint. The acoustics in the building are recognized as some of the best in the world. Perched six floors up, the first notes of the trombone from Sibelius' Symphony No. 5 have our hairs standing on end. It is an experience not to be missed and one of the few bargains to be had in town at fifty dollars a pop.

After the concert we go for a wander around the entertainment district, turn a corner on to a quiet side street, and uh oh! We see a column of paddy wagons, complete with roof top mounted water cannon. Scores of riot police in full kit milling about restlessly. Shoulda checked the news before we went out, I guess. Political protests and demonstrations and clashes with police are pretty common. We retrace our steps and beat a hasty retreat. Once we are a safe distance away, we intercept a young man and quiz him about what is going on.

"Oh, ees nothing, ees Saint Paddees deh todeh."

It is estimated that there are about one million Argentinians of Irish descent. I guess with the Irish reputation for whooping it up, the authorities aren't taking any chances. After all, the biggest Argentinian troublemaker of all was of Irish descent. His name? Ernesto "Che" Guevara Lynch. Stranger than fiction?

Now on our way back to our hotel, we cross over the Avenue 9 De Julio. We should have packed our supper. It is B.A.'s main drag, its name commemorating the nation's date of independence. It is a whopper of a street, the largest in the world they say, 452 feet wide, twelve lanes of traffic, two dedicated bus lanes down the centre, plus another two-lane road on either side, separated from the main artery by treed medians for a grand total of eighteen lanes. It occupies the width of a whole city block, which was torn down to make way for the construction of the thoroughfare between 1930 and 1960. Nothing like a few coup d'etat to hold things up. Maybe they will get the bike lanes in faster.

Close to the hotel by now, we stop in at a restaurant for dinner and join the queue waiting for a table. It is eleven o'clock on a Wednesday night in March! How they get by without a siesta, I don't know. Wonderfully fed we lurch toward home and our beds, but fail to resist the final temptation, a trip to the heladeria. You scream, I scream, yes, we are going for ice cream. There is a lot to thank the big Italian influence here for, try the traditional dulce de leche or go out on a limb with a Malbec frutos rojos (Malbec and berries).

On our last day as our final outing, we visit, appropriately, the Recoleta Cemetery. A necropolis, an impressive city within a city. Since 1822, it has staked its claim to fourteen acres of prime downtown real estate. Home to family tombs, vaults, crypts, mausoleums and sepulchers, numbering nearly five thousand.

This the final resting place of the who's who of the Argentinian elite. To be honest, I only recognize one name, Eva Peron (craftily disguised thanks to her maiden name, Duarte, being used on her tomb). The other residents being a selection of presidents, actors, wrestlers, poets, etc.

Foreseeably, this graveyard is on the list of ten best cemeteries in the world. On what basis these paragons of peacefulness are assessed beats me. The folks in the best position to judge are already slumbering in marble pajamas. Maybe they get to cast a vote via Ouija board or something. And on what criteria would they be rated? Granite countertops, non-smoking units, pet unfriendly, free Wi-Fi? Check these out preferably before you die.[13]

Anyway, someone's going to have to shove over a bit pretty soon. With a couple of Argentinian megastars hovering just off stage, the Pope (eighty-one years of age) and Maradona (fifty-eight dissolute years), something special is going to have to be done.

Dining in B.A. is unfailingly a delight. For our last supper we visit the Rodi bar. We have no expectations. It is a simple no-frills traditional restaurant-come-bar, oozing authenticity from the black and white checkered tile floor, walnut panelling, middle-aged male wait staff who know their shit and with a glare that

---

[13] https://www.mentalfloss.com/photos/504533/12-most-beautiful-cemeteries-around-world

says they aren't going to take any guff from any decaf, soy latte, drinking pseud. They don't care who you are or in our case, aren't. There won't be any "how are the first bites" here. We are a barely tolerable inconvenience.

I had been warned about the steaks tending to be overdone in Argentina, but rather than second guess the chef, I ordered my usual, medium rare. Already suitably intimidated by our waiter, I decide not to engage in a discussion about the finer points of how I like my meat cooked. There is an air of simmering belligerence bubbling beneath his stone-faced mask. The eye contact spoke volumes, it telegraphs, "I've been serving steaks for twenty years, pal, just you try it..." He is on a hair trigger and enjoying every moment of it.

The clientele is a mixed bag: Investment bankers at the table next to us going down market. Talking in self-important tones, there are always deals to be had/made in basket-case economies. Some tourists with open guide books. Office workers stopping on their way home. A guy from the apartment above the restaurant coming down in his slippers to collect his supper. Deliveries going out to other customers in the neighbourhood.

Thinking back on some of the best meals I've ever had, I realize that it is as much about the whole experience, the company, the surroundings and the unexpected, as it is about the cuisine.

The meal itself is straightforward simple food made with excellent ingredients and cooked to perfection. Steak, boiled potatoes and red wine. One of the best I've ever had.

The next day, I pass our waiter in the street. He greets me with a barely perceptible upturn at the corners of the mouth and there may have been a hint of a nod. I guess that I had passed the test, whatever it was.

After our decadent interlude, our plan is to fly 1,300 kilometres to the northeast of the country for a sampling of nature's wonders. An early morning flight demands an even earlier taxi ride to the airport at four in the morning and the Portenos are still making their way home from their evening's socializing.

By mid-morning, after an uneventful flight, we are welcomed by the sticky heat of the tropics and catch a cab for town. It is only just approaching fall when we leave B.A., and we know that the tropics don't have seasons in the way that the temperate zones do and yet the air seems to be filled with a cherry-blossom blizzard. The answer to the puzzle gradually becomes apparent, these are actually thousands and thousands of small yellow butterflies that blur the windshield like a fog. What a welcome.

Checked into our hotel, we go meander around the town of Puerto Iguazu. It is situated where the borders of Argentina, Brazil, and Paraguay all meet. The natural barriers of the River Parana and the Iguazu Falls have made for peaceful relations and many Brazilians and Paraguayans come across the border in the evening to enjoy the market nightlife.

But this is South America, so inevitably there are cops. They seem pretty chill compared to their city counterparts.

Sitting at a street side juice bar, I have the luck to watch a couple in their police cruiser having a mate break. Mate is the steeped leaves of the caffeine rich yerba plant, brewed a bit like tea but different. It is more popular than tea or coffee in Argentina and the ritual is as important as the ingredients.

The officer sucks on the bombilla (a metal-like straw), one end of which sits in a gourd about the size of a small cup, which he cradles in his hand. He is a handsome fellow and he looks a bit like Daniel Craig doing an impersonation of Basil Rathbone doing an impersonation of Sherlock Holmes and his pipe.

Being careful not to drain the gourd, he passes it over to his partner, no slouch in the attractiveness stakes herself, all Charlie's Angels ringlets. It is an experience meant to be shared. She reaches forward and gently takes his gourd in the palm of her hand, bends forward and encircles his bombilla with her full lips, taking care not to touch the stem with her fingers (considered seriously bad form) and sucks until the warm elixir starts to flow.

Sherlock looks on with a contented look on his face, clearly impressed with her technique. Farrah's craving satisfied, she returns the cuia to him. Holmes adds some more hot water to the gourd from a thermos, he is going for a second. Farrah has had enough though, she leans over gives him a kiss on each cheek and exits the car, another shift over.

Brilliant. Sure, the food safe people would probably have a fit, but it certainly ticked all the environmental boxes. Reduced containers, reused straws, recycled yerba leaves. It probably does more for the esprit de corps and waistline than sharing doughnuts and drinking coffee out of cardboard cups. As always with progress, some things gained but some things lost.

The next day, we visit the waterfalls of Iguazu, Guarani for "Big Water" no kidding. Fantastic! Experiencing it is a lot more fun than trying to come up with superlatives to describe it. Well I always say, when in doubt adopt the modern ploy and mash a few words together to come up with an escape. Failing to find the apoca-hyperbole- geddon of all apoca-hyperbole-geddons, it was impressive, maybe even armalyptic.

Suffice to say the measurements are splendid, it is three times the height of Niagara, wider than Victoria but with a smaller 1,600 metre curtain, to use the composed words of Wikipedia.

The Iguazu curtain, the final curtain for our first trip to South America; it won't be the last.

Chapter 15
The Island That Shall Remain Nameless

Afflecus Gargantua on TITSRN

"ISN'T LIFE A SERIES OF IMAGES THAT CHANGE
AS THEY REPEAT THEMSELVES?"

– Andy Warhol

"THERE'S SOMETHING REALLY GREAT AND ROMANTIC ABOUT
SLEEPING ON COUCHES."

– Ben Affleck

As portended, we come to the Pacific postscript to our Austral adventure and fly into Mataveri, the most remote airport in the world, on the island known variously as Rapa Nui (the name given by the Polynesian first settlers somewhere between the seventh- and twelfth-century), and Isla De Pascua, (the Spanish translation when annexed by Chile in 1888), and my own personal favourite, "the navel of the world." However, this tiny paradise is more commonly known as Easter Island (the name given by Dutch Explorers in 1722, who had been sent to find Terra Australis). The Rapa Nui were no doubt mystified when the Dutch tried to explain why they had named their home Easter Island, given that they hadn't seen a tree in over two hundred years, let alone a crucifix.

So what to say about this multi monikered motu? Well, it is hot though sub-tropical, you can't drink the water, it is a five-hour flight to the nearest Starbucks, there is no golf course, it is expensive, there isn't as much as a two-storey house, you can rent a car, but you can't insure it. So maybe the less said the better, a rock to be avoided at all cost, left alone like some Pacific backwater only to be referred to as "the island that shall remain nameless," TITSRN.

Having given TITSRN short shrift, I will fill you in on our sojourn to its second self, Affleck Island (the name given by Raccoon Sixty, retired civil servant on a trip in March 2021, and after reading this, I am sure that you will agree that it was a trip and not a holiday). It is an island similar in all respects to TITSRN. It lies approximately 3,700 kilometres west of Chile.

Affleck Island was created about 750 thousand years ago, when three volcanoes erupted out of the ocean, like three zits on the right cheek of the mighty Pacific, it must have been quite a show. The molten mass gelled into a single island roughly thirty-four kilometres long, the shape resembling a turtle facing eastward. The craters of the volcanoes each four- to five-hundred metres high define the eastern head, northern hump, and western tail, where the big city Hanga Roa lies, home to 95 percent of the island's six thousand inhabitants.

It is all very peaceful and rustic, our little cabana faces an empty ocean, no boats at sea, a dog might bark, a car may pass by every half hour or so, a rooster might crow at any time of day just to provide some conversation material, you might hear a distant nail being hammered in for a few minutes just to prove that industry though not a priority is permissible, there are no traffic lights and the stop signs are merely a suggestion. The skies are also empty, unless you are unlucky and spot one of the two flights a day that bring the ninety thousand visitors a year to the island, less than arrive on a slow 41C August day in Las Vegas. Internet is a community event here (signals are on island time), so the town has installed a free site in the town square. Good for a whopping fifty users at a time. It's an interesting social experiment, it remains to be seen if the folks continue to get more entertainment out of their neighbours than pleasuring themselves with their handheld devices. The old wisdom used to warn that if you overindulged in your handheld device, you would go blind. Given the ominous omnipresence of the new handhelds, is there anyone qualified left to caution about the potential dangers of going deaf, dumb and blind?[14] In any event, the locals seem to have at least as much faculty with their senses as their Western contemporaries.

There are no Walmarts, no McDonalds, no chains of any kind and no trash (they usually travel as a package). There is no vandalism, unless you count the devastation caused by falling coconuts as they turn the boardwalks into kindling when they fall from the trees or the toppled moai. There is no graffiti, corporate or home grown, it is all very quaint. Little open-front restaurants dot the seafront, no plate glass or shining steel (this

---

[14] https://psychcentral.com/lib/does-masturbation-cause-blindness/

includes the cutlery), instead all they have are locally-painted murals and carvings to invite you with their own individual albeit tumble-down charms.

OK, so this is a one-horse town, but a one-horse town with a difference. There are horses everywhere. The island has thousands, some say more horses than people, and are all apparently given the run of the place. Roads, farmland, archeological sites, downtown and in any phase of life/death. Foals/skeletons, yearlings/rotting corpses, pregnant mares and stallions with glints in their eyes and a spring in their step. It seems that the missionaries were so successful in converting the Rapa Nui to Catholicism, they had plenty of spare time to devote to breeding the horses they brought with them.

So enough of the Fodor's guide to the island commentary and on to the riddles of its alter ego. Of course, the 64,000 puka-shell question is, "How did Affleck Island get its name?" Come down the rabbit hole with me to have the mysteries of Affleck in Wonderland revealed.

As is usual with questions stretching back before written history, many mysteries, legends, and scientific puzzles surround the answer. But in a coconut shell, there are about nine hundred of the world-famous moai dotted around the island and they are all carved in the image of Ben Affleck. These iconic moai stone busts measuring anywhere from two to ten metres in height and weighing up to eighty tonnes (Stonehenge mere Lego bricks at less than half the weight) bear all the well-known indicia of Affleckism. Slightly defiantly upturned lantern jaw, small forehead, deep set eyes, thin stern lips, largish ears, perfect nose, and flat head. But what about the top knot (pukao), the rock that can add another two metres and twelve tonnes to the edifice? "What does that have to do with Ben?" I hear you ask. I have a theory, but that will have to wait for now.

A more glaring non sequitur in this connection would seem to be in the timing of events. How could the Polynesians carving away between 1250 and 1500 have known what Ben, born in Berkley in 1972, would look like? The answer may be more obvious than you think... the fifth dimension, time, and time travel. The Orono volcano crater at the west end of the island is more than just the navel of our world but a portal that leads to other time continuums and parallel universes.

It is unlikely that Ben himself travelled back in time to initiate this great endeavour, as he has demonstrated no artistic ability whatsoever so would have been ill-suited to provide the islanders with the necessary direction to fulfill the task. All evidence leads to the conclusion that Andy Warhol had indeed spearheaded the venture. Andy and Ben met at a save-the-chicken conference in Kampala in 2097. Andrew, always the innovator, had pioneered the use of the Orono connector to get there, whereas the means of Ben's transtemporal travel to the Ugandan capital remains but another unanswered question in this supernatural account.

All this was shortly after Andy had produced his famous diptych of Marilyn Monroe in our reality year of 1962. Andrew was at the peak of his creative talents and was hell-bent on delivering his next breakthrough work in three dimensions, 5D art still being in its theoretical infancy. The etymology of moai is scant, obviously Affleckius Gargantua would have been too highbrow a handle and given the Polynesian language only has ten consonants, none of which are an F or a B. Andy probably went with the name the carvers repeatedly yelled out. The shouts usually caused when the chisellers hit their thumbs with their hammers. MOAI!!!!! MOAI!!!!!!!!!

Travelling back to Affleck Island in 1249, Andy got to work with its skilled and willing populace, numbering 16,000 in those days. Before long, Ben's chiselled good looks were ubiquitous. He would be mounted on a plinth, or Ahu in the local lingo, which could be up to one hundred metres long. Sometimes singly, or in groups of up to fifteen. The feats of engineering required to transport eighty-tonne statues from the "nursery" (a quarry/mountainside near the centre of the island) to the perimeter of the coast, in some cases a distance of twenty kilometres, provide fertile ground for many wacky theories.

Anyway, back to the facts. So the moai direct their gaze inland and each site has its own name. We have one in front of our cottage, which faces directly into our room. It is called Ahu Akapu, which translates into "Peeping Ben." I have a staring contest with him every day, to no avail. I don't feel bad, as he has had six hundred years more practice at it than me. Apparently, the moai were erected facing inland so as to reassure the citizens that as long as they were under the watchful eyes of their ancestral leaders, no harm could come to them (we all know how that turned out), so it's a bit like CCTV in more than one respect.

Andy started to wear out his welcome when he started putting the funny topknots on top of the hunky Ben. Eyebrows were certainly being raised, the islanders suspected that he was mocking the moai. Things worsened, by the mid-1800s, food shortages and clan warfare gripped the island. The islanders, just recently introduced to the wheel, realized that they were rapidly coming off. Ben became as popular as reruns of Gigli. The moai were toppled and the era of the birdman cult took over.

As a test of Andy's godliness, the islanders made him participate in the "Birdman" competitions. The bravest and strongest of each tribe were challenged to climb the cliffs above the crater of the Orono volcano in a challenge to be the first to bring back an egg from a nest of the returning sooty terns. Many fell to their deaths attempting this feat, Andy fell too, five hundred metres down into the pool of water that fills the cauldron of the cinder cone. It was quite a spill; his hair was a mess, lost his glasses and everything. Down and down he went, to the bottom of the crater, through the bottom of the crater, through the navel itself (fortunately an inny). The portal, with its cosmic energy field just on the other side, pulled Andy through, like he was in the spin cycle of a top loader on the speed of light setting into the time space umbilical cord.

He popped out into the parallel universe we call reality—if you can call East 47th Street, Manhattan, 1962, reality. Andy landed with a thump physically and artistically. Having tasted the delights of three-dimensional reproductive art, he was crestfallen by the banality of length by width. Sure, he probably had more devotees in reality than on Affleck Island, richer too, but they were lazy and showed no aptitude or appetite for chiselling volcanic tuff under the hot sun. Even a trip to the hairdresser and a new pair of glasses didn't cheer him up. He couldn't even enjoy the spin-off benefits from having lost his spectacles when being pulled through the portal. His crystal-framed Miltzens being further immortalized as they were sucked into the cosmic single sock belt for all eternity.

After 250 years of churning out moai, his prescription was seriously out of date and without new glasses, he would likely have permanently damaged his sight, with or without the additional optical degradation caused by the impending arrival of handheld devices.

Andy, however, was never the same. His work suffered, his art reflected his contempt for two-dimensional representation. He abandoned his quest for fifteen minutes of fame in every century. He resorted to painting Campbell's soup cans. Each was thematically the same, like his moai, but each a little different, the label describing each of the thirty-two varieties available at the time. Revealingly, amongst the thirty-two, he included chicken noodle soup even though through the ages he had been a lifelong advocate for chicken rights (see Kampala 2097). When you are a genius of imagery and metaphor, you don't need to lop off an ear to get your point across.

Yes, that is the history, some would say stranger than fiction, but that's it in a cowrie shell. Well, enough of the history of the island. Other more contemporary delights include a visit to church, something for everyone, where the priests, decked out in headdresses and feathers, look like they've just stepped off a carnival float in Rio. They sing a song, with all hands linked "Auld Lang Syne" style, and instead of a church organ, a ukulele band and choir give the hymns big licks. It takes all my willpower not to applaud at the end of every number, and at the end of the service there are sporting handshakes with every congregation member that you can stretch to.

There is plenty of sightseeing to be done, including visiting the Tongariki Ahu at sunrise, the biggest collection of standing moai, at fifteen. An intimate affair as these things go, about two hundred or so other worshippers spread across a field of about ten acres. As the day warms up, we head for a refreshing dip at the beautiful white sand Akena beach, where seven Bens have their backs turned to us. Then we hike up one of the volcanoes, take picture after fabulous picture. This one is going to be the one I have on my computer as screensaver for the rest of my life, but then it is the next one and then the next and next... They say a picture never lies, but they don't feel like they tell the whole truth either, the images never fully measure up. How times change. It used to be so much fun in the seventies and eighties to disparage the snap-happy Japanese tourists, turns out they were the pioneers and me but a late adopter.

The hues and combinations of greens and blues and reds are unattainable, still I click away. They also say a picture is worth a thousand words, which in my case is hitting too close to home and yet even a thousand good words wouldn't begin to describe the vistas. Who would have guessed that ecological collapse would result in such amazing beauty?

Whether you believe this all to be a Rapanuan legend, children's bedtime story, alt truth, or a peep into a parallel universe, never utter the name of "the island that shall remain nameless," this is just between us, the secrets stop here.

PART III

REEDUCATION RWANDAN STYLE

Chapter 16
The Beer Necessities

Are you sure that this thing is going to have eight billion seats?

"Those who make peaceful revolution impossible will make violent revolution inevitable."

– John F. Kennedy

"Friendship and money: oil and water."

– Mario Puzo

In the spring of 2022, with COVID-19 on the retreat and our bank balance experiencing a revival, we figure that it is the perfect time to get back to Rwanda. It's an ill-wind that blows nobody any good.

The marvel of long-haul air travel isn't just about the speed with which you get to your destination but the jarring snapshots of the world's paradoxes that confront you along the way.

The delights of central Africa aren't easily accessed from Western Canada. Our long journey there begins with a hop from Victoria to Seattle. SeaTac an airport that is continually in a state of confused construction. Built in 1944, when America was in its ascendency, its infrastructure is now crumbling, much like the Republic itself. Our connecting flight is on Qatar Airlines, to their home base in the capital Doha. It will take us eighteen hours. We will fly bearing 359 degrees virtually due north, firstly over the Rocky Mountains, before passing just south of the Pole. (West would be more accurate but doesn't convey the same feeling of proximity given that everything below the Pole must be south of it.)

It seems questionable to be going over the Arctic to get to the desert. Once we start heading south, the route takes us through the not-so-friendly skies over Russia, skirting Moscow a couple of hundred kilometres to the east, perhaps a bold choice when there is a "special military operation" (aka war) going on. The US and Russia have blocked flights from their respective commercial carriers from their airspaces. Our passage bisects the Caspian Sea and then transports us over some more dodgy real estate, Iran. It could be the nearest that I will ever get to visiting that conflicted but fascinating country. We shimmy past Teheran and cross the Persian Gulf (also called the Arabian Gulf by other local human rights abusers) to Qatar.

We approach the airport in the dead of night. It's as if each one of Qatar's 2.7 million people have left their porch light on to welcome us. A glowing sci-fi sea of light surrounded by the pitch-black emptiness of the desert and Gulf Sea that encircles it suggest an otherworldly civilization.

Twinkling suburbs built on man-made islands the shape of palm trees extend into the Gulf, the city centre rises directly from the flat lands to nearly one-thousand feet, shining like a flood-lit Mount Everest. Scores of skyscrapers, nearly all of them constructed in the last fifteen years, form the outline of the central pinnacle.

A tiny country less than the tenth of the size of Greece but rich enough to host the world's biggest event, the World Cup of Football. A featureless land whose tallest hill tops out at twenty-eight metres. Less than half the wingspan of the Airbus 350 that we are arriving in. A country with nothing but sand and the good fortune to be sitting on massive oil and gas reserves provides the inhabitants with the highest GDP in the world. If the tournament isn't a success, it won't be for the lack of money, the budget being a whopping $220 billion, or to put it another way, eighty thousand dollars per person. $10 billion for stadiums and the rest for infrastructure projects intended to benefit the population long-term.

Who will benefit from this extravagance isn't readily apparent. When only 13 percent of the 2.7 million people currently resident in the country are Qatari citizens, the math becomes a bit more revealing. Something more like $628,000 will be spent for each of those roughly 350,000 citizens. Most of the other inhabitants, migrant Nepali, Indian and Philippine construction workers, can expect long hours and dangerous work in a tortuous climate at minimum pay grades for the equivalent of $275 per month. The average organic chicken is assured of better working conditions.

The Qataris are doing quite nicely, but there is more than a monetary cost to all this luxury. As well as being one of the most obese societies on earth, "Worldometer" tells me that Qatar is the undisputed champion at emitting CO2, weighing in at a whopping 37.29 tonnes of CO2 per capita. Canada is an embarrassing seventh worst polluter in the world at 18.58 tonnes, nearly four times more than the global average of 4.79 tonnes.

We touch down at Hamad International Airport. The terminals deliver all the opulence one might expect from a miniscule country that is home to 13 percent of the world's LNG reserves. Faux main streets dotted with shops glittering with brand-name temptations assault the senses. Travellers are teased by the likes of Harrods, Versace, Cartier and Rolex storefronts. The airport's internal rail system has more track than the entire country of Rwanda.

Our seven-hour layover gives us ample time to watch the firework display for the World Cup opening ceremony over and over and over again on the IMAX-sized screens that are inescapably placed throughout the ultra-modern complex. It's a simulation of the real event that will happen nine months hence, a display so played out by now that it inspires as much awe as a McDonald's ad. It is as good a way as any to get it over with without having to expend any energy oohing and aahing.

Qatar continues to flog its resources to a world that doesn't care. It turns its oil and gas into money, which it turns into glass and steel and concrete and roads and plastic and water. Water, which is more precious than anything here. A country without so much as a puddle of surface water creates its drinking water by desalination, producing 1.5 litres of effluent for every one litre of potable water. The polluted waste finds its way back into the Gulf.

A scant hour and a half after taking off from Hamad, our Boeing 737 is over Ethiopian airspace. The world economy has worked its magic by turning Qatar's oil into water. Water abundant enough to supply their fountains and swimming pools. But as we begin to acknowledge the interconnectedness of our world, we are also aware that it turns Ethiopia's rains into droughts, which starves their children. Where is the legitimacy in any of this?

The rainy season has failed to arrive for the fourth consecutive year, leaving sixteen million people in the region struggling to find food. The average Ethiopian produces a meagre climate friendly .1 of a tonne of CO_2, close to four hundred times less than the average Qatari. Who will the world show its gratitude to? The global North is Qatar's biggest customer, that probably says it all.

The looming question is, what happens when the Global South figures out that 20 percent of the world's population produces 92 percent of the world's excess carbon dioxide?[15] It won't be long before some small Pacific nation, whose islands are vanishing beneath their feet, or some African tribesman, whose crops fails again and again because of drought, or some Bangladeshi farmer, whose land is flooded, start resenting all this and come calling with their pitch forks for you and I dear reader. Desperation breeds militancy and who could blame them. We get into a lynching mood when our cell phones go down for the day. Maybe nuclear winter will seem to some especially aggrieved victim to be a justifiable measure to have their plight addressed. There is nothing like a common enemy for a call to unite. Better that we start to make amends now, if not out of a sense of altruism but our own selfish self-preservation motives. This is not a population problem but a greed problem.

A further four and a half hours on our connecting flight sees us arriving in Kigali, a tidy city with some stylishly modern architecture on a modest scale. We are welcomed by Justin, one of the directors of the organization we have come to visit. He ferries us to our hotel in an oldish Toyota Corolla that he has rented for the purpose. We sleep like the dead, travelling for thirty-six hours will do that to you.

---

[15] https://inthesetimes.com/article/climate-change-wealthy-western

While in town, we take the opportunity to have dinner with a group of urbanite Rwandans in their thirties, who we had made friends with on previous trips. They, like us, are now more worldly than ever due to the relentless reach of connectivity in their lives. Despite or maybe because of exposure to social media, they seem to have become somewhat less satisfied with their lot in life. Not being plugged in to their social media networks, I am pretty clueless as to what they have been busy with in the intervening years. It is noticeable that their standard of living has improved over the four years that we have known them, maybe not dramatically but steadily.

Strangely, I feel as if I am witnessing some sort of social experiment, where these friends are living life as a control group in a time-elapse study. I check in on their condition every few years. Back in Canada amongst my regular crowd, where changes in lifestyle aren't so marked, I am too immersed in my own feedback loops to notice shifts in my own attitudes.

Expectations here though, are changed. Being educated, having a house with plumbing and electricity, having access to renting a car on special occasions, for example, don't rate with them as being signs of middle-class anymore.

Middle-class has become a global standard. No matter which country we live in, we assess our worth as individuals in relation to the most affluent as promoted by media and the marketing industries. Your peer group is no longer your own village or your own country for that matter. Our goals are being driven by the hyping of consumption and the bar is always being raised. Any hope of being content with what you have has been subverted. The whole system depends on us never being happy. The onslaught to disseminate dissatisfaction and stress will lead nowhere good.

As the number of empty bottles of Mutzig on the table grows, we opine on what we see as the most important issue for Rwanda right now, each sticking pretty much to our home turf.

Justin, a businessman, sees an urgent need for security to protect the country from the instability of its neighbours and from disruptive elements within the country. Several of the henchmen that promoted the genocide escaped overseas but continue to foment rebellion amongst the many Hutu, who also fled the country. As many as a quarter of a million of these emigrees still live in refugee camps in the neighbouring countries of the DRC, Tanzania, Uganda and Burundi. It may be a coincidence but the impact of the Holocaust and the Rwandan genocide seem to have had a similar effect on the country's attitude to defence. Rwanda, like Israel, has become a regional military powerhouse. Well-equipped, well-trained and capable of prevailing over their much larger neighbours.

Danny, an engineer, sees investment in technology as the way forward. The potential to be a hub nation in the centre of the continent with a stable, if somewhat autocratic government, plentiful options for clean energy from solar and rivers engorged by the tropical rainy season. Located close to the mines where the rare metals required for computers are found. The Singapore of Africa maybe.

Trixie, a romantic, sees compassion as the fundamental building block needed for a successful society. This element an essential ingredient not just for Rwanda but for all countries given our ever more tightly-woven connections to each other.

Olivier, a teacher, naturally enough chose education. His pupils are enthusiastic and motivated to learn. Knowledge entertains and provides a self-perpetuating need for intellectual stimulation. He is optimistic that through teaching critical-thinking skills and debunking unfounded myths, the country will be able to escape backsliding into irrational paranoia based on ignorance.

Marcus wants sustainability for all of the people in his village and the country. His philosophy guides the way that the social enterprise works. They have recently shelved plans to buy a tractor for the farm. He cannot justify replacing the twenty-three villagers who tend the fields with one tractor driver. Paying jobs are scarce and those that have work are respected and admired.

Precious, who has won a scholarship to attend a liberal US university, sees the protection of the environment as the number one priority. He educates us on a few facts regarding the 200 million-hectare Congo Basin forests, which spreads across six central African nations. It absorbs even more carbon than the Amazon region. Frighteningly, recent reports show that 35 percent of the Basin has been earmarked for oil and mineral exploration.

The Bezos Earth Fund pledged over $100 million at the 2021 COPP for environmental projects in the area, a rather callous demonstration of generosity, when a couple of months earlier, Mr. Bezos had spent four minutes up in his "Blue Origin" spaceship. The cost of the enterprise reputed to be $5.5 billion.

Precious, his ire rising, stabbing the table with his index finger, remonstrates that while all this is transpiring, Bezos's Amazon empire hammers away at pushing as much merchandise as possible to as many people as possible. And what are the major elements in that merchandise? Oil and minerals.

Then rather than letting us get complacent about our own contributions, he warns us about congratulating ourselves on how much we recycle.

"The only reason there is more recycling is because we are ignoring the best hopes for addressing the problem "reducing and reusing." We are consuming more and more. We are still making the problem worse.

When we are still stuck in the old thinking that money can buy our way out of this mess, there is no motivation to reduce and reuse because there is no profit in that. No one in the world of commerce has any incentive to help us change our behaviour."

Danny has seen this show before, he thrusts another beer into Precious's hand before he bursts into flames. These guys go way back, since they were kids. They take one look at each other, tilt back in their chairs, stare at the ceiling for a millisecond, then simultaneously erupt into fits of laughter.

After the hilarity dies down, it is time for my two cents worth. Me, being an ex-bureaucrat, has to agree with everyone that they are all important. But to me, all of those initiatives can only be addressed if the demographics are tackled.

Too many people is the big problem. To use the patois of 2022, Rwanda is going to have to pivot to address the unprecedented birth-rate explosion that is spiking like an Omicron contamination rate graph.

Rwanda's population is thirteen million, nearly doubling from seven million at the start of the 1994 genocide. Terrifyingly, the populous is forecasted to more than double again to twenty-seven million by 2050. Rwanda is currently one of the most densely-populated countries on earth already, it seems that every hillside is dotted with homes and every patch of land is cultivated. Life expectancy has soared to seventy years of age and ominously, the average age of a Rwandan is just eighteen.

Our thoughts generate a daunting list of diverse priorities. Revealing in one way, not by what was a common theme (there was none), but revealing in what they all omitted, which is that none of us put material wealth as the top priority. In its own way an unveiling of the things that really mattered most to us.

The true test will be to see if we can reject the distractions that fill our days and go after what we really want.

The next day, having solved all the world's problems, we hire a car to take us to Shagora, Marcus's village, but there is no escaping the conundrums. It is market day and goats are being transported into the city in wheelbarrow buckets lashed to the back of bicycles, feet in the air, heads lolling over the rim, limp and lifeless, skulls dangling macabrely. Apparently, they are only asleep, reminiscent of passengers sleeping on an eighteen-hour airline trip i.e., they couldn't look deader if they were dead. No point in killing them when they might not sell at the market.

Whether the airlines have learned these tactics from the farmers or vice versa, the principles are the same. Restrict the passenger's movement, deprive them of light, squeeze them into inadequate space, add mechanical vibration and tell them to relax and enjoy the trip. A convoy of probably two hundred of these cargo bikes pass us, heading in the direction of town. There are plans to have the road paved and those two hundred cyclists will be replaced by one truck driver. It seems like the more you pollute, the better you are paid. There is nothing like progress. I am beginning to think that it is pointless to believe in anything at all when it always ends up being wrong anyway.

It is dark when we arrive at the village, hugs, smiles and chatter ensue as we get reacquainted with old friends and are introduced to new members of the team. The house is unfamiliar to us, bigger than the last one we stayed in, with more but smaller rooms. The ever-growing family of clients and staff means that accommodation arrangements are always changing and as a result, JHA now has a boy's and a girl's house. For now, Trixie and I will be staying at the girl's house.

But I am getting ahead of myself. The team are keen to show us the progress they have made since our last visit. On consecutive days we are given a tour and are awed by what they have achieved in the last two short years.

We take a visit to the farm, replete with fields of corn, peppers, amaranth and pens housing goats and cows, tended by the caregivers and beneficiaries, where we are handed shovels and put to work for a couple of hours, until we cry uncle and are chaperoned to the now completed preschool and some cooling shade.

We are introduced to the school administrator Bosco. He is a recent recruit and this is his first stab at welcoming visitors. Bosco seems intimidated as much by the size of his desk as the enormity of his responsibilities. Beads of sweat forming on his brow. Here he is, new to the job and expected to provide an impromptu tap dance in a foreign language to a couple of strangers who might help provide for his students.

The issue of money always lurks at the shadowy fringes of these initial encounters. We know and he also knows that we could drop enough dollars to feed his 350 children for a day without it registering any more financial impact for us than a trip for two to McDonald's.

We will be here long enough to form a friendship with Bosco, one where we can leave the stereotypical roles of scrounger and scrooge aside. One where we can accept that we are all only trying to help in whatever way we can.

His torment finally at its end, he takes us to the classrooms and introduces us to Mabel, the head teacher.

Mabel a dynamo, supremely comfortable with authority and a take-no-prisoners teaching style, who could care less whether we sit in on one of her classes or not. We wouldn't have missed it for the world. She seems to have trained to be a Marine Corps drill sergeant rather than a teacher.

Her forty or so pupils, all five years of age or younger, sit quietly on the concrete floor and hang on her every word. Her authority is absolute. In between teaching "the cat sat on the mat" and "how many beans make five" she maintains absolute discipline and decorum with a mix of tyranny and seduction.

"What is all the noise? We are not at the market."

"Where are your manners? We are being ladies. I don't want to see your knickers."

"Who is coming to America with me this October?" I am totally hoodwinked by this one. When I ask her after class where in the States she is going, she looks at me as if I have horns on my head.

And with an imperious, "And how do you think I can afford that? I've never been out of Rwanda," burst my bubble. With that, we adjourn for lunch.

There are over 350 tykes quietly sitting cross legged on mats in the school playground. Eyes as big as saucers awaiting their biggest, perhaps only meal of the day. The children wait patiently and are each served a plastic plate heaped with porridge and a cup of milk. Not a drop is spilt, not a crumb is left.

Not every child in the village is this lucky, though, as the preschool is filled to overcapacity. Scores of those less fortunate turn up at the gate each lunch time in the hope of being fed. Depending on the funds available on any given day an extra sack of rice may be bought. The sacks weigh twenty-five kilograms, cost the equivalent of about twenty dollars, and can provide about one hundred children a meal.

The school staff let as many of these kids as they can feed into the compound, while the others gaze through the chain-link fence in hopeless silence.

Mealtime over, the children placidly file forward in rotation, neatly stack their plates and mugs, then tear off at great speed full of childish glee.

The next morning, we are invited to go on a ride-along with the emergency team, "Uncle" Andre, Samira and Norbert, that goes out into the village. Not as you might expect, in a tricked-out SUV driven by muscular first responders in uniform. This motley band of Samaritans head out on their rounds on Mary Poppins era bicycles. We assemble at the school, jerry cans are filled with milk from churns brought from the farm. The jerry cans are strapped to racks on the back of the bikes, a plastic jug is tied on, and off they go.

We tag along on cycle taxis that they have arranged for us, (regular bikes that have been modified to accommodate a cushioned oblong seat in place of the usual rack). My unit and driver, decked out like an escapee from a Saint Patrick's Day parade, resplendent in white and green rather than the typical black. I dub it the Celtic cycle.

We weave our way along dirt lanes and paths, stopping regularly to deliver a jugful of the precious cargo to the seniors who occupy the dimly lit mud brick homes. Andre is on first name terms with the elders. They welcome him into their homes like a son who hasn't been seen in months.

Each home has its own story to tell and Andre takes the time to hear them all. One lady, an irrepressible centenarian, tells us that there are four generations living in her tiny home. She and her daughter look after her greatgrandchildren while the granddaughter works, it's a common scenario. An ever-present pool of roaming kids two to ten years old surround us.

Further along on our rounds, I try to engage in conversation through Samira's translations. I ask the woman of the next house how old she is. She doesn't know, but dashes inside her house and emerges with her ID card, which she passes to Samira. Samira reads aloud "Fifty." The lady seems surprised but pleased.

Production from the farm is steadily growing and the milk round grows with it. We stop at another hut, a new client. She is initially suspicious about her good fortune. Disbelievingly, she asks, "How can this be free? Who do we have to pay?"

And so it continues until all of the milk is given away. The gratitude of all the residents is humbling.

Even the most skeptical, that would be me, slowly sheepishly raising my hand here, can't but be stunned by the selflessness of the volunteers. That and the pervasive poverty in the village will have you seriously thinking about selling your house and putting that money to more productive use. Fortunately, a little distance and time will have you reconsidering the extent of your magnanimity.

I have come to the realization that I am addicted to comfort and convenience. Even though it doesn't provide much emotional fulfillment, I can't kick the habit. One of the side effects of being an addict is the feeling that you are letting loved ones around you down as well as yourself.

Maybe I need a twelve-step AA style intervention to bring me to my senses. Maybe by confessing this in front of others, I have started on the long process to recovery. In the meantime, cooler heads and insanity prevail and our house stays off the market. The milk-run experience is only the first of many instances when I am unable to shrug off my own shortcomings.

On another occasion, I go to the shops in the centre of the village, accompanied by one of the beneficiaries, Princess. Princess was rescued from the streets. Despite only being fourteen, her attractiveness and naivety has already been taken advantage of. Yet those hard times on the street gave her an assertiveness beyond her years. On more than one occasion, I see her have no trouble dealing with cat-calling oafs. Silencing them with a scowl and a withering tirade.

For a snack, I buy each of us a mandazi. A deep-fried doughnut-like confection, a rare treat for Princess. We start eating our goodies as we walk down the street, me forgetting that it is bad manners to eat in public unless you are willing to share. Realizing my mistake, me the last of the big spenders, surreptitiously stows the mandazi in my bag, just as I am spotted by a little kid. The tyke runs up to Princess and without even being asked, she hands the rest of her treasured delicacy to the resourceful youngster.

It wasn't a begging situation, it wasn't a donor and donee, it wasn't a gift. It was pure sharing.

I have some, you would like some. I have and you need.

Childlike and yet with her life experiences she is so far from being a child in so many ways. Completely unfazed, not expecting any thanks. There was none. One human to another as natural as twins sharing a mother's bosom.

Why this chance encounter strikes me so forcefully is because of how ashamed it makes me feel, how small it makes me feel in the aura of Princess's selflessness. Me, whose first thought was to stow my twenty-cent doughnut out of sight. Why is it that those who have the least are the most generous? Why is it that the more we have, the less we are able to share?

Perhaps bringing the technologies, medicines and commerce of the "developed" nations is a better gauge of our ability to share. But even there, there are troubling signs. Help can be welcome and unwelcome at the same time.

Portuguese workers that are building the new international airport nearby throw candies and small change out the windows of their trucks as they speed past children standing by the roadside. Well intentioned gestures, but one that predictably leads to a demeaning scuffle in the dirt as kids scramble for the dregs. Selling sexual favours for dollars is becoming a growing problem.

Is it the jet lag? Is it the company? Is it the heat? Is it village life? Is it the beer?

Whatever it is, it feels like I am seeing things that should have been obvious to me long ago.[16]

---

[16] https://www.nightviz.ca/single-post/michael-apted-wanted-to-go-from-seven-up-to-70-up-and-more-but-his-time-was-up

Chapter 17
Art For Art's Sake

Equals Fake News

"Art is never finished, only abandoned."

— Leonardo Da Vinci

"Rice is great if you're really hungry
and want to eat two thousand of something."

— Mitch Hedberg

We do our best to get comfortable in our six-by-six room. The room that the girls have surrendered, provides us with two bunks. The three displaced girls will snuggle up in the big eight-foot square room, four bunks and six girls. It isn't as grand as it sounds.

The girls, beneficiaries, range in age from twelve to eighteen and are grateful to have security, regular meals, a roof over their head and companionship. They have been poor, traumatized too, but remain uncowed. Utensils are in short supply but even when having to eat with their hands, they are polite, delicate in an almost elegant way. I expected something feral, with appetites sharpened by months perhaps years of hard living on the streets, not knowing where the next bite, never mind meal, might come from.

They cook and clean prior to leaving for school and must be home before ten. Despite the structure, they retain a fierce sense of independence and self-preservation. The caregivers try hard to provide just the right environment. Too much Club Med and the girls will never leave, too much Colditz and they will be back on the streets in a flash. Some of the caregivers are barely older than their wards. The bulk of this responsibility falls to Samira. At the tender age of twenty-three, she seems to have found the middle ground. Between servings of Cleopatra's cunning and doses of Nurse Ratched's steeliness, decorum is maintained.

In the predawn, the bolt of their room is shot and with the scrape of wood on cement, the door creaks open. This alarm clock gets us all up at 5:30. Shortly after that the slop, splash and splat of a mop on the concrete patio outside our bedroom window signals that a new day has begun. Having had our fill of airline rations, we are thrilled with the delicacies we are being treated to. It is a special breakfast, served on a platter. A feast bristling with goodness, fresh mini bananas, tree tomatoes, passionfruit, mango, paw paw and pineapple that have been picked for us.

We have arrived in the last week of March. The last Saturday of each month is named Umuganda Day. An occasion that brings Rwandans together to work on a shared community based task for a morning.

This week's project relates to Kwibuka, a national holiday held on April seventh each year. The event commemorates the day the genocide started and promotes reconciliation and remembrance. We join with scores of villagers in sprucing up the memorial site in preparation for this most significant day of the year.

The tasks involve cleaning up litter, whacking away at overgrown foliage with machetes and trimming unruly grasses. It seems macabrely ironic, given that the machete was the weapon used to slay so many of the victims. It is a surprisingly upbeat affair, unlike the solemnity on Kwibuka itself.

Perhaps the buzz is because of the gathering of international celebrities on hand. That is if you believe the T-shirts being worn—Armani, Neymar, Versace, Mr. Abercrombie and Mr. Fitch are all there, as are several Guccis. Other more dated luminaries also strut their stuff on the green carpet. Notable among them, Mozart, Rooney, Batman and Marilyn Monroe. There's no spectacle without sponsors and this occasion is no exception. Guess, Vancouver 2010, Scotiabank's "You're richer than you think," The Indiana Pacers, Dunkin Donuts and Al's Garage add their market share exposure to the event. Minority activists the likes of "Science Matters" "Kiss Me, I'm Irish," and Sponge Bob mingle with the "A" listers.

All this branding I should admit became a bit of a crutch in our attempts to recall the numerous individuals that we were introduced to each day. Kinya Rwandan, like most languages, has its favourite letters. U, B, M and Ws get the most airplay and with the speed of their delivery, I have the devil of a time trying to keep up. Family names reflect this etymology. Mercifully, first names provide some relief from the Uwimanas, Mushimiyimanas and Uwimbabazis. They are often French or

English in origin, with liberal sprinklings of biblical and royal links such as "Charity," "Patience," and "Angel," and "Queen," "Princess," "Prince," and "Elvis." Others just as enchanting have more obscure derivations, "Juvenile," "Stressful," and "Innocent," to name a few and "Che Guevara," the most famous Argentinian revolutionary to come out of Africa.

In surrender we resort to creating mnemonic aide memoires to keep track of the ever increasing cast of characters. For example, Georgina becomes Prada because of her fetchingly branded ball cap. All very clever in theory but far from foolproof in practice. The next time we see the hat, it is on Ishimwe (or was that Sonia or Science Matters?). The girls do like their fashion and what clothes they do have, they trade constantly. Their shared rooms festooned with their communal inventory, like a Milan change room in fashion season.

So successfully have the ad companies colonized my subconscious (or maybe even my conscious), that I have forgotten the names of the real flesh and blood living souls who wore the T-shirts. Without my permission, the marketers have suffused my scant mental CPU with information that I don't want or more to the point, actively try to avoid. The logic is all back to front as usual. If by some accident I were to find myself using those implanted messages or logos, it would somehow be incumbent upon me to pay them for the privilege.

I should be charging Apple and all the rest one dollar a month for dumping their trash onto my mental cloud. Our laws are so far out of touch that they now only reflect what is morally justifiable by coincidence than specific design. It's like we all collectively nodded off at the same time and started sleepwalking. As we slowly emerge from our slumber, only to find that we have embarked on a series of small steps that turn out to be heading in the wrong direction. I will use Mozart and Science Matters in this story, as hopefully they will be less likely to sue me than Armani and Abercrombie if I were to "violate their rights."

On the day of the memorial, we are invited to attend the ceremonies. The garden of remembrance is packed with villagers. The mausoleum sits mutely in the corner of the grounds, casting a heavy presence over the proceedings. The crypt containing the remains of many thousands of the victims, family members of these same villagers. Speeches, personal recounting of memories and prayers are offered up by dignitaries and survivors hold the somber crowd spellbound. The grief holds fast, still visceral and vivid for so many.

After the formal proceedings have finished, Marcus asks us to join them in the visitation to the crypt. Each year Marcus arranges a private remembrance in the tomb. All the caregivers and any of the beneficiaries older than fifteen are allowed into the tomb to confront the grim history. An object lesson about what could happen if racist hatred takes hold again.

A stone staircase leads us down twelve feet to the floor of the dark tomb. The only light comes from a couple of flashlights and a small, grimy skylight above us. Row upon row of dusty glass display cases are arranged around the perimeter of the floor. Each case secured with a tiny padlock. These flimsy tributes provide more protection in death than the humans inside the cases got in life.

A warehouse full of human suffering. Each case contains the same inventory, three skulls wide, eight skulls long, two skulls deep. Compared to human form, how small those skulls seem. Their humanness further diminished by the deep gashes and crushed bone that many of them bear. All this but a tiny testimonial to the lives ended in this one of the most severely hit provinces in the country.

Exiting the memorial is through a small museum, essentially a room. Piles of clothes salvaged from victims are stacked floor to ceiling. Most now faded and disintegrating, more resembling rags rather than recognizable as garments. And yet even now family members of victims recognize bits of cloth as belonging to loved ones who vanished during the madness or who they may have seen slain before their eyes. A shred of a connection to the past or a memory too haunting to fade.

As the services wound down, folks made their way to their homes. Return to normal routines would be gradual. Commemoration week immediately follows Kwibuka. A week where many businesses and sporting events see reduced activity. The official one-hundred-day mourning period a tribute to the one-hundred-day genocide being recognized with another public holiday on July fourth each year.

My own everyday life includes plans to build some furniture for the gallery but while I am waiting for the stars to align, I find myself at a loose end. Restlessness gets the better of me and I forget my government conditioning and the cardinal rule. That would be, never volunteer for anything.

One afternoon while sharing a silence with Amza, I offer to help with the kid's art classes. Amza, the lead artist and instructor, is a bit of a mystery man. He doesn't have much to say, which seems odd given that he is quadrilingual, French, English, Kinyarwanda, and Swahili. His appearance begs more questions than answers. Likely in his thirties or forties, perhaps twenties. His coiffed dreadlocks sprouting like the coiled antennae on Sputnik.[17]

Skin texture and colour like patent leather shoes. A man with a pointy beard and a spectacular mustache, taciturn in four languages. He lets his paintings do the talking, impressive.

His assistant Gervais, sports the favoured Van Dyke beard, which is by no means reserved for artists in Rwanda, does most of the speaking. He replies to the offer that I have posed to Amza by dropping a bombshell. Marcus would like one hundred picture frames made by tomorrow morning. Two of the

---

[17] https://www.cbc.ca/radio/thenextchapter/full-episode-feb-8-2020

classrooms in the preschool are having windows installed and one hundred or so tykes will have to be entertained elsewhere for the day. An art class at the gallery will provide the perfect diversion.

"We are pleased to welcome you," says Gervais.

We adjourn for supper and agree to reconvene at seven to get down to business.

Our meal plan pays homage to the latest trends in Western cuisine. A vegan sampling that gets its inspiration from the Monty Python "Spam" skit. Our evening repast might be an infusion of rice, rice & cabbage, rice and rice, or a rice, cassava, rice, cassava and rice chiffonade, or a concasse of dodo, rice, rice, dodo and rice. Flippancy aside, most of the people in town would envy the variety of our diet. Rice is their essential staple and much too often the difference between eating and going hungry.

After my carb loading, as a digestif, I work my way through one of the daily crosswords that I brought with me. Satisfied with my efforts, I toss the mostly completed scrap of paper into the waste basket, a container about the size of a medium flowerpot. Small as it is, it dawns on me that we probably won't fill it in the six weeks of our visit, such is the absence of packaging and scarcity of goods to be bought. It's just as well, as the village has no garbage collection service. Be that as it may, our bin is emptied daily.

At seven sharp, we three musketeers (me the miscast beardless one) assemble. We are on the second floor of a partly constructed workshop. It has no roof yet. Our space is illuminated by a work light that dangles from an overhead beam. The floor of this makeshift tree fort has gaps in it as wide as a finger and is as uneven as a washboard.

Our equipment comprises one handsaw, four claw hammers, two with handles made of repurposed pipe, one with its original wooden handle. The fourth handle-less artifact is used as a paperweight to stop Gervais's cap from being blown away. We have a piece of string to use as a tape measure.

Our supplies consist of a Jenga pile of irregularly sized wood offcuts left over from construction of the floor. A torn paper bag of nails, which tips over and spills half of its contents. An aggravating number of them find the gaps in the boards and fall through the slits in the floor, lost forever.

And so to work. To break the ice, I ask Amza what we will do with the hundred canvases that will be produced by our first-time painters?

"Will they take them home?"

"No."

I suspect he thinks, hopes, that we will take them to Canada to sell.

I try explaining to him that our own kids also used to churn out masterpieces by the ton. What does he think the chances are that if we brought them to Rwanda that people would pay for them?

No reaction.

Trying another tactic, I suggest we could reuse the canvases by painting over them. Offended, he comes out with,

"Oh no, never! We are making memories of today."

Makes no sense to me, but hey, I am no artist. Art for art's sake.

Progress is slow. The saw is as sharp as a butter knife, there are no benches to work on and even the floor can't be relied upon to provide a flat surface. Things aren't sped up by Amza's ongoing attention to the media devotees on his phone and Gervais's preoccupation with getting his favourite playlist on the stereo.

At last, Gervais is done putting the finishing touches to his musical Mona Lisa and Amza's followers have all been led.

Gervais's masterpiece blares forth and production ramps up. Obviously, what they were lacking was inspiration and motivation. This army marches on its ears, so crank up the beats.

This happy state of affairs lasts a good half hour, until we are plunged into pitch-darkness thanks to a power outage. Unpredictability is the mother of self-sufficiency. We all reach into our pockets and pull out our solutions.

Picture framing by Petzl light. But without the tunes, morale again flags. Amza manages to hammer in two nails in the next half an hour. Gervais spends his time sorting through the pile of offcuts rather than do battle with the insufferable saw.

I peevishly amass a collection of about a dozen frames. By now it is 10.30 p.m. One hundred is a futile goal. Fed up, I give up. Very bad behaviour.

Getting up from my workstation on the floor, I totter. Off I go, stiff-legged, as if doing my best Joe Biden impersonation of C-3PO, heading toward the ladder, and thence to my room.

As I slip beneath my bedcovers doing my best not to waken Trixie, an earthquake trembles around me. A thumping bass shakes the unshakeable mud brick. The power is back.

Discretion being the better part of valour, I pull the covers over my head and attempt to pull up my auricular drawbridge. Porthos and Aramis can take it from here.

The auditory assault continues throughout the night. Senses are mercilessly bombarded with "music" full blast. This must be like the psychological torture tactics the CIA used on Noriega when they tried to flush him out of his compound.

A new level of cruelty is added to the torment. Fleeting elements of hope are introduced just to be snatched away. The constancy of the music becomes unreliable. Songs break up into bursts of sound punctuated by unpredictable intervals of silence. Just to keep you guessing, they vary in length from thirty seconds to over two minutes. If there is a God, maybe this is another power cut.

To add to the symphony, the cow next door is literally having a cow and it doesn't sound like she has been to a Lamaze class.

I curse when the racket plays and then pray that it doesn't restart during the lulls. My mind explores twisted scenarios that might explain the cause of this music interruptus. A brief image strikes me. Am I missing out on some sort of sadistic local cultural epic version of musical chairs? Where they drop their hammers every time the music stops, run around the heaps of picture frames, pick them up when it restarts and start bashing away when it begins again? Very strange. At about 6.30 a.m., someone or something decides to turn off the music for good.

I rise late, at nine a.m. the next morning and go next door to check out the progress. I am astonished to see heaps and heaps of picture frames. There could easily have been one hundred.

But there are no kids.

I return to our unit and knock on Amza's door. Presently, his groggy countenance appears between the door and the jam. His antennae as erect as ever but his half-shut eyes a bloodshot testament to his all-night labours.

"Wow, you guys did it, but where are the kids?" I say, genuinely impressed.

With a casual shrug, he replies, "Yeah, I like to work late at night. Marcus just texted me that the kids aren't coming. The windows won't arrive today. It will have to be some other day. I am going back to bed."

This, I was beginning to realize, would be a recurring theme.

I am starting to figure out that when one door closes, opportunity knocks. Instead of playing Picasso 101 with a throng of pixies, we can head up to the village soccer pitch and catch a game.

En route, we encounter a field littered with scraps of garbage. Underfoot lies the still unanswered thirteen across, my discarded crossword beginning to rot in the red earth. The heat and rain will soon see it absorbed into the soil. I can't say the same for the plastic and foil packaging from my malaria pills, which also deface the ground. Even a little garbage can end up as permanent garbage.

We arrive in time to watch the girls taking the field. Some of the JHA caregivers and their charges are on the yellow team. Everything goes better with music in Rwanda and a stereo system is set up on the sideline. The equipment includes a couple of loudspeakers that might have been abandoned at the end of The Who's first farewell tour in 1981, behemoths the size of fridges delivered on the backs of bicycles. Somehow, the hodgepodge of electronics blasts out true stereo. From one speaker Dolly Parton twangs out "Jolene" at full pitch, while the other belts out a gospel version of "Amazing Grace."

We are escorted to our place of honour five feet from the touchline at centre field under a shade tree. Two goatskin covered chairs appear and we are invited to sit. I install myself like Mobutu on his throne. All I am missing is the fly whisk and the leopard skin hat.

The pitch is readied, FIFA would be impressed. The village driving instructor takes a bit of persuading to bugger off. He reluctantly vacates the north-end goal mouth when the kick-off whistle blows, his pupil using the goal posts to practice her reverse parking until the last second. The local peculiarities continue when a guy on a bike gets hit by the ball as he crosses the field amid the action and some goats invade the pitch when the yellows score their second "goal." Another blatantly offside score that the referee seems oblivious to.

By this time, the crowd has increased to about thirty. It has grown so much so that we can't see the pitch. The "fans" are a bunch of kids who stand between us and the field. The spectators, it becomes apparent, aren't here to watch the match. They are all turned quizzically facing us, trying to figure out where these aliens came from and what they want? What could possess a couple of white folks to watch a bunch of girls playing soccer under the hot sun? These people are clearly mad. Having made their diagnosis, the kids soon become bored and wander away.

Meanwhile, the travesty on the pitch continues, both teams netting dubious tallies. By half time, the beleaguered official has outlived his welcome and the teams unanimously decide to send him off. An ironic justice I'd never before encountered at a football match.

I find out later that he was a teacher's aide at the school. He had been, recruited to ref the fixture not for his knowledge of the game, he had none, but because he had a whistle. The only previous "refereeing" experience he had was rounding up the kids at the end of school recess. He was magnanimous enough to lend out his Acme Thunderer for the rest of the match. The second half, though short of controversy, evolved into a nail-biting contest, with the blues scoring the equalizer in the last minute.

I will probably spend an unjustifiable number of hours watching the World Cup, but I would happily have spent another afternoon or two critiquing the classic 4-4-2 formation used by the yellows. The fixture list is blank, though, another one of those opportunities to make your own amusement.

After a sleep filled with dreams of biriani, risotto and sushi, I awake with a hankering for physical work. Rousing Amza, we head back to the gallery. Our mission is to get going with our project to create a business-like-setting fit for his stunning artwork. To display the canvases at their best, we plan to hang them from picture rails.

"This is going to look professional," says Amza. He is becoming quite the conversationalist.

"That's because we are professional," says I.

Aziz happens to be passing by and offers to give us a hand. Aziz is a lad who is pretty sure that he is sixteen years old, he comes to the village to go to school. Every moment that he doesn't spend studying, he devotes to volunteering with the JHA. Despite his youth and humble background, he has become a leader amongst his peer group. Amongst other things, he and his team, "The Miracle Workers," devote countless hours planting crops and tending fields to be shared with the community. An impressive example to us all.

Logistics present their usual challenges. With some trimming of the floor offcuts with the accursed saw, we create the rails. A few screws to attach them to the walls are scrounged up. A rummage through the tool kit produces a screwdriver. It would be the perfect size if I was trying to fix a Rolex Oyster, but not much use trying to drive home a number two Robertson. About as much use as a toothpick. With much swearing on my part, we attempt to improvise with my Swiss Army knife, to no avail.

It is our good luck that Aziz is the proud owner of a multibit screwdriver. It is not so lucky that the tool happens to be at his house. Undeterred, he and one of his pals borrow a couple of motorcycles to take us to his home in the neighbouring village of Rilima, to pick up the tool. It is a convenient reason for him to show us where he lives and introduce us to his family, so he also invites Trixie along for the trip.

By this time one of the monsoon-like drenchings that are so frequent at this time of year has thankfully stopped. Aziz informs us that we won't be using the roads but slaloming along the network of paths that connect the adjoining fields and farms in the area. He explains that this is because it will be a shortcut. I am pretty sure that the real reason is because he doesn't have a driver's license and is worried about being collared by the police on the main roads. I'd rather have taken my chances with the constabulary after experiencing the ride, which was like crossing the Somme in the aftermath of a barrage followed by a torrential downpour.

Fifteen slithering minutes later, we pitch up in front of Aziz's house, nerves a little jangled, clothes somewhat mud spattered, but otherwise none the worse for wear. He invites us into the simple structure, mud brick, corrugated-iron roof, barred windows and wooden door, with a padlock typical for the area.

Introductions are made in the cool gloom of the un-electrified main room. As our eyes adjust to the low light, we can make out a clutch of individuals of various ages and sexes and extend our hands to the greetings. In the middle of the group sits Mama Aziz on a three-legged wooden stool. She is clearly the centre of this small universe.

We buy some Fantas and mandazi as treats, settle in and start telling each other our life stories, the common theme being family. Despite sharing this interest, our parenting choices couldn't be more mystifying to each other. She is just as incredulous about us having only two children despite our vast wealth as we are about her choices. Here she sits proudly surrounded by her riches, eight hungry but smiling faces.

She has no regrets about the path she has taken, despite all of the sacrifices she must make every day. Mama Aziz owns her own house, which she is able to rent out for seven thousand RWF, about six dollars US a month. She and her children live in this home for a rent of five thousand dollars and so as to earn a monthly profit of about two dollars US. To add to her meagre income, Mama fishes at the nearby lake. Sells her catch to buy rice, which is a cheaper source of nourishment. She is unable to obtain a permit because of the overfishing of the lake. Even a crime as minor as fishing without a license could result in jail time. She has no choice but to tempt fate in order to feed her kids.

During the course of our chat, there is a clatter from the far corner of the shadowy room. Princess has passed out. There is surprisingly no flurry of alarm. Mama Aziz blithely observes, "Oh, it's OK, she's just hungry she hasn't eaten in two days." A couple of the children prop her up in the corner of the room and give her a glass of water and another mandazi. Problem solved for the moment.

Due to some disagreement or perhaps some misdeed at the girl's house, Princess now finds herself back on the streets of her home village and it's a hard, hard existence.

Our get-together draws to a close and we must take our leave. Amza will be anxious to get the picture rails installed, so we say our farewells, jump on the backs of the Yamahas and off we go. The heat of the day has dried out the paths and fields and on the return trip, Aziz takes us through the grounds of RICA, a US-sponsored agricultural college, where we pass by its lakeside glass-and-chrome recreation centre. There it sits empty but for rows of the latest fitness equipment lined up in air-conditioned solitude.

Minutes later we are back at the gallery, where Amza wastes no time in putting Aziz's screwdriver to good use.

A couple of hours and a few twists of the wrists later, we are able to stand back and view our handiwork, the glorious art now commanding the room as it should. Pleased with our efforts, we shake hands and decide to celebrate with a cup of coffee and a game of darts.

I was never big on helping my kids with their homework. I preferred to help their education by playing games. The darts set that we brought with us from Canada has been a big hit. Games are ideal vehicles for introducing essential life skills such as addition, subtraction, multiplication and cheating. I hope to promote those same talents here through darts.

As if by some sort of telepathy, a cluster of excited youths inevitably gather as soon as the dart case makes an appearance. I ask Abercrombie (or was it Abdul or maybe Al's Garage) to keep score.

We divide ourselves up into four teams of two persons. Mozart, Sam and Patrick, our alleged project manager, are among those that I recognize. As the objective of the game, to get the most points, becomes clear, the competitiveness and engagement increases. Each recording of the score devolves into a group exercise. Arms waving, bodies jumping up and down, raised voices and fingers pointing, until the suitable number is arrived at. The less numerate stand to the side, mystified and hopeful that their partner is alive to any score rigging that might be going on.

Some of the mathematical problems prove too tricky to reach consensus on. When Samira hit triple nineteen and began chalking up her fifty-seven points, Mozart begins chanting something I can only assume is the Rwandan equivalent of "Stop the steal."

At this point, Patrick chooses this opportunity to reinvent himself into a problem solver. He whips out his cell phone to do the three times table. Africa is on the fast track for sure; it took the West a generation to forget how to do multiplication. The assembled captivated, drunk with anticipation.

Even here there is total belief in the new Google God so much so that when Patrick does the computation, no one bats an eye when he pronounces the score to be fifty-four. The reliably unreliable Patrick having keyed in eighteen instead of nineteen. Garments would surely have been rended, if they weren't already mostly in tatters. Tensions mount.

Sam, sticking to her guns, eventually prevails after several recounts, an inquest and an impeachment. Conspiracy theorists still muttering their disbelief.

I've never enjoyed a livelier game of arrows, this is the way the game should be played.

It has been a totally different experience from the two years I spent as a young man in Liberia in the late seventies. Whether Africa or I have changed more in those forty plus years can be argued equally convincingly either way. What I do know is that, back in the day, I enjoyed the ex-pat life, my air-conditioned office, comfortable apartment, free car and driver, nice restaurants and good pay. I was delightfully ignorant, completely insulated from the larger community.

Here's the thing, though, here in Rwanda, I have enjoyed my time every bit as much. I know that compared to the majority of the villagers our life here is enviable and that creates a divide. Despite that, I do feel a close connection and that connection feels good. It's a connection that has me asking questions of myself.

It used to be that I was sure that less was bad and that more was good. That was until now, when everything is starting to get confused.

Chapter 18
Measure If You Like, Cut Once

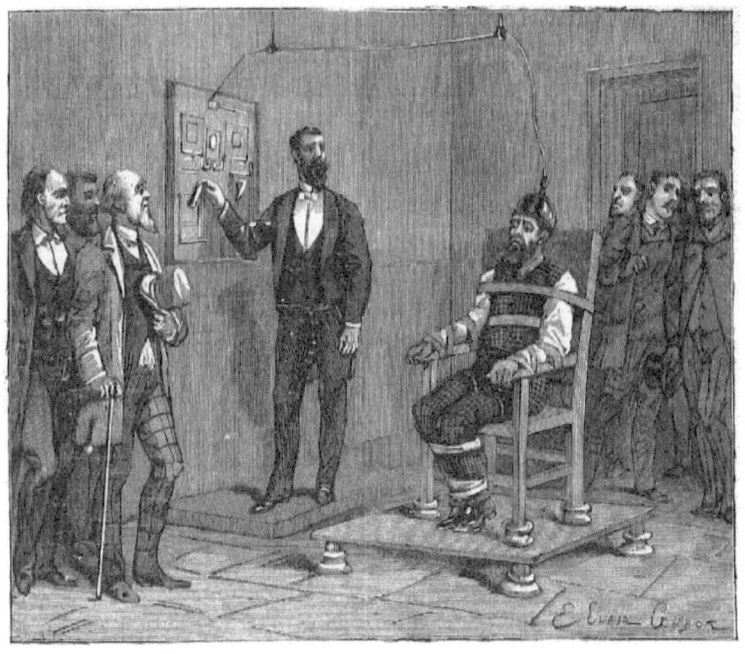

This is a lot harder for me than it is for you.

"In the beginning was the thing. And one thing led to another."

– Tom Robbins

"Rivers know this: there is no hurry. We shall get there some day."

– A.A. Milne

While Trixie's dance card is triple booked with many constructive tasks, like organizing shipments of handicrafts, negotiating with weavers, assisting with the launch of a women's sewing co-operative, coordinating the dying of the weaving materials in custom ordered hues for the market back home etc. etc., my immediate future stretches out lazily without much focus. Some reading, crosswords, walks to town, a bit of exploring on the weekends are all that's on my docket. I have brought a few chess sets and the dart board to entertain myself and the kids, but with school being in session, few of them are around during the day.

To escape the hurly-burly of the "girls' house," we have relocated to the "White House," otherwise known as "The Gallery." It has recently been completed, constructed with the usual mud brick, but in this case spiffed up with a stucco like finish and whitewash.

The property is about thirty metres square and surrounded by a two-metre-high perimeter wall. An interior wall also about two metres high divides the enclosure into two halves. On one side sits the gallery building, essentially a four-roomed house. One room will be used as a showroom for the artwork. To take advantage of the soon-to-be-opened new airport, which is located about a half an hour away, the other three rooms will be used for visiting guests and hopefully generate rental income.

The other half of the compound is multipurpose. The yard area is roofless and the ground hard-packed gravelly red earth. Along the back wall is a large shelter constructed from rustic, salvaged wooden poles lashed together and planked with ill-fitting roughhewn timber. The shelter provides a roof of sorts for the women of the sewing co-op. I suggest that we make some improvements to the roof so as to minimize the rain splatter that messes up the sewers' cloth. The kids get karate and gymnastics lessons there a couple of nights a week in their bare feet. The rest of the time it is used for construction projects and the storage of various supplies.

Our quarters, quiet and cool as they are, could do with some work. The walls have a first coat of paint. Each room has an en suite, more accurately an en chambre, literally a toilet, a shower and a sink. It is wall-less and is located in the corner, occupying about a quarter of the room. Luxury beyond belief for most Rwandans but an arrangement a bit too up close and personal for Western sensitivities. The lights work, but the water and plumbing are as yet unconnected. We will continue to make our ablutions at the girls' house, a twenty-minute round trip walk away.

The furnishings, simply a couple of mattresses on the spotless floor, inspire the Bauhaus minimalist theme. It is a perfect refuge for us.

The building is staffed by Immaculee, the cleaner. A miracle of perpetual motion, who appears to mop unceasingly for her entire eight-hour shift. I wonder if iRobot sent a research team to study her maneuvers when designing their autonomous Roomba vacuum cleaners. Immaculee's design is superior to the Roomba in every respect, except one—she has no off button.

Feeling vaguely like a twenty-something son living in his parents' basement and growing increasingly uncomfortable in my role as a freeloading layabout, I figure that I should make myself useful. Still suffering from the mental and physical constipation that I get from a thirty-six-hour journey, I plan to get myself unplugged with a course of laxatives and some physical labour.

I offer to coordinate the task of finishing off the interior work of the gallery and fund the materials.

These refinements will involve a second coat of paint and the design and construction of bed frames, night tables and shelving, which will double as supports for shower curtain rods to cordon off the bathroom areas. Trixie and Samira will beautify the space with bedding and curtains in colourful local fabrics. Marcus is initially cool to the idea, but I eventually convince him to construct the furniture out of steel rather than wood. I should have listened.

Even at a leisurely pace, four weeks should be ample time to complete this modest project. Before I know it, Sam has made calls and arranged to meet with a couple of local steelworkers to start negotiations on the project. In vain, I try to defer the confab until we have designed the furniture to be built, determined the number of pieces required and established what our budget is. We are not building an Olympic stadium here but having been born in Montreal, I am a bit twitchy about cost overruns. Dynamism having trumped pedantry, the meetings take place.

Conveniently, our first potential contractor Felix is already on site, just finishing off construction of some steel security gates for the compound. He is a charm-free gruff individual, a ball-scratcher, who distracts himself with a game of pocket billiards throughout the discussion.

Bafflingly, we start by negotiating a price before I have explained what it is that I would like made. I can only put that down to the fact that in this milieu, white and deep pockets are taken as synonymous. It could be that this potential jackpot is the cause of his excited state. Despite our best efforts, we are unable to get him to reduce his price and talks are abandoned.

Candidate number two Hassan arrives punctually, gracious of manner and clad in work overalls fit for the task. Reassuringly, he wants to know what the project involves. We make ponderous but necessary progress in explaining what is required.

As usual, there are obstacles to be overcome. Making a set of shelves in a poor village is a big event and becomes very much a committee affair. Before long, we are a group of about eight, including Bedu, who is Marcus's right-hand man and the team's mover and shaker when backsides and boots need to get acquainted. The welder and his six- year-old son are there, as is our procurement officer Patrick, the lead farmer Moses, and a couple of schoolboys, who happen to be passing by on their way home.

Some of the basic needs are in scarce supply. When a tape measure is eventually found it has both inches and centimetres on it, just to add to the confusion. We have to scrounge a scrap of paper and the nub of a pencil from the weavers. And yet nearly everyone seems to have a cell phone and a favourite internet example that they would like Hassan to copy.

At this point, a young man carrying a sack joins our confab. Uttering something in Kinyarwandan, "Abracadabra" maybe, he opens the bag and out leaps a monkey. The answer to my prayers as the surplus delegates become engrossed in the task of recapturing the creature, with the intent of taking it up to the boys' house as a potential pet.

Samira and my negotiations with Hassan resume, communication made tricky by rap music belting out from the adjacent sound system, Felix's power saw getting ever louder as he inches his way closer to the confidentialities, not to mention the language barrier.

At last, we are down to negotiating price with the contractor. Samira's forceful pitch belies her tender years and radiant persona. Hands on hips, leaning in, voices rising, tempo quickening, steely-gaze probing for weakness, the haggling is soon over. She has him signed up.

All, however, is not perfect. Hassan now decides to share with us that he has no tools to do the job. They have been stolen and he will have to see if he can rent some in the village.

At this point, our pickle-tickler decides to rejoin the conversation. It transpires that he is the proud owner of a spare set of tools, which he is willing to rent to Hassan. His only condition being that we also hire him at the same rate as we have agreed to with Hassan. What's not to like? In some fortuitous, roundabout way, we have magically doubled our capacity. The job should be finished in no time. Handshakes all around, it's a done deal.

I sum up our plan of action by informing them, "Let's get cracking the day after tomorrow, that's when the steel will be arriving."

It would be eleven o'clock on a rainy evening some two weeks later, that an old Toyota pickup truck lurches to a stop in front of the gallery, sagging under the weight of dozens of bars of metal angle iron. Better late than never.

At last, we have all the elements required to get this show on the road. Labour, raw materials, space, power and plans. And so to work. The reward, the high pitched whine of circular saws ringing like angel song in my ears.

Narrowly escaping ending up as roadkill under a truck laden with straw barrelling down the road, I head for my room and an early lunch. Nourished, the better part of an hour later, I return to the compound to check on progress. A local woman pushes by me with a pile of hay balanced on her head.

Work is continuing apace beneath the unrelenting hot equatorial sun, lengths of steel are scattered around the area, some half buried beneath mounds of tinder dry straw. Sparks fly off the scorching hot saw blades in all directions. Half a dozen weavers crouch alongside the metal workers working on their own projects. The work yard is now packed with stooks of dry grass which are being trimmed and bound with twine into mat like bunches of thatch which will be used to provide the roofing for the second story under construction above the workshop, a conflagration waiting to happen.

"Stop" shouts I, it wasn't Kinyarwanda but sometimes volume and intonation are enough to get the desired result. After a bit of pantomime, me stamping out imaginary flames easy to do in my current humour, Hassan and Felix grudgingly concede my point and move the steel and their tools to the street outside the walls.

Before work recommences, Felix checks his watch and announces, "Sasita!"

That translates to, "Lunch!"

Back go the tools and steel inside the compound, there are light fingers to contend with in the neighbourhood and off they go for sasita.

An hour later I return to the worksite, no sign of the lads outside the wall, so I peek inside the gate. There they are, welding together the steel they cut this morning, still surrounded by mounds of the tinder dry fuel. I deliver an even more frantic version of my fire dance and the welding mercifully stops.

We lug the steel and tools back outside the wall and Felix attempts to start up his saw.

Crickets.

Oh Buddha, what now? Maybe the electrical load of the tools had tripped the power breakers. A quick check rules out that possibility. But the sewing machines have also stopped chattering away, so maybe it is one of the common local power outages. Eh, nope, the neighbour's stereo still blares away loudly enough to be heard in the next province.

Smart phones are tapped to no effect, a search party, a half a dozen boys, are sent out in different directions to track down the landlord. A couple of hours later, we have the indignant owner in custody and challenge him to provide an account of his dereliction, which he does with a measure of righteous irritation.

"Yes, I am not surprised there is no electricity, you have not paid the electricity bill, you will have been cut off."

It seems a reasonable enough explanation.

Much discussion ensues about the whereabouts of the power bill as dusk approaches, and Felix and Hassan pack up after an inauspicious start. I would have a lot less white hair if I believed in omens.

After a slow start on the morrow, the teller at the utility office is late due to his goat having a toothache, or at least that is the excuse we are given, our project recommences.

But not for long. Again, we find ourselves without power. It transpires that on this occasion the use of the electric welding machine combined with the simultaneous use of the saw has overloaded the system and blown a fuse. Our landlord proves to be more elusive today. By the time we figure this out, you've guessed it, it is time to go home.

We must now accept the fact that the gallery's electrical system can't handle the draw of the tradesmen's equipment. It is now Friday. Time is of the essence, for we leave a week from next Wednesday.

Bright and early Monday morning, Bedu comes to the rescue again. There now being over thirty boys housed by the charity, it has been necessary to move to a larger house. No new tenants have moved into the old boys' house as yet. Bedu is convinced that the power supply there is plentiful.

Before I can say, "Let's test it out," Bedu has rounded up twenty or so of the lads and in short order, he arranges the Berlin airlift Shagora style. All the construction materials now located in the courtyard of the White House will be moved to the old boys' house and glorious power.

Small bodies wrangle ten-foot-lengths of angle bar steel, lads pair up and stagger under the weight of the transformers, cables are wrapped around small torsos bandolier-style, lumber is tucked under scrawny armpits.

A stream of hobbling youngsters spills out onto the street and weave their bedraggled way up the road. You would think that a steel plant was being looted by midgets. Within a couple of hours, work recommences. Progress, a little, is made.

The rainy season begins to build, the evenings are becoming cooler. I sleep well despite the cracks of thunder and torrential downpour that stir me in the middle of the night. Around 8:30 the next morning, I make my way up the road to the old boys' house to check in on the team, who assumedly started at 8 o'clock. As I draw nearer, I am not greeted with the reassuring rasp of metal on metal, why am I not surprised. But voices yes, I hear voices, boy do I ever.

On entering the compound, I am not greeted with the usual cheery "muramutzes;" my presence is as air. Bedu, Felix, Hassan, Patrick and some unnamed supernumerary, are gathered in a circle pointing fingers, waving arms and having a right old barney.

My eyes follow the flailing arms, which point in the general direction of the transformers that power Felix's and Hassan's welding torches. I try to figure out what's going on without the benefit of subtitles. I can discern "machine," one familiar recurring word that peppers the animated harangue.

It becomes clear that the machine in question refers to the transformers, which wouldn't look out of place in Dr. Frankenstein's laboratory. A bunch of bolts, twisted spirals of cable all cobbled together with yards of wire wound around oversized wooden bobbins. Exactly what vintage they might be is an open question. I will have them carbon dated and get back to you. They sit in a two-inch-deep puddle, where they drowned during last night's deluge. Here lies the source of the remonstrations.

Clearly accountability operates the same way here as back home—shit flows downhill.

From the contractor, Hassan, who isn't taking any guff from Bedu (if looks could kill), Bedu our contract manager, to our alleged project supervisor, Patrick, on down to the poor nameless sod who has purportedly been instructed to look after the equipment by some yet unidentified someone.

The unfortunate offender endures the entire brouhaha head bowed, staring at the ground, hoping for the earth to swallow him up and pondering exactly how deep his mismatched flip-flops might end up in the doo-doo flowing in torrents in his direction, how much of it might stick and for how long.

It soon becomes apparent that I am a catalyst in prolonging this agony, every time I make a comment or interject, the debate resumes anew, with even higher volume and raised voices. I learn to keep quiet.

After a full and frank exchange of views, détente is reached. The assembly begins to melt away. I try to innocuously reinsert myself into the conversation with a plaintive exasperated.

"So, what's going on?!"

The consensus that they have reached is that nothing is to be done other than to leave the equipment out in the sun for a few hours in the hope that the heat will work some magic on the compromised apparatus. Court is recessed until after lunch. The goats in the compound, glazed expressions on their faces, continue with their munching as skeptical about the prospects as I am.

But lo the sun shines brightly upon us, nature works its wonders and by one o'clock Bedu assesses the transformers as good to go. Calls to the welders are made, they ride up on their bikes fifteen minutes later, just as the rain starts again, take one look at the sky, turn on their heels and head for home, no more "work" that day.

I was born on a Wednesday. Wednesday's child is full of woe, so the old song says. Today is Wednesday, there will be woe. I arrive at the old boys' house, it is deserted. I can see through the grimy windows that the equipment has been put away overnight, nice. But where might be our esteemed crew? Patrick isn't feeling well and won't make it in today, he tells me when I phone him.

Next, I call the ever-reliable Bedu. "Leave it with me," he says. Minutes later, he phones back.

"Felix has gone to Kigali to get his drill fixed." As un-shocked as I am that he is unavailable for the day, I am more shocked that he has a drill, given that we have been searching for one all over the village.

"Well, where is Hassan?"

"There is a big soccer match this afternoon, so he is resting and so he can't come today either."

After learning more about the big game, I am more forgiving. It's a bit of an intervillage grudge match. Our guys will be playing the pretty boys from Karama. Their team attend the agricultural institute there. Warren Buffet's son Howard has dropped $500 million for philanthropic projects in Rwanda in recent years, all very magnanimous of him. Still, it does rub me the wrong way that some guy gets to splash around a ton of money that his dad won on the stock market. Another example of dynastic mega-wealth in action. Ironic in that some sort of nouveau monarchy gets to swan around the globe issuing largesse to the peasants after having taken too much out of the countries in the first place. All the while, the support of corrupt governments and exploitive corporations continues. What possible justification can there be for one individual to have that amount of money and what makes them in any way qualified to make judgements on where the best benefits are to be derived?

Take all the rest you need, Hassan, just beat the logoed pants off them.

Thursday all the basket-making materials must be moved out of the gallery to allow the walls to be painted before the shelving and beds are moved in. It wouldn't be a normal day unless there is at least one gaffe to deal with. On this occasion, a bag of powdered-dye used in the colouring of the baskets spills onto the floor. Before anyone becomes aware of the problem, many feet have left trails of magenta footprints throughout the building. An artful exhibit to be sure but not the look we were hoping for. An upsetting event for all involved. All except for Immaculee. Could this be the hint of a smile suffusing her Sphinx-like demeanour? At long last, a challenge worthy of her talents.

As my spot on the earth slowly turns itself away from the sun at the end of another colourful day, I resign myself to the thought that only the world knows what new mischief it might have in store for tomorrow.

Friday marks a milestone. We have the first prototype of a set of shelves and nightstand ready. The test will be to see if the boards that will slide into the metal framework will fit. The shelving has been designed with the same measurements as the width of the wooden planks so as to allow a snug fit. All that has to happen now is to cut the ten-foot-long boards into sections short enough to match the length of the brackets.

Patrick has made a spectacular recovery. I saw him playing centre back at Wednesday's soccer match, and his assignment is to arrange to take the planks of wood to the carpenter's workshop to be cut to size. Yeah, I know what you might be wondering, why is it that no one can find a wood saw blade to put on the metal workers' circular saws? It could be the language decoding deficiencies at work again, having been informed that, "I don't think we have the word 'circular saw' in Kinyarwanda." This gets me to thinking about words. They say the Eskimos (maybe that means the Inuit now), have fifty words for snow and the Scots, I'm guessing, have fifty words for drunk (more stereotyping), so how many words, I wonder, are there in Kinyarwanda that mean tomorrow?

Several phone calls later, Patrick has lined up a cycle taxi to transport the wood the fifteen-minute trip to the woodcutter. The planks are balanced on the bike's back rack, which acts as a kind of fulcrum, with six feet of timber pointing forward and six backwards. Patrick steering by the handlebars. Backlit by the sun and with the right kind of Cervantes imagination, the silhouette perhaps resembles a medieval knight about to joust.

Various cracks at lashing the materials to the bike fail. The banana fronds are still soppy from the recent rains and disintegrate when knotted. So, we try a bungee cord made from old car tire rubber. It fires its hook, an old bent nail, at an innocent pedestrian as it catapults itself into nearby scrub, never to be found.

A new strategy is required. The lumber is laid athwart the vehicle and now resembles some sort of weird land-based trimaran. Don Quixote would have been galvanized. Patrick, still at the helm, steering and yelling orders to a couple of kids that he has press-ganged into service, one at either end of the planks, supporting them like a couple of pontoons. Fortunately, there is no traffic as they trawl their way up the centre of the road, before they branch off onto a side path. The path weaves through a cassava field as they trundle full-tilt for what might turn out to be just another windmill, now reminiscent of a combine harvester designed by the Wright brothers.

We arrive at our destination, the workshop, winded but unscathed. It looks as if Mary and Joseph might have just recently left it. The edifice evocative of a vacant cow shed. Repurposed bare poles, a corrugated roof and some open fence rails define the working area. In the middle of it is Damascene, master of the domain. He stands barefoot, shin-deep in saw dust, he wears no glasses, ear protection or mask. Judging from his imposing girth, he runs a thriving business. After a spell of negotiation with Patrick, he beams a broad gap-tooth smile and turns to the task.

He eschews high-tech gadgetry, things like a tape measure and gets on with it. Forget measure twice, cut once. He merely hefts the four-metre-long beams of wood with density of lead onto the edge of his table saw, gives the fence a couple of whacks with the free end of the timber, a quick but highly accurate eyeballing of the material, a nod of the head from side to side of the wood and away he goes. Two perfectly butterflied symmetrical pieces of lumber emerge.

He works his way through our pile of nascent shelving with steady purpose. His three employees continue with their own projects and wrastle crude beams not much more uniform than tree trunks through saws and planers, only a couple of feet apart from Damascene. Amidst the mayhem a six-year-old kid darts about, gathering the offcuts and lending a hand wherever it is needed.

Soon enough our virtuoso has finished the job. Satisfied with his work, he sends the youngster to bring his tea-break beverage. The laddie returns with a mickey of gin, which is consumed so quickly that it can't possibly have touched the sides of his throat on the way down. As a final bonus Damascene insists on running the planks through the old behemoth of a planer, then whacks together a tabletop in a few seconds.

Our new friendship hits a bit of a wobbly when it comes time to settle up. Some good-natured but protracted negotiations result in raised voices and hand waving. An agreement is reached and a split-the-difference compromise price of $1.50 is the final tally. The original quote of one dollar plus fifty cents for the nails that we had to have special ordered.

We hail a couple of cycle taxis and make our way back to base with our now more maneuverable cargo.

Saturday

The wooden shelves fit snuggly into the metal framework, hallelujah. I provide my Raccoon Sixty seal of approval, for what it is worth.

Output ramps up and skeletal furniture starts to fill the compound. If we keep at it, we might just get finished before our departure in three days.

I confide with Bedu and ask him what he thinks are our chances.

Bedu informs me that tomorrow will present a new obstacle. The crew won't be showing up because "Tomorrow, they are playing God."

Barely able to contain myself, I respond, "Well, Bedu, it seems to me like these guys have been playing God all week. Or is Howard Buffet's team coming to town again?"

"No, no, tomorrow is Sunday, playing God."

Ah yeah, the old l and r transposition thing!

"Huh, oh, I get it, praying to God."

I deliver a few words in the direction of the Almighty myself.

Over a gloomy midday platter of rice, I fill Trixie in on the latest setback and let her know that she can cancel her plans to decorate the rooms on Tuesday. Ever the pragmatist, she announces, "Just hire someone else."

"Yeah, like where? Get real, how many welders can there be in this bump in the road in the back of beyond?"

"Well, we passed a man making window bars in front of the tailor shop yesterday."

"Hmm."

I inform Bedu of "my" flash of brilliance after lunch. His bullish outlook ripe for any and every challenge. He has never seen a goose wild or otherwise, let the chase begin.

We sweep down main street to the tailor shop and begin a parley with the welder. Or to be more accurate, Bedu briefs our potential saviour in the local lingo. It all is going swimmingly until the cost negotiations begin. A stalemate is reached. It appears the problem, as usual, is me. My muzungu presence has grossly inflated the price. Even the fact that a BIPOC is doing the negotiations isn't going to earn us the local price. I let Bedu know that at this stage of the game, I will gladly pay the NITNOC rate, which in this case is an extra twenty dollars for the day.

But no, principle and precedent are at stake and Bedu disengages.

We head back toward home, Bedu, a force of nature not used to being denied, is disconsolate.

As we pass the bicycle repair shop, a now familiar "dzzzz, dzzzz... zap... pop" catches my attention.

As I contemplate the mechanic fashioning bike racks out of rebar, I have my own incandescent moment of inspiration... it can happen. How much different can it be welding rebar onto bicycles for bike racks compared to making steel shelves, I wonder.

I don't need to convince Bedu that the recruitment drive isn't quite over. Before you can say maybe, he is embroiled in negotiations with the entire staff of the shop and a few passersby to boot. Not taking no for an answer from the head mechanic, he inveigles the shop owner's phone number from the reluctant employee, punches the numbers and makes contact.

Bedu gleefully ends the call, mission accomplished. He has worked a deal with the owner, who will send his guys with their equipment to the boys' house at 9 a.m. tomorrow.

"So how many guys?" I ask. "Two? Could we maybe try to get three?"

"Oh no," says Bedu, "there will be six of them."

"Six!" I say, my voice grimacing and my mind quavering. Swiftly recalibrating into default mode, I revert to thinking inside the box.

"Where are we going to put them all? They've probably never seen a set of shelves let alone built them. What do you think will happen when six transformers fire up at the same time? We will probably blackout the entire continent!"

Bedu, unperturbed, beams his "it will all work out smile," and all he says is,

"Boy, I am thirsty." No explanation is required, we head for a beer.

Sunday—I arrive at the appointed place and time. Tape measure and plans in hand, ready to greet the troops and provide my tutorial. It transpires to be another solitary start to the day. By 9:30, I have contacted Bedu and enlisted his skills to bird-dog our new recruits. Pronto he gets back to me with the news that only three of them can make it, but that they are on their way. Paradoxically, I am disappointed that there are only three of them. Expectation is a funny thing. Why should I be disappointed when I didn't really want six guys to begin with?

At 10 a.m., two newbies show up. Or maybe it would be more accurate to say one, Evode and a half, Ronnie, as they only have one transformer and one bladeless steel saw between them. The younger of the two, Ronnie, it soon becomes apparent, knows as much about welding as me but helpfully does speak a few words of English. In true work-safe fashion, he goes about readying the worksite.

He takes the plug less cable from the transformer, twists the frayed ends of the bare wires into something of a point and then wedges them into the power outlet with the aid of a twig. I don't think that the fluorescent safety vest, one of the many that some NGOs seem to have, liberally sprinkled throughout the community, that he is sporting will save him. It will just make his body easier to find. The machine buzzes and hums, coming to life, sounding like it is preparing to deliver an electric chair coup de grace to someone on death row.

Come to think of it, these contraptions have probably electrocuted more people in the last fifty years than old sparky, which was invented by a dentist in 1881 in New York. By now I am ready to do a few extractions myself without the benefit of anesthetic.

In the meantime, Bedu has rustled up a blade for the saw. I point out the safety logos on it to Evode: mask, goggles, ear protectors, gloves and boots' hieroglyphics. He shrugs and gets back to work in his short sleeves, bare hands, flip-flops, and his sunglasses on the top of his head.

Given that this is a new line of work for them, progress is fair and they are quite willing to do whatever is needed to get the job done. After taking great pains to stress the importance of getting the dimensions right, I stick around to check on things and answer any questions. To kill some time, a couple of the kids and I set up the chess board for a game. Predictably enough, I suppose, in the time that it takes to get to checkmate, the shelving framework manages to shrink from the desired thirty-five centimetres to thirty-three centimetres wide. Too narrow for our recently cut wood to be slotted into.

How in the heck did that happen? I check the measurements, the spacing on the top and bottom are dead on, but the three in the centre have tapered in markedly. As I step back, I can see that it is due to warp in the steel that our apprentices haven't compensated for. Not a problem they encounter welding rebar to bikes, I guess.

Monday—The final push with the finish line in sight gets off to a sluggish start. I near the compound just after 9 a.m. and can hear several voices. This sounds promising, as Felix, Hassan, Evode and Ronnie are all supposed to be here. Curiously, I also pick up the yap and yelp of a dog. As I walk into the compound, a couple of boys are headed out. They are about twelve years old, walking single file, with a long pole between them resting on their shoulders. Slung below the pole feet in the air dangles and wriggles a mid-sized dog, wrong side up. The unfortunate canine is unmistakable.

The creature is a local stray that has adopted the compound as his home.

It would be a mistake to say that he is ugly. Hyenas are ugly. The grisly visage on this mutt is in a league of its own. He has a face that looks like Michael Jackson's plastic surgeon has put it together using leftover parts from Mr Potato Head. In the dark, when he had a hangover, using one of Picasso's portraits as a template.

Stepping over the clutter of construction debris, steel, wood, boxes and old rope, I hesitantly ask Bedu for an explanation.

When will I ever learn?

"Oh, the dog was with the watchman to stop the steel from being stolen during the night. It caught a sick monkey, killed it and started to eat it. This is the only way we can get the dog away from the monkey. We will keep it tied up until we bury the monkey."

Unshockable by now, I ask, "Where is the body?"

"There is a leg behind the house, and the tail is over there," he says, pointing to the piece of "rope" that I stepped over earlier.

Oh great, thinks I. I hope that dog doesn't bite one of those kids or lick someone's open wound. It wasn't on my bucket list to witness the next animal-to-human health epidemic outbreak firsthand. Now that we are all part-time virologists, I ponder whether it is time to dust off my pandemic protocols. I must remember my COVID etiquette and start singing "Happy Birthday" five times again when I am bucket washing my hands every evening. Immaculee, not only being a hewer of mop but a drawer of water, replenishes our fifty-gallon drum daily.

The welders, having finished their job, show remarkable promptness when it comes to collecting their pay. Samira has the unenviable task of figuring out how much to pay them. Without a hint of irony, she asks me what we should do to show our appreciation? I nearly choke on my tongue... take a deep breath, count to ten and try as tactfully as I can to provide my team-building performance appraisal.

Felix, a curmudgeon who delights in presenting problems, who comes and goes as he pleases, Evode, who's rectangles come out like rhombuses, Ronnie, a complete novice, who should get danger pay and nothing else; and Hassan, a bonus, as you never want to burn all your bridges.

Finally, into the home stretch. Our posse of mini-movers collect the completed components straight off the production line and heft them back to the patio in front of the showroom. There, the painting of the metalwork and varnishing of the wooden shelves will get underway while the metal workers finish off the last of the units.

The guest rooms are also getting big licks. The second coat of whitewash is being slapped on with abandon, the floor looks like it has been strafed by seagulls. A trifling inconvenience to our human Roomba.

It is becoming an all-hands-on-deck event. The boys must paint the rooms and they suggest the girls do the painting of the furniture. A great idea, except the girls have vanished and aren't "picking" (up their cell phones). The boys threaten to down tools. A last-minute sortie sees the fugitive helpers rounded up and put to work.

Africa goes from zero action to a hypersonic melee in the blink of an eye. With our workforce, a contingent of about a dozen by this point, firing on all cylinders, our luck has surely turned.

It is at this time that the ex-lax chooses to live up to its claims. I will get to have some alone time when I reach the thunderbox sanctuary, a twenty-minute walk away. I take my leave to go powder my nose.

Mission accomplished, I make my way back to the gallery to check on progress. If I thought that things were chaotic when I left, I am to be greeted with pandemonium on my return. More than thirty kindergartners are tottering around amongst the shelving, paint pots and workers. A single teacher is valiantly trying to find places for the wide-eyed kiddies to sit and do some artwork.

Apprehending Samira, I demand an explanation as to how this sit-in has come about. As is often the case, the motives are embarrassingly well-intentioned. Marcus thought it would be a treat for the kids to do a painting and have Trixie and I sign them as a sort of a going-away keepsake. No one thought to tell him about the circus already in full swing behind the madhouse walls. Just as this debriefing is taking place, our seamstress turns up to do a fitting for our latest tailoring.

One of the painters comes by to tell us, "My mom is sick, so I have to go home."

Princess interjects with, "I think that I am going to faint. Please bring me some water."

The head weaver arrives to give us each one of her handcrafted bracelets as mementos. By this time, there is nothing missing but The Simon Fraser University Pipe Band, The Terra Cotta Warriors of Xian and a few stilt-walkers.

Amid these multifarious interactions, Immaculee does another fly by, deftly weaving her brush in and around a forest of legs. My sandal-shod feet receive the merest whisper of a refreshing spritz as she continues on her program. Imperturbable as ever, she threads her mop in and out of our animated group, delivering a light flossing between my toes as she goes.

It's just another day.[18]

---

[18] https://www.youtube.com/watch?v=ahVsa0jAdy0

Chapter 19
Everyone Has A Story

"Punishment is now unfashionable... because it creates moral distinctions among men, which, to the democratic mind, are odious. We prefer a meaningless collective guilt to a meaningful individual responsibility."

— Thomas Szasz

"As I walked out the door toward the gate that would lead to my freedom, I knew if I didn't leave my bitterness and hatred behind, I'd still be in prison."

— Nelson Mandela

A longer visit changes the dynamics of our interactions with the team and their associates. Trust, acceptance, personal relationships and friendship don't happen overnight. We are fortunate to have gradually progressed from the status of suspicious alien to novelty b list celebrity and sometime confidante amongst our immediate circle.

Language is still a significant barrier and although Trixie tries valiantly to learn some basic Kinyarwanda, relations are mostly with those who speak some English. On more than one occasion, improvisation is called for.

One evening a cockroach the size of a small Westphalia motors under our bedroom door. OK, more like the size and shape of a jumbo prawn. Trixie calls our night watchman for help. Robert, whose job it is to repel all unwelcome intruders, gives dispatch with a few swift blows from the squeegee, which leans redundantly in the arid corner of the shower area, eliciting a reassuring boot steps-on-gravel kind of a crunching sound in the process. A satisfied twinkle in his eye, mission accomplished, our cherubic seventy-something exterminator bids us a "mwiriwe neza" goodnight and leaves the room.

Robert returns to his mat outside our bedroom window and within moments is snoring like a freight train. Before any new crustaceans decide to pay us a visit, we turn off the light.

Tomorrow augurs to be an emotional day. Marcus has suggested that we visit Mama Ella and talk with her about her harrowing escape from the genocide. Mama has been hired by JHA and cooks the lunches at the early childhood centre.

Until now our discussions about this horror have been limited to dispassionate recounting of dates, circumstances and overviews of the events. The subject is by no means taboo, but dialogue has had an impersonal almost academic quality to it.

Everyone has their own private memories and stories about that time. Thus far, no one has felt inclined to share those experiences with us and that desire for privacy deserves respect. Nevertheless, Marcus thinks that hearing a firsthand account will give us a better insight into the day-to-day personal traumas and societal challenges that his team confront as they go about their work.

In the morning, Blaize, one of the caregivers, takes us to Mama Ella's house. He has a good grasp of English and will translate for us. We have met Mama Ella a couple of times before but out of politeness, we reintroduce ourselves to her and her mother Honorine.

The home is neat and tidy, mud brick with a metal roof and a concrete floor. The garden is in rough shape, but this afternoon a work party made up of JHA volunteers, neighbours and friends will arrive to install a series of kitchen gardens. For now, the five of us sit on the cement stoop by her back door in the shade provided by her modest home.

Mama, who is now forty-two, recounts her story. Her voice is steady and unemotional, but her gaze is distant and almost unblinking, there is no eye contact.

At the time of the genocide, she was thirteen. Her father was a Tutsi. Her mother Honorine was a Hutu. One night in April 1994, her policeman uncle Bab and a mob of bloodthirsty Hutu descended on her home and proceeded to butcher her father and three younger brothers to death with machetes. This happened right in front of her own eyes. Her mother managed to distract her brother long enough for Ella to flee. She took sanctuary under a bush inhabited by a colony of bees. The murderers chased after her, but the slashing of their clubs and machetes only succeeded in incensing the bees. Driven back by the bees, the frenzied mob abandoned their attack and moved on to another part of town to continue their slaughter.[19]

---

[19] https://www.perfectbee.com

Knowing that there was no safety in the village, she made her escape alone and on foot to the Burundi border some fifty kilometres away, travelling only at night. After several weeks existing like a hunted animal, hiding during the day and scrounging or stealing food at night, she found shelter at the Gikongoro refugee camp. By this stage of the civil war, French armed forces had arrived. A strategy called Operation Turquoise was intended to try to stabilize the situation. The French established a safe zone in the south of the country, which then became a haven for fleeing Hutus. Paul Kagame's RPF army of Tutsi by then had overwhelming success in crushing the Hutu forces to the north.

Mama was now confined to a camp almost entirely populated by distraught Hutu refugees. Keenly aware of her own mixed-tribe status and with the images of the recent massacre of her family at the hands of the Hutu still haunting her soul, she would spend six more months fearing for her life every waking moment.

By February 1995, some semblance of calm was restored to the country. The refugee camps were being closed and the displaced citizens were encouraged to return to their smashed communities. Mama would return to her village with Papa Luc, a Hutu man whom she had met in the camp. Papa Luc had given her some level of protection from the ever-present threat of violence. Papa Luc impregnated her. Ella, barely a teenager, naïve and unenlightened, was unaware that she was pregnant until a neighbour commented on her growing belly. Mama became a mother at the age of fourteen. Papa Luc was forty-eight years old.

Mama Ella was trapped in a no-win situation. Being of mixed race, and discriminated against for being a single mom, she was looking at a life of stigma and abuse. Luc had found some manual work and so could help provide for her and the baby. In due course they were "married," a village arrangement with no legal papers. The relationship soon deteriorated. Living with an abusive and alcoholic husband was a desperate choice, but she had no other option being little more than a child herself. They had four more children together.

To make matters worse, when they returned to their village, they found nothing but destroyed homes, that her mother had disappeared and that all her familiar friends and relatives had also fled.

As Mama Ella tried to rebuild her shattered life, she came to the realization that Papa Luc's drunken and cruel behaviour was poisoning her family's future. Showing remarkable bravery, she threw him out. Several years later she found companionship with another man in the village, they now have a seven-year-old daughter together.

In the aftermath of the war, her barbarous uncle had been arrested on suspicion of being a genocide "super killer" and incarcerated. Bab and his accomplices had been charged with killing an estimated fifty Tutsi, including seven babies. They had been in jail for years awaiting their trial. The court system was at a virtual standstill as many of the lawyers and judges were themselves implicated in the killings, still more had fled the country.

The quasi legal assemblies known as Gacaca courts were used to try and address the backlog of cases. Tens of thousands of these trials took place. One of those tried was Mama Ella's uncle, who had been waiting for over ten years for his day in court.

Respected leaders in the villages were called upon to preside as judges. These judges had no legal training and in many cases were illiterate. The proceedings varied from court to court and village to village. The government did encourage reconciliation and clemency. The penal system could not sustain the staggering rates of incarceration.

At Mama Ella's uncle's trial, many witnesses were called, the judge would allow the mass murderer to walk free if a survivor of the attacks would openly forgive the killer in court. Bab's guilt was never in doubt. Several villagers had lived to tell the court what they had seen him do. No one would forgive him, and he was sentenced to thirty years, with no possibility of early release.

At this point in the recounting of her story, Mama Ella hesitates for the first time. She quietly confesses that even after the conviction, the bitterness and hatred that she had held for her uncle ever since that hellish night still burned as strongly as ever. Knowing that his sentence would effectively see him die in a horrifically overcrowded jail, somehow didn't provide her with any sense of closure.

Over the course of the next five years, Mama Ella came to the realization that there was only one thing that she could do to bring herself some measure of peace of mind. She made the decision to approach the judge who presided over the case and offer to forgive uncle Bab. The judge approved her proposal and in 2014, at a gathering in front of friends, neighbours and fellow victims, she proclaimed her forgiveness of her uncle. The judge approved his release.

Her change of heart had been as much about casting off her own emotional shackles as it was about releasing her uncle from jail. As she put it herself,

"For me to step back into the light and free my heart, I had to forgive. There is nothing left to talk about. It is over, that devil thing that happened is in the past. I wanted to be an example to my community. I rebuilt my house and I rebuilt my life. I am happy to live back in my family home, where I can be close to my father and brothers, who are buried just across the street at the genocide memorial. This way I can honour them. I now have a good life. They now live close by."

Her uncle now lives not far from Mama Ella and comes to visit her and her children and grandchildren, like their families did before 1994.

Honorine, the mother, has sat silent and motionless throughout her daughter's story, saying nothing. She just sits stone-faced and seems to watch as much as listen to the words spilling forth from her child's lips. Honorine herself has her own story to tell (or not) in her own good time. Being a Hutu, she had feared reprisals from the conquering Tutsi army and had escaped to a refugee camp in the Congo, where she met a man and had five more children. She was only reunited with her daughter by chance. In 2002, they had both been visiting a neighbouring village at the same time and literally bumped into each other in the street. Each had assumed that the other had perished sometime during the troubles. The reunion brought Ella five new half-siblings and Honorine five new grandchildren, with another to follow. Honorine, now sixty-five, lives with Mama Ella.

I can't begin to comprehend what she must think when her brother comes by. Her brother, the killer of her husband and her sons. Does she share Mama Ella's belief that generosity of heart is the only way to find inner peace? Has she found her own way to put the past in the past? So many stories, so many questions.

It is Mama Ella that realizes two hours have elapsed since she started her story. For us it had been as if time had stood still, as if we had been invited into some unbelievable parallel universe. We are drained of emotion and in a numbed state of incredulity, and yet Mama Ella, who has just relived what was a real reality, seems to be able to disconnect herself from the events, like mentally being able to close a photo album and put it back on the shelf. Her pragmatism, forgiveness and indomitable spirit are her only defences against the nightmares of the past.

Like everywhere, life must go on in Rwanda and Mama Ella has work to do, she must prepare a lunch of rice for the crew that will come later in the afternoon to create her vegetable garden. She knows a thing or two about catering for the masses. First, she must build a fire, suspend a huge caldron above it, then fill it with water collected from the village pump. One of her pre-teen sons has already collected two jerry cans for this purpose, each one as big as he is.

We say our temporary farewells, as we will return to help with the garden project later in the afternoon after a quick drive into the nearby town to replenish our supply of cash. Blaize walks us back to the gallery. We ask him what he thought of what he had heard with us that morning. He dispassionately commented.

"I have heard many such tragedies. There was much hatred, even before the genocide. My own family ran to the Congo in 1992, fearing that it was unsafe for us as Tutsis in Rwanda. Once the peace talks began in Arusha and the UN peacekeepers came, my mother thought that things would settle down. She returned home to Rwanda at the beginning of 1994. I was the oldest child and she left me in the Congo to finish my high school exams. Soon after she went home, the president's plane was shot down and the genocide started. I never saw her again or any of my six brothers and sisters. I found out later that they were all killed."

We offer our sympathies, for what they are worth. Condolences feel so inadequate in the face of such tragedy. We finish the rest of the walk back to our room in silence.

Back at the "White House," we are met by the aptly named Charmer. He will be our driver for our trip to town. We are lucky to have him, his usual beat is uptown Kigali, where he is popular chauffeuring around the more affluent city folks in his tidy Honda. He happens to be in the village after dropping off a VIP at the local regional office.

He is stylishly dressed, sports jacket with upturned collar, sleeves pushed up to mid forearm, pressed open-necked royal blue dress shirt, spotless chinos, tan dress shoes, with no socks. Voguishly chic, like he is about to step on to a chat show stage.

He needs no compere to prime him with probing questions. He readily provides an engaging recounting of the key points of his life. His English is good, although he is unable to read or write in any language. He is now thirty-four and having been born just before the genocide, had never gone to school. His mother had been raped during the war at a time when AIDS was rampant in the country. She had died of HIV when Charmer was seven. Education delivery, which was in its infancy before the genocide, was completely unavailable for the bulk of the population for many years after the war. In any event, the four orphans, Charmer and his three siblings, were too occupied with the challenges of finding food and shelter to be concerned about schooling.

He tells his story in a congenial almost proud manner, without a hint of rancour or self-pity. The fact that he has overcome so many obstacles has given him an unshakable confidence in his own self-worth and a conviction that he can overcome any hardship that life might send his way.

After our quick visit to the neighbouring town, he finds us an ATM lickety-split, and with his thumbnail of a biography over much too soon, he delivers us back to the village in time for the afternoon gathering at Mama Ella's house.

It is a lively affair, all of the JHA staff and their charges are in attendance. A regular shindig, even our watchman is there, neighbours and family too. The strapping young men and women soon have the yard transformed into productive shape.

The piece de resistance is a mystery sack delivered by pickup truck. Speeches are made, nothing unusual about that. Marcus asks the kids if they can guess what is in the sack. No one dares offer a suggestion. You can hear a pin drop.

The sack is emptied out in the centre of the yard. Dozens of sneakers spill out onto the ground. The kids go bananas, a screaming, leaping, hugging, dancing, clapping mass of ear-to-ear smiles. For most of them, this is the first time they have had footwear of their own other than hand-me-down plastic flip-flops.

After a semblance of order is restored, kids are selected at random to come up and choose shoes for themselves. The suspense is so intense that more than one kid literally pees their pants in anticipation. The caregivers help them excavate the pile in search of the often-errant matching shoe. They then have their picture taken, beaming with their new, maybe only, possession clutched to their bosom.

Another humbling experience for us to see how much joy can be experienced from having access to such a basic need as a pair of shoes. A day that will live in these children's memory for years to come.

A big lad comes over to us to proudly show us his new prized possession, a pair of gold plastic canoe-sized runners. The kind of odour incubating footwear that would have any mother reaching for the fumigator. He is probably in his early teens, rangy and already not much short of my six feet in height. The kids love to practice their English, and so we are soon engaged in a laboured conversation. He is embarrassed to tell that he is the oldest and tallest kid in his class, which is grade four. His family has been living in a refugee camp just across the border in the Goma region of Congo. When still a pre-teen, he was separated from his mother and five sisters. A marauding militia, bandits really, had kidnapped him and conscripted him to be one of their child soldiers. He figures that he spent three or four years living that violent existence, his only education during that time was in murder, looting and lawlessness. Now his struggles are with his ABCs.

As the festivities draw to a close, we go to say our farewells to our host Mama E, who is standing beside our night watchman. As we are about to start our goodbye hugs, Ella's daughter, who is close by and speaks passable English, says,

"I would like to introduce you to my Mama's uncle Bab."

My consciousness can't make the connection between what my ears are hearing and what my mind is trying to comprehend. As Bab, Robert, our night watchman, grips my extended hand, the smile on my face freezes as shards of details, pictures and emotions stall my brain with conflicting messages.

The moment lasts mere seconds and before I know it, I am enveloped in Mama Ella's farewell embrace.

We make our way home in stunned incredulity. Could the affable old man that sleeps outside our bedroom window, our cockroach hit man, really be a mass murderer, a "super killer?"

Have I shaken hands with the devil? Is it possible to think about his actions without passing judgement on him? Do we condemn him just to reassure ourselves that we aren't capable of such evil?

It is not just that he has paid his debt to society and been accepted by the community, but the family that he decimated has tea with him. Why should it even be an issue for us? Better that we simply remember Mama's words: "That devil thing that happened is in the past."

She is right. We will sleep well again tonight knowing that he is doing what he does every night... keeping watch over us.

Chapter 20
Overthinking the Last Supper

Twerking for tweets

"She lowered her lashes until they almost
cuddled her cheeks and slowly raised them again,
like a theatre curtain. I was to get to know that trick."

– Raymond Chandler

"The human brain is a wonderful organ.
It starts to work as soon as you are born
and doesn't stop until you get up to deliver a speech."

– George Jessel

Village life provides few luxuries or opportunities to indulge in canned entertainment. It has been a lesson for us that happiness is not dependent on these advances. The team doesn't decree "an all work and no play" philosophy. Fun, laughter and lively banter is the cheery daily soundtrack. Once a month the lightheartedness extends to party time down by the lake. This month's festivities promise to be a pull-out-all-the-stops affair due to our imminent departure.

It's a universal convention that the less well-off will roll out the red carpet for the elite. I remember as a kid being giddy about standing on the sidewalk in the hopes of getting a glimpse of the queen as she drove past in her Rolls Royce limo motorcade.

Somehow, we all feel more important or more respected if someone famous, in power or wealthy has come to see us. And maybe intuit that by seeing the glamour, we share in it somehow or enrich ourselves by projecting ourselves into those roles. As celebrities more and more frequently reveal themselves to have feet of clay. It is now common to scoff at such notions. Unless of course we are talking about Taylor Swift.

But here in this village there is no escaping the fact—we are celebrities. We are greeted like muckety-mucks wherever we go. And there is such gratitude that somehow someone with influence (crazy to think that they think that about us!) has come to visit and rub shoulders with them. It all feels undeserved, a bit daft, a bit discomforting. I wonder if the royal family ever feel similarly awkward.

The comparison may not be as self-aggrandizing as it appears at first. As far as material wealth is concerned, we probably have more in common with Chuck and Camilla than the villagers have with us. Something that bears thinking about, lest we drift into a "let them eat cake mindset."

Royalty is now a decidedly retro second-class strata of celebrity. Quite different from the new multi-billionaire tech sovereigns who seem to feel that their wealth requires them to pontificate to the masses. Somehow, they have bought into their own propaganda that they are a different breed, uniquely gifted and enlightened. They've earned their fortunes through hard work and brilliance so if only we would listen to their wisdom and let them do what they want, the world would be a bed of roses. We will stick to just waving to the children.

Preparations for our jubilee are well underway down at the lake. The roadies have lugged the sound system down the dirt paths bisecting the planted fields of the farm, batteries are humphed into position. Once the budget stretches to some cabling, things will get easier. They will be able to connect to the solar system that powers the pump for the well. Glastonbury better watch out.

Firewood has been collected. Some makeshift benches are cobbled together on the grassy shores of the lake. A couple of goats are given the last rites. Lighting is barely in evidence; timing is everything, as you must coordinate your actions with the flash of the strobes. Crates of pop will provide the kids with their once-a-month treat. Bottles of locally brewed potent banana beer and a few commercially brewed options are available for the grown-ups. I should mention that the local suds pack a punch triple that of domestic brands, strong enough to knock out a horse.

By now it is early evening, which being near as dammit to the equator means it's already pitch black. The retinue of staff, helpers, volunteers and caregivers are there as well as the children that they look after. Friends and family from the village round out the throng of around one hundred. Folks chat, enjoy a drink and generally socialize. Kids toss around an illuminated ball and they are more bothered by their partners poor throwing aim when they retrieve the ball from the shallows than they are fearful of the hippo and crocodile that are rumoured to inhabit these marshy shores.

As the volume of the music ramps up, the appetite for conversations declines. The partiers don't have a problem with the decibels. They are more than willing to amplify their own voices. What they really want to do, though, is dance. And this they do with unconstrained spontaneity. Clusters of men, boys with old ladies, three girls to a circle, man and a baby, woman with handfuls of children, nephews inviting wives, soloists, grandchildren asking strangers—I doubt if the word inhibited exists in this space and time.

We are caught up in the energy and enthusiasm of the boogying mass and join the mosh pit. The darkness and the odd beverage probably spur our abandon. As the night wears on, the children and the older hoofers start to run out of gas and retreat to the fringes, content to snuggle and watch the moves of the others. The "moves" by this time don't leave much to the imagination, everything from foreplay to climax is on display. Couples swaying groin to butt snug as a condom. Others showing beyond doubt that if it is possible to conceive fully-clothed in the vertical position, this dance would be the way to do it. And there alone, the fourteen-year-old Princess, gyrating like a spaced-out sexpot, dangerously oblivious that she is the object of a feast of hungry eyes. A fourteen-year-old with a body that could spell trouble even for a thirty-year-old.

One of the adult supervisors from the "girls' house," let's call her Mata, who I have spoken to maybe twice, clamps a vice-like grip on my wrists and drags me back into the mayhem for an encore. The strobes are mesmerizing, the sound thunderous and our space on the perimeter of the dance floor intimate in the gloom. After a few get to know you bumps and grooves, she yells above the music into my ear.

"I love you so much, I am going to miss you!" then pirouettes her back to me before reversing her splendid cushions into the region that might generate the maximum reaction. By this time, if I had been dancing any closer to her, I would have been in front of her.

Old stirrings start to stir, fanciful, not to mention reckless thoughts start to percolate. Ideas about recommissioning the decommissioned start to formulate.

She spins again, this time to face me. She maneuvers two of her most precious assets into position, orienting them toward me with sensuous purpose. I didn't need a hashtag to spell out the message that was being sent my way.

Then seductively gazing up with come-hither eyes, she cozies up to me, her warm breath on my neck, her lips millimetres from my ear. No longer able to deny her carnal yearnings, she purrs breathlessly,

"Please buy me a cell phone."

I've known odder conversations on the brink of intimacy but nothing of the kind in recent decades. Cowardice, or was it a sense of morality, already having reared its head, this new development provides me with a handy escape route. Despite, or maybe because of, the banana beer, I ad lib with the inventive if not somewhat mealy-mouthed excuse,

"Well, we don't (note the use of the word "we" here, cunningly inserted so as to hide behind my wife's skirts) give gifts to any of the beneficiaries without asking Marcus (name dropping the big boss provides another shot across her impressive bows) who is the most in need of help at the moment."

If it was daylight I wouldn't have seen her for dust, as it is a bob of the head, a swivel of the hips, and two brisk steps would see the African night smothering her as comprehensively as a cloak.

I do enjoy the rest of the dance, even if by now I am all on my own, flattered in a strange way that as long as I am not old and broke at the same time, there can still be choices. Was it through some sort of altruism or something baser, the fear of losing something cherished, that formulated my response. Clearly, some sort of cognitive dissonance was going on. The devil on one shoulder reminding me of a missed opportunity, which may never come my way again. While Jiminy Cricket is on the other, flattering me for taking the honourable path. It's curious that Jiminy always seems to punch above his weight. One wonders what the state of society would be if he didn't.

Why jeopardise a relationship of forty years and risk encouraging prostitution in the process? The world's oldest profession is probably not one of the institutions that the heritage preservation people are hoping to perpetuate.

Funny that Jiminy's voice in my head bears an uncanny, nae terrifying, resemblance to Trixie's. Our thoughts are seldom simply black and white. Fortunately, with age, these conundrums don't linger or vex the mind the way they did in the days of my youth. Still, it's nice to have options, even if you know you won't cash them in. You take your amusements where you can.

Marcus has called for an intermission in the revelry. Being a largish gathering, I know that there will be speeches. Marcus takes every opportunity to encourage everyone in the group to practice their public-speaking skills and expects them to talk with confidence and conviction. I make my way to the cooler for another bottle of conviction. On my way back, I am intercepted by four young Rwandan men. Thirsty, as they make me aware with their theatrics. I let each of them take a swig of my brew, trying to take a lesson from Princess's example in generosity the other day. Having finished passing the bottle around, I don't get the warm satisfying glow that I expect from having shared with someone less fortunate.

I wouldn't even share my beer bottle with four strangers at home. So why here? I can't make up my mind whether I am getting smarter or stupider. What am I thinking? Later, I check in with Doctor Google and COVID aside, find that it's less risky than I thought to share a bottle. Anyhow, I promise myself that I will find out the Kinyarwanda for "no backwash" before I do it again.

Before the speeches, an impromptu debating contest is held in the centre of the gathering. A spotlight is rigged up and two microphones are handed to the first two orators. They are introduced as Henri and Robert, aged four and seven. They loudly quiz each other on who their favourite girl is and what they will do for the country when they grow up. Like a couple of old pros, self-assured and persuasive, they have the crowd in stitches. Two more pairs of debaters, teenagers this time, follow and provide similarly impressive performances, equal parts entertainment and food for thought. I've never seen anything so encouraging in my life.

Bedu, the second in command, provides the conclusion to the production and provides an effusive if embarrassing thanks to Trixie and me for coming and being part of their community for the past six weeks, before heading toward us. Trixie dodges the mike thrust in her direction and generously suggests that,

"It's time for you to give it a go, I've been doing reruns for the last two nights."

Playing the hapless Prince Charles role to Trixie's Diana, I am tagged with the undertaking. I kick off by expressing my sincere and heartfelt thanks to the assembled. Then vainly attempting to come up with some original content for a change, I veer into untested territory. What possesses me to do this?

Performance anxiety is a real thing, put yourself in my position. We were, of course, supposed to be top of the bill. What would you have done faced with the inevitability of being outshone by a couple of pint-sized Ciceros? I go for broke and try my best to deliver a JFK-like address.

"Ask not what your country can do for you but..." that sort of stuff.

"Ich bin ein Rwandan, etc., etc." and other hopefully crowd-pleasing refrains. Luckily, my memory has blotted out what other pearls I may have imparted on the unsuspecting bystanders.

At the time, a run for office didn't seem entirely out of the question. Up until now, I've never really fancied myself in the Roman mould, striding about the floor of the forum, thumbs in the lapels of my toga, the laurel-wreath crown, a nice touch, conveniently accenting the obligatory bald patch. The insightfulness of my oratory enthralling the assemblies. My investiture surely now merely a formality.

That was all until I realise that I have lost my thread, or more to the point, that the speech is missing something, something it was missing right from the start. Maybe something like a topic or a theme. But before I am given the thumbs down, and all that that might entail, what with lions just having been reintroduced to Rwanda, there is reprieve.

Not only have I lost my thread, but I seem to have lost the audience, who are becoming increasingly restless too. The volume of the mike does little to compensate for more fundamental communication problems. Most of the crowd are non-English speaking and to make matters worse, my hybrid Glaswegian Canadian accent makes my full volume soliloquy sound as if it is being processed through a garburator.

Before I get in any deeper, Marcus rescues me from myself. He takes the mike and primes the eager partygoers for a resumption of dancing. With great relief! I head back to my seat and anonymity, oblivious of the greater grief yet to come.

Before Marcus has eased far into his segue way, the DJ begins the fade in of a song that is to turn into a musical equivalent of waterboarding. Unbeknownst to Trixie and me, the current karaoke favourite of the group is "Lean on Me," A tearjerker if ever there was one, made even more mawkish given that it was the Michael Bolton version, a performer who could make me weep, even if he was singing "Jingle Bells." Give me a root canal any day.

Marcus and Bedu are only too willing to lead the crowd in a rousing rendition. What they lack in polish, familiarity with the words and talent, they make up for with enthusiasm, good humour and inclusiveness. Not comfortable with monopolizing the limelight, they start brandishing the microphones, blanch, in our direction.

Trixie in devious humour (Perhaps she had witnessed Mata's phones for favours overtures. Not that I hadn't spotted her enjoying a bit of a renaissance herself), deftly parries the offer, proclaiming that,

"You are the one that is supposed to know the words to pop songs."

So unable to resist some insane urge, hers not mine, I blame Trixie as I always do in these sorts of situations, me a guy whose happy place is at the back of the room, two steps from the nearest exit, closest to the door, take up the gauntlet. What possesses me? I can only speculate that I can somehow hope to rescue Bedu and Marcus from their predicament and repay their extrication of me from the speech debacle. I might as well be throwing a drowning man an anvil.

Realizing far too late that I don't actually know any of the words save the chorus, I chip in with plenty of volume. As far as the lyrics go, I got nothing. I improvise as best as I can. Making up words as I go, experimenting with things that might rhyme with "lean" like "spleen," "submarine," and "baked beans." Rapidly running out of options, I somehow drift into "He ain't heavy, he's my brother," before realizing my mistake and switching inexplicably to some heavily-accented Bob Marley, "No woman, no cry," for the coda, just to cement my pro-Africa bona fides.

By this time, the crowd has receded further back into the bushes. Simultaneously transfixed and terrorized, unable to look away, as if they are watching a dumpster fire. The whites of their eyes the only clue as to their whereabouts.

The DJ, sensing that the headliners have effectively annihilated the mood, swiftly cranks up one of his undeniable dance beats and soon has the traumatized emerging from their safe havens. The place is heaving again in no time. We are graciously provided a last banana beer, what am I thinking, and plate of delicious barbecued goat, before being driven home and packed off to bed. Our hearts brimming with gratitude to have been feted with such a loving last supper.

Dawn breaks cautiously the next morning. It eases out gingerly, one eye at a time. Consciousness comes with all the trepidation that a bomb disposal expert might experience. 5,4,3,2,1, slowly open the left eye. OK, so far so good, now close. 5,4,3,2,1, slowly open right eye. That isn't so bad. Now open both eyes at the same time. God it's bright. That beating that I am feeling isn't in my heart, it's in my head.

It is a remorseful awakening, filled with too much remembering. It is the kind of resurrection that only a tumbler of Glenlivet or a Colt 45 could provide immediate relief from. But no, life must go on, no matter how painful it is at the time.

It is a morning full of only one question. A question circling in my brain that only amplifies the throbbing in my head. A question I ask myself too many times.

What was I thinking? What was I thinking? What was I thinking?

Despite all this angst, my little spot on the earth close to the planet's midriff continues to turn inexorably toward the sun at a speed of one thousand miles per hour. Even with all this speed, it carries me no closer to home, so I must prepare myself for another cruel reality.[20]

Shrinking from the harsh light of day, I pull the sheets back over my head and try to distract myself from thoughts of... packing.

---

[20] https://earthsky.org/earth/why-cant-we-feel-earths-spin/

EPILOGUE

"The use of travelling is to regulate imagination by reality, and instead of thinking how things may be, to see them as they are."
– Samuel Johnson

"Who are you going to believe, me or your own eyes?"
– Groucho Marx

Still mulling the question, why do we travel? I will end by taking a look at a plausible cause that gives us the urge to travel.

Could it be about storytelling and the tales we have absorbed from an early age reading books, watching movies, hearing friends and family recount their travelling adventures both near and far?

I would argue that it is more about conditioning (nurture) rather than genetics (nature) that provides the spur for us to go. Genetic predisposition would seem an unlikely cause, in my case at least. Even though my father was descended from a line of seafarers, I think the travel bug was passed on through words rather than blood. He was a seaman fitting the Star Trek stereotype of Scottish Chief Engineers. A man of few words, brought up in Glasgow, where the gift of the gab, eloquent storytelling and reasoned argument were admired. A good silence ruined by mindless prattle, however, was subject to any number of condemnations. A blether, a blowhard, a patter merchant, a blatherskite, a gas bag who could blow the hind legs aff a donkey.

My enduring memory of him is as a newspaper with legs. Two massive oven-mitt-sized hands sculpted by years of hefting massive tools and the persuader (the ball-peen hammer) on recalcitrant marine engineering. Now used unflinchingly to support the Glasgow Herald at eye level. Me, barely a teenager, on the floor in front of him, thumbing through the atlas and asking questions like, "I wonder what it's like in India?"

"I've been there," would come the disembodied voice from behind the headline, The Queen Opens Glasgow Airport.

"Fiji is so tiny."

"Aye, been there too."

So conditioning doesn't seem to hold much promise either as a genesis for wanderlust, at least in my case. Even so, the odd tale would often dribble out by the time that he reached the sports section. If I was lucky, the newspaper would crumple and sag down onto his grey-flannel pants, which rested on highly-polished black leather shoes for a minute. A full head of white Brylcreemed hair would emerge, then a pair of black thick horn-rimmed glasses would appear, the white dress-shirt collar, maroon (not red!) tie peeking out above the yellow V-neck sweater, reflective for the moment.

"Aye, Fiji, there were no container terminals in those days. The locals would paddle out to us in canoes and we'd lower the cargo with derricks down to them, and away they'd paddle. It was a paradise, some of the boys would go ashore on leave. McPhail, my second engineer, had an awful liking for the drink. He had his pajamas monogrammed... said it was so he could remind himself in the mornings what his name was. Anyway, he went ashore and didn't come back that night. Arrested he was... drunk and disorderly, put in the jail. I had to go get him at the magistrate's court. The judge found him guilty and fined him two pounds for his drunkenness and five shillings for damage to government furnishings.

"Five shillings for a bloody piss pot," says McPhail.

"And another ten shillings for contempt of court," says the judge.

"Ah, that McPhail, he was a character, his mother did fret so. She'd write and write, "We're worried, son, we haven't heard from you," and all he would send back would be, "Don't worry, haven't written." What a handful he was."

248

But where all had my father been? And what all had he seen? And all what adventures had he experienced? Maybe the spareness of his storytelling created the allure, like a trailer for a Hollywood blockbuster, just a few teasers are enough to arouse interest, just leave it to your fancy to fill in the rest.

Dad had been "deep sea" sailing all over the world for most of his early career, until getting married and taking a shore job in ship inspection in Canada, where I was born. But the sea—or was it the experience of travel?—was in his blood. Transatlantic jet airline travel had only just been introduced in 1958, so we returned to Scotland in 1959, on the ocean liner Lismoria, all eight thousand tonnes and 455 feet of her. She could carry fifty-five passengers and many crates of whisky. How far we have come, or maybe how silly it has all gotten. The largest cruise ships now are nearly a quarter of a million tonnes and can carry over 6,500 passengers.

Dad then joined the Ocean Weather Service, whose ships were based in Greenock. Their job was to head out into the North Atlantic at all times of the year and position themselves for a few days at a given set of coordinates in the middle of the ocean. These stations were given the uninspiring names like Alpha, India and Lima.

Month after month, year after year, for a decade and a half, he sailed out blindly into some of the fiercest seas in the world, the mission to go and find out what the weather was going to be. There were no satellites, doppler radar, internet, etc., back in the early sixties. The option was to venture out into the unknown and once on station, send up a few balloons, and take some measurements amidst all the fury of the elements that Mother Nature would throw at you and report back.

All this was done on the smallest of repurposed WW2 warships, known as corvettes. His ship, renamed the Weather Ship Reporter, was built in 1944; a tin can of a mere 252 feet and a feather-light 1,358 tonnes.

Being of the strong, silent type disposition, the family wasn't to be alarmed with details of the life-threatening conditions.

A rueful shake of the head and a somberly delivered, "It was a hell of a trip... a hell of a trip," was as dramatic an account as we ever got.

It wasn't until long after he had died that thumbing through an old 1982 Guinness Book of Records, I came across an entry under the caption: "Highest Wave."

"The highest instrumentally measured wave was one calculated to be exactly 86 feet high, recorded by the British Weather Ship Reporter in the North Atlantic on December 30th, 1972, at Lat. 59N, Long. 19W."

It's impossible to imagine how anyone could endure those monstrous mountains of water pounding down on you for hour after hour. Relentless onslaughts of eight-storey-high waves, which threaten your very existence.

We are all captivated by the drama and daring of heroic exploits, the rescue of a helpless child from a burning building, the brave raid on a terrorist cell. But there are many anonymous heroes among us. My father was one, I never told him that he was one, to be honest, it never even occurred to me that he was a hero until long after he had passed. A different sort of a hero. An everyday hero.

So you might say that this book is a dedication to my dad, if you like, but more so, I think that it is a thank you for the nooks and crannies of our minds. Our memory banks, where we store our remembrances. A wealth of sounds, pictures, smells and emotions on hand for whenever we might need to recall them. Or that even more magically may come percolating, unbidden, to the surface when you least expect them.

Travel provides firsthand context to so much of the academic, the grand theory politics, the trending information and international affairs that our virtual world swamps us with. It provides time to connect to the more mundane dramas of day-to-day life, the reality of sensory-lived experience, in all its glory, confusion and immediacy, the feedback loop of instant cause and effect.

The preservation of those experiences in memory makes coming home easier and after all, who among us wouldn't want the chance to reacquaint oneself with family and friends and the luxuries of home, even at the cost of reverting to your more distracted, more stressed but less fit and less trim self.

It is usually spring when we return to our home in the temperate Pacific Northwest. Arrival at the airport is the first true reintroduction to the familiar looks and feels of our routine life. The difference in the appearance of people always provides the biggest impact. Sure, we are inevitably coming to the realisation that we are all the same species, but despite that and the emergence of multiculturalism in the West, travel confirms that we are still many, many tribes.

Whether you can call it a tribe or not, I am always struck by the attire of the younger travellers at our local airports. It is as if Robin Hood is continually holding a convention for his band of merry men and women. The attendees sport tights and tunic-length Gortex jackets, in all the colours of the forest. Hunter greens, beaver browns, moss, olive, sage, with the odd sky-blue thrown in. Their appearance may evoke medieval England, but their locomotion is semi-robotic, with an extra-terrestrial vibe about it.

Silently, these young folks propel themselves along, right arms half-extended, clutching disposable coffee cups, left arms tucked in close to their stomachs, cradling iPhones, a silhouette like a Dalek from Doctor Who. Heads bowed, non-looking automatons, seemingly tracking some invisible route map embedded in the concrete concourse beneath their feet. It is all so different from the chatter and human-face-to-human-face interaction that we have left behind in the less connected worlds. Clichéd occurrences in themselves, but revealing in their own way, all our expanded capacity for connection has cost us a diminished capacity to actually connect with one another. There is no gain without something being lost. Our planet provides the perfect example of that, individuals have never lived longer and the price for that is that humanity has never been closer to extinction.

What isn't so simple is to reconcile the experiences gained over the weeks away and the miles travelled with life at home. If you have been travelling light and away long enough, culture shock will make itself felt. It will actually hit you travelling in either direction, much like jet lag, it gets you coming and going. The poverty in parts of Africa that we visited is incomprehensible and yet the luxuries we are met with on our return to Victoria, cavernous fridges, closets bursting at the seams, cabinets filled with gadgets that do everything from balling melons to finding studs, a house with a separate room for every human activity and some that are hardly used at all, suddenly seem quite superfluous.

I guess that you don't have to tolerate stomach bugs, hard beds, heavy packs, cold sleeping bags, bad/non-existent plumbing, dodgy transportation, language barriers, unreliable food and smelly socks to get a sense of a country, but I have to rationalize that it should add something. If nothing else, it is an opportunity to look within and discover something about yourself that you did not know.

The wealth and the poverty seem equally unfathomable, at least for a while, it's a lot easier to adapt to wealth methinks.

For myself, those experiences have given me a growing appreciation of my privileges, which are noticeable enough at home but totally un-ignorable when you are away and out of your bubble. The inequities cannot easily be dismissed and the questions that these experiences evoke can no longer be so easily dodged.

There are never simple answers to the big questions, but I now have for sure an increasing appreciation that for travel, time is the more critical factor, not distance.

EPILOGUE

Now beginning my eighth decade, subtle changes have corrupted my life, time works in devious ways. Topics of conversation have regressed from baby formula and mortgage payments to bowel movements and doctors' diagnosis.

Whole sets of previously only once-in-a-lifetime events threaten to become the norm.

Oops, forgot to pack my shirts (again)!

Where are those damn glasses? I spend more time looking for them than wearing them. Oh yeah, they are on the top of my head.

Is there an antidote to these declines? No, probably not. But they do say that time slows down when you are making memories. Are there any better ways to create memories than through travel? There are enough wonders "out there" to fill a lifetime of lifetimes, so use your time wisely and remember...

It's never too late to kick over a piss pot or two.

"The time you enjoy wasting is not wasted time."

– Bertrand Russell

BE PREPARED

The cardinal rule: we all need to remember
to pack clean underpants.

"The best laid schemes o' mice an' men Gang aft a-gley,
An' lea'e us nought but grief an' pain for promised joy."

— Robert Burns

The pleasures of travel and the trip itself is only half of the fun. Planning the trip is also half of the fun. Sharing the experiences that you have had with family and friends is another 50% of the fun. And right there lurks the all-too-common problem. If we expect to get that much pleasure out of our carefree holiday, is it surprising that things don't measure up to the idealised concept that we have contrived in our mind's eye.

To help avoid this pitfall, here is a checklist of things to consider:

1) Don't take any medication with you.

In most less developed countries, many medications can cheaply be bought over the counter from hole in the wall operations. It is often easier in these places to buy pills than M&Ms, as long as you have the money. Of course, you may in fact be buying M&Ms but heck, it's estimated that placebos have been effective somewhere between 17 and 72 percent of the time (maybe it depends on what colour of M&M).

In more developed countries, try out the local health care system. It will be more of an insight into the country than a shopping trip to the mall.

2) Don't read lists on what to take or how to prepare (especially this one).

Create your own list and when in doubt, leave it out.

3) Do buy local.

Say you arrive in Kathmandu and find that you forgot your hat thanks to my advice in number two. Pick one up in Thamel for maybe three dollars, and have it personalised with embroidery of your own design for another three dollars. You saved yourself forty dollars from buying a hat at home that probably came from Asia in the first place.

4) Don't look at pictures of your destination before you go. Tough I know, but rewarding.

There is no more of an anticlimax than getting to your idolised destination and the best thing you can say is, "Wow, it looks just like the pictures." You just spent thousands of dollars to find that out. Treat yourself to the thrill of seeing something for the first time.

5) Do use guidebooks, but be discerning.

Tear out the pages that talk about "the dangers and annoyances." These pieces of advice are like having Cheezies in the house, they are bad for you, but you are unrelentingly drawn to them. I have the habit of reading them first and then spend the first few days of the trip getting used to the fact that they really are the worst-case scenarios. And pitfalls that generally won't happen to you unless you forgot to pack your common sense.

6) Don't over plan.

Insource your creativity, you will be amazed at your ability to improvise and impress yourself with it.

7) Do read travel accounts.

They are fuel for your imagination. All kinds of unique perspectives will percolate in your mind, none of which will turn out to be the same for you. Your actual travel experience will be much different from that which you have conjured up. Enjoy the surprise

8) Don't over glamorise.

The "just one night syndrome" is OK, but try going down market for a change. Try a hostel or a tent, or sleep in your car. It will stick in your memory long after the fancy meal in the 3-star Michelin restaurant

9) Do consider volunteering while you are away. First ask yourself some questions about your motives, though, to avoid falling into the voluntourism trap.

Will I make money from this? Would I still do this if I couldn't take a camera with me? Would I feel confident doing this work at home?

If you should find yourself having the opportunity to upload the TED Talk you give to a group of Kalahari bushmen on the benefits of taking OxyContin as a prophylactic against malaria onto YouTube, while staying at a five-thousand-dollar-a night safari lodge paid for by Purdue Pharmaceuticals, give pause and think about the optics. While your intentions may be entirely altruistic, there are always a cynical few who delight in diminishing the efforts of the venerated.

Better that you leave these sorts of assignments to the experts and true humanitarians like Bezos, Gates and Bono.

If you are short of cash, try dipping into your daughter's Girl Guide cookie collections rather than selling out your objectivity to the highest bidder.

10) Don't try to do too much. Give yourself free days and go with the flow.

11) Be romantic. You are far from home in a strange land, that's why you came, so enjoy the unexpected.

12) Be sensitive to the health risks that you may present to the people and animals that you meet on your travels. If you have to sneeze, sneeze under your arm, then promptly lower your arm, trapping the offending germs in your armpit. The armpit's naturally occurring elevated temperature will neutralise the harmful effects of the pathogens.

Do not casually aim your sniffles at your elbow, for as you straighten out your arm, you risk catapulting potentially lethal viruses at unsuspecting victims. You do not want to be the one responsible for wiping out an entire civilization.

13) Consider adopting a new name in order to fit in better but choose wisely. When visiting Israel, Hitler would be a no-no (or mostly anywhere).

Maybe use a number, sorry sixty is taken, but do not use an odd number, as this would be insensitive to the feelings of those that our society has labelled as odd in any way.

14) Take any opportunity to drink with the locals, but don't stay until the end.

15) Go to places where English is not usually spoken. You will find out that you really do have a gift for comedy.

16) Don't wait in lineups. If your destination is that popular, you will be able to find all you need to know about it on the internet. You will be better off spending your precious time getting lost... anywhere.

17) Remember, it's about life, liberty and the pursuit of happiness—not the pursuit of safety, so get your will in order before you leave home and then take a few risks.

18) Don't be afraid to appear dumb. Believe me, you will astonish yourself how dumb you really are. The more developed your home country is, the dumber you will find yourself to be and the locals will love you for it.

And finally,

Take only memories and leave only memories, good ones.

ABOUT FACE | APOLOGIA

"If there is anyone here whom I have not insulted I beg his pardon." **Brahms**

I realize that as time passes, what is socially acceptable and also as one ages time passes more quickly. So having been unable to keep up with the mores of the day I would like to apologize to everyone for everything in this book. Getting this apology out of the way up front will save us all sometime later on. So here it is:

I made those decisions and they were my mistake and I am here to say that I am sorry, I convinced myself that the normal rules didn't apply, I was out of control and am deeply ashamed and can only ask that you can find room in your heart to believe in me again as I receive guidance to conquer my demons . I have taken necessary steps to ensure my return to health, reached out to the medical professionals for help, to tell me why I did what I did and I will have that help.

I learned that things have happened here that never should have happened . In the darkness we found the light. Only 10 employees . . . are involved in making napalm this was a big mistake on our part. Our goal has always been to create products that our customers love. Generally, the suicide rate in a society will increase when its GDP rises. A painful but important reminder of the progress we still need to make. I'm just very, very sorry that it's come to this, that a small personal matter has been able to be blown out of all proportion, and with such venom and such gore, I mean it's just terrible.

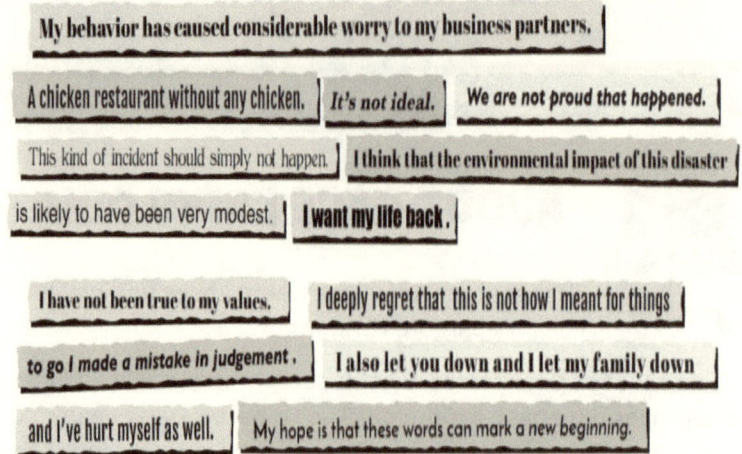

My behavior has caused considerable worry to my business partners.

A chicken restaurant without any chicken. | It's not ideal. | We are not proud that happened.

This kind of incident should simply not happen. | I think that the environmental impact of this disaster is likely to have been very modest. | I want my life back.

I have not been true to my values. | I deeply regret that this is not how I meant for things to go I made a mistake in judgement. | I also let you down and I let my family down and I've hurt myself as well. | My hope is that these words can mark a new beginning.

And some more apologies if you have noticed that in preparing my mea culpa that I have borrowed a word or two from my fellow transgressors (and apologies if I am offending the trans community by using this word. It was not my intent to weaponize it. Nevertheless, we must all be vigilant and sensitive to potential PTSD triggers), but I would be remiss if I did not give a tip of the hat to the masters of the apologia art form. My thanks go out to: Tiger Woods, Bill Clinton, Justin Trudeau, Mark Zuckerberg, Bill Gates, Google, Volkswagen, Du Pont, Martha Stewart, Mike Tyson, BP, Kentucky Fried Chicken, Ellen DeGeneres, Dow Chemical, Harvey Weinstein, Foxconn, Apple, Mel Gibson...[21]

Health Alert

If any readers have been triggered or re-traumatized by any of the content in this book they should follow the following guidelines which Boondoggle Legal Department has developed in collaboration with the WHO. This three stage protocol is intended to stabilize readers who may be suffering from LITS

---

[21] https://sorrywatch.com/category/celebrity-apologies

(Literary Induced Trauma Syndrome). Should symptoms worsen or persist seek the advice of a health care professional immediately.

Protocol level I

Proceed immediately to the safe space on the next page

Protocol level II

Proceed to page 265. Remove Calming Device (cut out with scissors). Place cutouts over eyes, attach with celotape (not included). Note: If you are using the audio book, roll the paper up and stick it in your ears.

Protocol level III

Climb into a cryogenic chamber and come out a) when humanity has ceased to exist, or b) even more dull when everyone shares your point of view.

Maybe this is also the time for me to confess that I once went to a seventies-themed disco party dressed as Barry White. To my eternal shame, I dyed my white hair and beard black and, probably, flouted some other cultural boundaries when I also put on black face and stuck a pillow up my shirt. Still, I can't help but wonder what confusion I may have caused without the padding and colouring. People would have been justified in wondering what Santa Claus was doing at a disco party. And why is he wearing a leisure suit?

Anyway, I won first prize… they were less enlightened times. I also seek your blanket absolution for the other scandalous skeletons that are doubtless rattling around in my closet.

PROTOCOL LEVEL I
SAFE SPACE

PROTOCOL LEVEL II

Calming Device

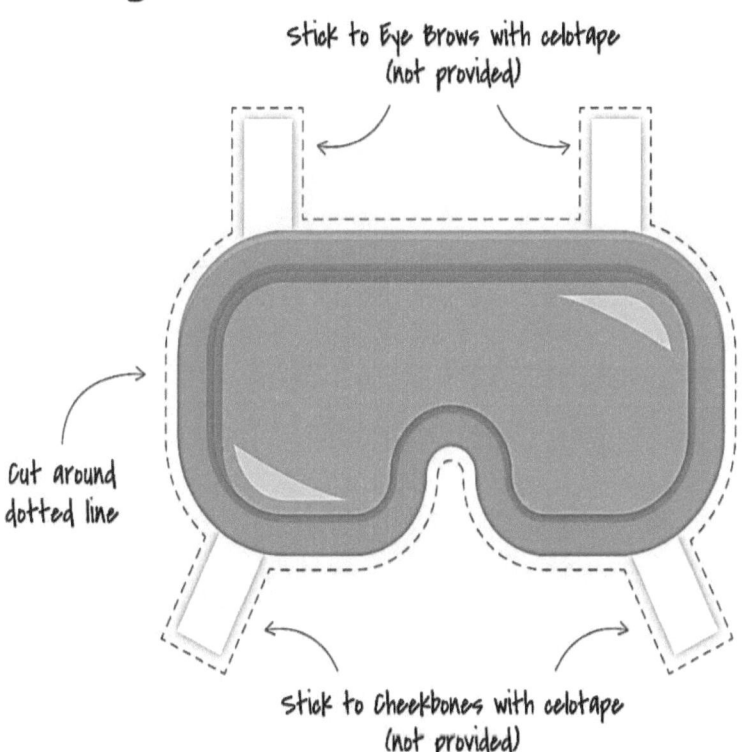

Stick to Eye Brows with celotape
(not provided)

Cut around
dotted line

Stick to Cheekbones with celotape
(not provided)

WHAT DID WE LEARN
- A QUIZ

The following questions could test a variety of things:

Your general knowledge, your powers of deduction, the state of your memory, or whether you found anything of interest at all in the book.

Listed below is one question per chapter arranged in numerical sequence.

All you have to do is match the answers listed on page 269 with the questions asked on page 268. Each answer may only be used once.

Hint: If you are struggling, you can refer back to the chapter in question, where you should find the answer somewhere in the narrative (or if you are like me, look at the solutions key on page 270)

The answer to number 1 has already been filled in to get you started.

TOMORROW THEY ARE PLAYING GOD

CHAPTER	QUESTION		ANSWER
1	Science meets slacks in which South American city?	I	Santiago
2	The tuxedos were all out when we visited which town?		
3	Which taxi service was a dinosaur even before Uber took over?		
4	Name this Irish descended revolutionary's home town?		
5	These three zits became home for which colonisers?		
6	This detective story didn't originate in Columbo, but where?		
7	African climate change could use some coverage from which guy?		
8	How many inches of rain can these gorillas expect in a wet afternoon?		
9	The WPP advertising agency earns more revenue than the GDP of which two countries combined		
10	Which of our closest relatives is one happy camper with his twenty-five times a day appetite?		
11	Which country had over three times the number of elected women politicians as the US in 2016?		
12	Which group were too small to be a factor in the genocide?		
13	You should have NO PROBLEM finding the Swahili answer to this question?		
14	If you find "no points of interest" interesting, where should you go?		
15	Per capita, Canadians produce 180 times more CO_2 than which nationality?		
16	Whose flight of fancy cost $5 billion?		
17	According to QANON, who is Joe Biden cloned from?		
18	What did this dentist invent in 1881?		
19	Which insecta of the hymenoptera order saved a life?		
20	How fast are you travelling when standing still at the equator?		

WHAT DID WE LEARN – A QUIZ

Match these answers to the questions listed on the previous page:

MATCH ANSWERS to QUESTIONS	
A	three
B	Rwanda and Malawi
C	Butch
D	Rwanda
E	the Twa
F	Hakuna Matata
G	Bugasera
H	Malawians
I	Santiago
J	Punte Arenas
K	Myladon
L	Buenos Airies
M	Polynesians
N	a computer lab
O	Anderson Cooper
P	1000 MPH
Q	bees
R	the electric chair
S	C3P0
T	Jeff Bezos

TOMORROW THEY ARE PLAYING GOD

Solution key by chapter number and answer letter:

CHAPTER	ANSWER
1	I
2	J
3	K
4	L
5	M
6	N
7	O
8	A
9	B
10	C
11	D
12	E
13	F
14	G
15	H
16	T
17	S
18	R
19	Q
20	P

GLOSSARY
A Guide to Foreign & Obscure Words & Phrases

Affleck Island - Perhaps a fabled island of Polynesian lore, see also TITSRN.

African Massage - A jocular term referring to the effects of driving on Rwandan back roads at speed.

Ahu - A stone platform (not to be confused with Air Handling Unit).

Arusha Accords- Failed last attempt to reach a power sharing agreement between Hutus and Tutsis before the Rwandan genocide.

Asado - An iron crucifix where dead meat is brought to life over hot coals.

Ay Caramba - A phrase that just stops short of saying something unprintable, by golly.

Banana Beer - A remorse inducing beverage.

BIPOCs - The only people we meet in Shagora each day

Bombachas - Harem pants worn by gauchos, baggy trousers. Mock them at your peril.

BOME - Bank of Mother Earth, no bail outs available.

Booty - Precious cargo, buns or junk in the trunk for example.

Boozerman - A person with a predilection for fermented bananas.

British Central Africa Protectorate - An invented land mass to protect the British settlements from Portuguese encroachment.

C-3PO - Bumbling stiff legged humanoid robot modelled on a stiff legged humanoid president.

Carmanere/Malbec - The grape divide between Chile and Argentina.

Cassava - A root vegetable ubiquitous in Africa originating in Brazil

CCTV - A talisman prevalent in primitive cultures thought to ward off evil.

Cerulean - Commonly used in such phrases as "He talked until he was cerulean in the face". Blue.

Coffee -A new cash crop in Rwanda a plant originating in Ethiopia not Brazil.

Cojones - Balls testicular, a measure of male bravery.

Cuia - Rhymes with "ooh-ya", a hollowed-out gourd used as a drinking vessel.

Cultural Appropriation - A recent concept yet to provide guidance on the Coffee/Casava issue.

Dulce de Leche - A heavenly confection wafted to Buenos Aires ice cream parlours by way of Indonesia, Philippines, Spain and heaven.

Dalek - Robotic extra-terrestrial life forms who invade earth. Nancy Pelosi? Mitch McConnell?

Fitz Roy - A South American mountain range named after the British Captain of Darwin's ship the Beagle, who in his spare time refined the crossing the equator hazing ritual.

Flycatchers - Sounds funny the first time you hear it. Touts and hawkers that pervade downtown Arusha. Not so funny.

Franc Afrique - French neocolonialist policy of the 1960's to 1990's which included clandestine military and economic activities. Also sarcastically known as "Franc a fric" – a source of cash.

Furious Fifties - Drafty latitudes sandwiched between the roaring forties and the shrieking sixties.

Handheld Device - An apparatus which facilitates onanistic practices leading to sensory degradation

Heimlich Maneuver - now cancelled and reestablished as the abdominal thrust. Known in some circles as the Weinstein maneuver.

Heladaria - Argentinian ice cream parlour, tapas schmapas.

His Excellency - A title given to the current president of Rwanda. Oddly enough bestowed by the voters without derision.

Interahamwe - Murderous Hutu militia during the Rwandan genocide.

In Absentia -when the people with most at stake aren't invited.

Irish Potatoes - A racially stereotyped tuber

ISIS - A new cooking style taking hold in Patagonia.

League of Nations - Predecessor of the UN, both later eclipsed by the English Premier League.

MG and T - Mothers ruin, a Malawian beverage made from sugar cane of all things.

Mattock - A farm implement half shovel half hoe, playfully also known as an African laptop.

Moai - A monolithic bust carved from igneous rock in the Affleckus style.

Mzungu - A word originally used to describe a white person who wanders around lost, more confusingly can now also be used to refer to an African America. Unknown whether this signifies true equality or subversive cancel culture terrorists at work

NITNOC - A nonindigenous traveller not of color, Trixie for example.

Orono Crater - The entrance to an umbilical cord connecting all the washing machines in the parallel universes together.

Pant Hoot - Obviously onomatopoetically simian greeting, featured in every Tarzan movie ever made.

Pseud - An unflattering description often applied to overly knowledgeable advisors.

Puka Shells - A less iffy monetary system than crypto currency

Ponzi Scheme - An entrepreneurial business model currently popular with billionaires

RPF - Abbreviation for Real Person Fiction, perhaps applicable to this book. Oh, and also substitutes for the Rwandan Patriotic Front

Ralf Urgh Blugh – When accompanied by the relevant facial expression a less than poetic reference to vomiting

RWF - Rwandan francs, not to be confused with the Royal Welsh Fusiliers.

Stanley (Henry Morton) - Illegitimate Welsh explorer of the Nile and Congo regions who aspired to make good with his birth certificate which described him as a "bastard".

Terra Gloopa - Possibly the Latin translation for mud.

Thar She Blows - an almost poetic way of describing our closest living relatives going pee-pee.

There be Dragons here - Cartographic shorthand for "who knows what shit goes on there".

TITSRN - The Island That Shall Remain Nameless that has many names.

Tree Tomatoes - The local version of tamarillos whatever they are.

Westphalia - A vehicle made by the makers of the Beetle that resembles a cockroach.

Wu Han Flu - A flu-like ailment publicized by racists. Then cancelled, then rebranded by virtue supremacists, then no longer trending but likely still reinventing itself.

GLOSSARY

Woke - awake to social issues not necessarily connected to Awoke from a slumber or?

Yerba - Informally grass but really used to make Mate a herbal caffeine rich tea.

BOOK CLUB QUESTIONS

1) Raccoon 60 and Trixie were profoundly affected by Mama Ella's recounting of her escape during the genocide. Do you think that Mama Ella's forgiveness of the perpetrator was justified, or would punishment be more appropriate in circumstances like these?

2) As the book progresses, it includes more commentary on the history of the destinations visited. What do you think are reasons for this trend? Do you feel that this context is important? Is it important that we become more aware of the impacts of colonialism?

3) How does the outbreak of the pandemic represent a turning point in relation to Trixie and Raccoon 60 attitude to travel. Are there changes to the way that they travel before and after the outbreak? Has it changed your attitudes to travel?

4) In several places the author touches on travel as being a sort of endorphin prompted addiction. Do you agree? Do you share that obsession? What obsession do you think ranks more highly than travel?

5) Is Miss Stella a good boss? If the calling, in her case educating children, is laudable enough, do "the ends sometimes justify the means?" Would you have tried to get her to change her ways?

6) Raccoon 60 had a few "Ah ha" moments and more than a few "WTF" moments during the various escapades. Discuss examples where the author felt that he was learning something new from these experiences. Who do you think benefitted more from the personal interactions between the author and the local people? In what ways?

7) What was the best travel tip that you picked up from reading the book? What behaviour, concept or idea did you disapprove of?

8) How would you contrast the luxury of the safari experience with the improvised party at the village lakeside? Which appeals to you more and why do you think that that is?

9) Do you think that Trixie and Raccoon 60 are being irresponsible by travelling to poorly serviced and remote locations? What factors should people consider when thinking about limiting the extent of their adventures? What role should age play in shaping those decisions? Are the considerations the same for men and women?

10) Is there one particular event or set of circumstances in the book that to you epitomises the challenges and rewards of independent travel?

11) The book features glimpses into societies of vastly different wealth and sophistication. One of the recurring undercurrents in the stories is that of inequality. In which scenarios did you find those inequalities most glaring?

12) While writing Tomorrow, They are Playing God, author Raccoon 60 kept a diary of the events that made the biggest impressions during his visits. When he returned to Canada, he transformed those notes into the stories that you have just read. Did the characters and sense of place feel authentic to you?

IMAGE CREDITS

Chapters 1, 11, 15 by the author

Chapters 2, 3, 4, 5, 7, 8, 10, 12, 17, 19 Adobe Stock

Chapters 9, 14, 16, 18, 20 Public domain

Images sourced from Wikimedia Commons with attribution

Chapter 6 The African Examiner

Chapter 13 Felippe Dana

THANKYOUS

To my book designer Dan for his persistence in finding solutions to the quirks inherent in the design of this book and especially for his tips on boating, anchors away.

To my editors Emily M. for the early drafts and Patty F. for the later versions.

To Freyja not only for being my graphics designer but also accommodating my Procyon Lotor proclivities and assisting me in my fledgling merchandising efforts. Coonadian or Coon and Crossbones flags anyone? Anyone?

Phillips for their excellent beer, even if I did have to buy it. I am hoping to parlay this plug for them into a free case, or wait how about Zorro lager? I always fancied myself on a beer can.

My friends Russell, Bolen, Ivy and Munro for their support. Each one of them a Victoria bookstore packed with literary treasures, drop in on them! Not only are they revered local icons, but they are home to dedicated knowledgeable staff who make each visit an experience.

Special thanks to Zoe, Jennifer and Todd for humoring my fur-brained marketing ideas.

To my 20-month-old granddaughter Hailey... just because.

And to you dear readers, you should know that the proceeds from the sale of this book will be used in the village where many of these tales took place. A big thank you.

And last but never least to Trixie for pretty much everything but in particular for introducing me to the wonderful humans in the Rwandan village I have renamed Shagora. Their dedication is an affirmation of what any of us can do if we put our hearts maybe more than our minds to it.

ABOUT THE AUTHOR

Raccoon Sixty is a retired civil servant living in Victoria, Canada. He was formerly known as the symbol "Don't let your baby put their head in a bucket in case they might drown."

He is married with two adult children. He is a cisgendered trans-species who identifies as a Raccoon but has not come out yet.

Tomorrow They are Playing God is his second book, it was winner of the prestigious Boondoggle Travel Book of the Year award in 2025.

It follows up on his 2024 smash hit *It's All Because of the Virgin*.

His hobbies include travel, emptying the garbage, and climbing trees.